THE QUIET GUN
A WESTERN DUO

LAURAN PAINE

SAGEBRUSH
Large Print Westerns

First published in the United States by Five Star

First Isis Edition
published 2017
by arrangement with
Golden West Literary Agency

A catalogue record for this book is available
from the British Library.

ISBN 978–1–78541–376–6 (pb)

Published by
F. A. Thorpe (Publishing)
Anstey, Leicestershire

Set by Words & Graphics Ltd.
Anstey, Leicestershire
Printed and bound in Great Britain by
T. J. International Ltd., Padstow, Cornwall

This book is printed on acid-free paper

Editor's Note

Recently Lauran Paine's *Open Range Men* was filmed as *Open Range* (Touchstone, 2004), starring Robert Duvall, Kevin Costner, and Annette Bening. Many years ago an earlier version of his story titled "The Quiet Gun" was filmed as *The Quiet Gun* (Twentieth Century-Fox, 1957), starring Forrest Tucker and Mara Corday. "The Quiet Gun" has not been otherwise collected, and, since the film version is still shown frequently, it was thought that readers might like very much to read the original story on which that earlier film was based.

Contents

Montana Manhunter

CHAPTER
ONE

The geese were overhead in great, sweeping Vs, sending down their sad autumn calls as they went southward, the aspen leaves were the size and color of old gold coins, white tree barks making striking contrast, and the pale, high panorama of flawless blue sky had an austerity to it raffish summer never possessed. Autumn was close. The first killing frost had drained out the varying green shades from plants that now hung, slack and discolored, and a soundless, steady wind brought winter's breath and the promise of more black frost, without more than touching rooftops and fence fronts in passing.

The squirrels rarely showed now, sage hens ruffled their feathers in underbrush windbreaks, and the crows were gone until another season's warmth summoned them back. Old mossback cows, exhausted from suckling big fat, sassy 400-pound calves, stood with their bony tails to the silent wind, but younger cows with good grinders and smaller calves grew abundant hair so that cold did not trouble them much. But the grass was tasteless, in some places downright bitter.

The marmots, rock squirrels, weasels, grass mice were not quite ready to dig down and burrow in yet, but even so they showed rarely. Wild horses with muffled manes and splayed tails, rough-coated and whiskered, faced into the steady cold, noting scents. Although most large animals feared wolves, with sound reason, wild horses feared panthers more; they could outrun wolves but not big cats, and as a rule big cats stalked them unseen.

In the high country bull moose made their hollow-sounding great trumpeting less and less, the elk and deer came lower to escape ten-foot snow piles, and now finally wolf packs prepared to eat well, down along the snowline where animals congregated, and as winter came on and progressed, where the older creatures got weaker. It would be a time before snow yet, and the warning signs would be abundant long before, but the smell, the soft scent of snow would be in each fall dawn and dusk from now on.

In the towns the preparations were something of a community affair, but the plans for winter in the countryside varied according to requirement, and differed according to temperament. In Hidatsa cordwood began to grow tier after tier, around the schoolhouse particularly, because they had two cannon heaters over there, and also at Wilkinson's General Mercantile where they also had two of those big iron stoves. Elsewhere around Hidatsa, summer-gathered hay was covered — an old canvas, usually, with four big stones placed crosswise and held in place by wires — storm shutters were dowelled into place along the north walls, porch benches were stored, barrows full of manure were wheeled up back alleys from Beacon's livery barn to be mounded protectively around plants and flower bulbs.

In the countryside the cow outfits got ready, generally by moving livestock to winter range — kept stock-free all summer so the feed would be tall when it stalk-cured — and pulled shoes from the horses after the seasonal riders had been paid off and sent on their way. Men hunted in the autumn, hunted hard and worked days away from home at it, so when the meat was salted and barreled to be preserved there would be a great variety of it.

A lot of people left, drove over to Hidatsa, got on a stage, and went south almost as far as the birds also went. Some returned in the springtime and some never returned, ever.

It was the time, Grant Shelby said, sitting his horse in the high-slope pines and watching, when one real bad Montana winter could freeze immigrants to their beds in fireless shacks, or could drive them out, abandoning everything, willing to exchange whatever they still had for a coach ticket far off and forever. He was comfortable inside his sheep-pelt coat, his lined gloves, and his wool throat muffler of brilliant red. So was the other graying man, beside Grant Shelby, perpetually narrowed, long eyes pale in the ruddy, weathered set of his lean features.

He said: "She's at it like a beaver, pilin' straw and dead vines around the roots. Gettin' ready just like she figures to hole up and last it out."

Grant Shelby did not take his sardonic gaze off the bundled woman down the hill and out through the open grassland working sturdily in her patch of vegetable rows inside the high paling fence. He shook his head, but gently. "That-son-of-a-bitch's never comin' back. She's mighty stubborn to go on livin' out here expecting it."

"She'll leave," Shelby's companion said. "She's tough. She's pig-stubborn and tough. You can't tell her a darned thing, and lately even when a man tries, she's out there on the porch with that shotgun before you cross the yard. But the weather'll do it for her. It'll convince her." He pointed with a gloved fist. "Look in the woodshed. She'll make it last until first snow."

Grant sat a while, watching. The distance was fair, and the intervening trees that hid the horsemen also inhibited the view. But he knew what she looked like — taffy hair with thick undulations to it, broad, low forehead, and dead-level gray eyes, a full, heavy mouth above a jaw of granite. She was maybe twenty-five, maybe twenty-six or -seven, big-breasted, strong-bellied, powerful in the back and legs and arms. He did not have to see her without all those mufflers and old coats. He knew what she looked like — so did his wife.

Grant sighed. Not very many truly handsome women came up to the Montana cow country. Those that did, either did not stay through one winter, or, if they stayed, they weathered and aged and changed in outlook and got to know fear of everything from the winters to the wolves, and to men.

The last really handsome woman Grant Shelby had seen had belonged to the freighter named Sevrinsen who hauled between Fort Hall and Miles City. A statuesque, high-headed, black-eyed, and golden-skinned Hidatsa Sioux woman, and her man was big enough to throw a saddle on, so she was plumb safe in any town of the high cow country.

But this one mounding those dead old rusty vines around her perennials in the fenced garden patch, she didn't have a man, and she was also tall enough and strong enough, and a lot prettier than some blanket woman.

Grant said: "I guess they're tough where she comes from. And strong put together. You ever see her up close in the heat of summer?"

The other man nodded with a faint smile. "Strong," he agreed. "Strong and put up exactly right for a gal."

Grant's gaze never left the moving figure down in the open. "You wouldn't need much of a bear robe this winter, Galt."

"For a damned fact a man wouldn't. Well, we'd better head back."

Galt Hays was one of those men who showed humor around his eyes, even long after something had amused him. It seemed as though once an expression settled upon his hawkish features, it lingered to some degree until a fresh mood brought up some other lingering impression. Galt was tall and spare and heavy-boned, the kind of man who seemed to live forever. He was dark-eyed and had sprinklings of gray in his black hair. He looked as predatory and weathered as a bronzed Sioux, but in fact there was not a drop of Sioux blood in him.

He had been Grant Shelby's range boss for six years now. They got on well. Galt was a taciturn man most of the time, watchful, prudent, a man who weighed things, who arrived at no snap judgments, an individual range riders respected. He could have been thirty-five or fifty-five. If Grant Shelby knew, he did not say, any more than he would have admitted to his own age of crowding sixty.

He had been married forty years and the sap, like the humor — which had always been thin anyway — Mrs. Shelby once possessed, had withered along with the many autumns that had passed. She and Grant spoke, but that was the extent of it. She had her interests. He had his interests. As they turned now to trace out a buck run along the uphill slope among the trees, he looked back, and, although the distance and the bundled clothing obscured the woman, he sighed. He knew what she looked like. A lot of menfolks around the Hidatsa cow country knew. Her name was Margaret Fulmer; she had been out here now about three, maybe four years, and the last anyone had seen of Tom Fulmer had been two years back. Since then, a lot of riders, owners, and range bosses, a lot of townsmen and haulers, drifters and pot hunters had come along, had looked, and had twisted in the saddle to look again. Folks knew she was out there.

The weather was turning. Galt snugged on his lined gloves and studied the roiled, high-layered, gray-bellied clouds that the silent, but searing wind was hurling altogether. It was too early, maybe, but once a rider saw his first russet or yellow leaf, winter could arrive any time. That same day even. Montana very often showed only a glimpse of autumn colors before winter fell. Unlike Wyoming and Colorado, where weather was largely predictable, Indian summer in high Montana was a specialty, a rare time of momentary lull before the hammer blow of full winter came.

CHAPTER
TWO

The nights were clear and cold, the days warmest from noon until mid-afternoon with winy air and perfect visibility for as far as a man could see. The underbrush rattled when a horse walked through it, each stalk withered and brown, but the old bull pines stood as rugged sentinels, impervious to whatever winter sent against them, and their centuries' accumulation of scented needles were spongy soft to muffle sounds of heavy animals up where the wraith-like rider came carefully around the north slope where coppery autumn sunlight reached thinly. He had been drawn around there to look southward by two quick glimpses of brilliant red.

He had waited with a gloved hand over the nostrils of his horse for the pair of cowmen to ride past, one with a red muffler wrapped snugly around his throat, then he had swung up to backtrack and seen what had held them over there so long, looking down through the trees to the wide meadow.

The cabin had a fire in the stove. There was thin gray smoke rising rope-like to be torn at by fitful gusts from the higher, colder northerly mountains. A woman wrapped in two coats with an old range rider's hat holding her wealth of taffy hair stood motionlessly gazing toward the northwest. From that distance the stranger could only make out her bulkiness, thick strands of light hair, and square shoulders. She was not old, he guessed, and she was sturdy, strongly set up for a woman.

Otherwise, he saw little to interest him. The house looked to have maybe three rooms; it was made of adzed-square, notched fir logs and had two porches, one in front, one in back. There were three outbuildings and a medium-size log barn, all of the same solid, sound construction. The woodshed was enclosed on three sides. From the front, facing the house, he could see very little wood inside, maybe a cord or a cord and a half.

He waited and watched, rolled and lit a smoke, and stood with his big bay horse, studying things. He was a thin, sinewy man with a week's beard stubble, dark curly hair, and dark eyes set weasel-close in a rather narrow, crafty face. He wore a six-gun that had ivory butts and rode a carved saddle. In some ways to knowledgeable eyes he would have seemed out of place for high Montana. He looked more like a southwestern range man, even to the silver cheek pieces of his half-breed bit and his silver-inlaid spurs. He was a hard man to place. He could have been a range rider paid off and heading south, except for the expensive saddle and the ivory-handled Colt, and the silver. Or he could have been a vain top hand, or maybe even a well-paid range boss.

The bay horse was leggy with powerful forelegs, a short back, and a fine head, young, maybe six, at the very most seven years of age. A valuable horse built for speed and endurance. Not a cowboy's kind of horse. Far too good for that.

The woman turned and looked up the northward, shielding hill, ranged her gaze left and right, then drooped a little as she latched the garden patch gate and trudged tiredly toward the house.

The man waited until his smoke was gone, then mounted and swerved around the side hill to come down in behind the barn from the east, out of sight of the house. He swung off back there and led his horse inside, the tie-down pulled loose on his six-gun. He stood and sniffed and studied things. Once, there had been horses here, but the scent was so faint it must have been a year or two ago.

He stalled the big bay, swung his outfit over the saddle pole, and climbed to the loft to fork down some dusty hay, climbed back down, and rubbed his hands together. The barn was like an ice chest, for although the midday was warm once a man was out of the icy wind, and the sun should have made a difference, the walls were of solid fir logs; there were only two openings to the barn, one from in back, one from out front, and the cold never really left once autumn arrived.

The bay horse did not mind at all. He detested wind; all horses did, but he was haired-up for winter and mostly he was grateful to be able to stand and eat, even if the hay was tinder dry and required twice as much

12

saliva as it should have required to fetch forth the sugar from the green joints. Whoever had put it up, long ago, had known exactly when to set out with his scythe.

The man stood a long while in shadows studying the house. There were ample signs to keep him from worrying very much. A man would have had that shed full of wood this close to winter. A man would also have had at least one horse, and he'd have left foot tracks half again as large as the only ones the stranger saw here and there.

A lot of settler men worked out during riding season, or on freighters, or at smithies in the towns, but by now they would have returned. This man hadn't come back; the stranger saw more signs of this. He made up his mind to cross over and see if he could get inside. People, especially range people, never refused a stranger food and warmth.

He beat his trousers with his dark hat, creased the hat again, dumped it on the back of his head, set his blanket coat to rights, allowing it to fall over and conceal the ivory-handled Colt. He rubbed a hand over beard-stubble, shoved both gloves under the shell belt, and struck out. He smiled, and kept right on smiling all across the yard, up onto the porch where his spurs *rang* at the same time his booted feet made a hollow echo.

He had a hand raised to knock when the door silently swung in and two black barrels of a shotgun were belly-high and twelve inches from him. He turned to stone, raising just his eyes to the woman whose solid jaw and pressed-back lips showed absolute resolve.

"Ma'am," he quietly said, "you don't need that thing. My name is Frank Helner. I was skirtin' around that side hill up north of your meadow when my horse lamed up in a badger hole. I put him in your barn and was hoping you might have some liniment . . ." He waited, dark eyes looking steadily across the gun barrel at her. He made a little smile of harmless guile, then shrugged coated shoulders. "It's all right if you don't have none. I'll lead him on until I find another place."

She neither moved nor spoke for a moment or two, stood with a finger curled lightly around the tang of one cocked gun barrel. Finally she said: "Do you ride for Grant Shelby?"

"Grant Shelby? No, ma'am. I got paid off up by Cardiff last week and am headin' down for the desert country to winter. I don't know anyone named Grant Shelby."

"Can your horse walk?"

"Well, yes, ma'am, but he's sure hurtin'. But that's all right." He slowly let the upraised arm go down to his side, and showed her a harmless, apologetic look. "I didn't mean to come up and scare you. I'd have skirted around and kept ridin' but for that dog-goned badger hole."

"I have some Kendall's tendon liniment," she told him. "And plenty of goose grease."

His eyes brightened genially. "I'd sure be obliged. If he could just stand overnight in your barn . . . I'll bed down out there with him and keep workin' the liniment in, and, as soon as he can walk a little without it hurtin' so much, I'll lead him off. We'd both be almighty obliged, ma'am."

She eased down the shotgun hammer, raised the barrel, and tilted the weapon against the wall as she said: "Wait here. I'll get the liniment."

He watched her move across and through a blanketed doorway, swiftly hoisted the scatter-gun, broke it, extracted both shells, snapped it quietly closed, and replaced it. He pocketed the shells and was smoothing his coat when she returned, wearing a sheep-pelt old rider's coat and a battered range man's hat. She paused to raise both arms and tuck in her muffler, which made the high, fullness of her upper body thrust forward. He looked, then swiftly turned to glance elsewhere. She was not old and she was as handsome a female-woman as he'd seen all year.

"The shotgun," she murmured, handing him the liniment and goose grease to pick up the weapon. "I take it with me everywhere I go."

He muttered something favorable about that and gallantly stepped aside for her to walk down off the porch first. He admired her strong stride and the solidness of her body under that bulky old coat.

At the barn she paused to find his horse, then went forward. The stranger loosened his coat, shoved it back, leaned in the doorway, and waited.

The bay horse turned, out of curiosity, neither favoring nor flinching. The woman stopped, watched, went up to lay a leaning hand lightly, and, when the bay yielded without flinching, she stood utterly still for a moment before turning, this time hauling back both dogs of the shotgun.

The dark-eyed stranger grinned, right hand ungloved and resting upon the cold ivory handle of his weapon. "Go ahead and pull," he softly told her. "Tug off both barrels at once if you're a mind, missus . . . it ain't loaded."

She did not pull either trigger; she eased off the dogs and sprung the barrels open. They were as empty as he had said they would be.

She said: "You do ride for Grant Shelby!"

"No, ma'am. I never heard of him before in my life." He remained loosely standing in the doorless, wide barn opening, gazing at her, his dark eyes signaling every thought that crossed his mind, and, when he finally jerked his head for her to precede him out of the barn, she said: "You're an outlaw, aren't you?"

He grinned again. "Yes'm, and a hungry, tired, cold one, so we're going over to the house an' get warm, and we're goin' to eat, and then, ma'am . . . we'll just have to see, won't we?"

Behind her the bay horse raised its head to stare in the direction of the rear barn opening, a half mouthful of hay held utterly still. The man and woman ignored him, absorbed in their own small drama. She felt scorn for the outlaw because of the dishonest way he had duped her. She felt a little contempt for herself as well for being so trusting, but it was her nature; she had been raised to believe there was inherent good in people. Only since her husband had not returned had she learned that men were not always to be trusted.

16

After the second year she was almost convinced no men were to be trusted. But it was still not her nature to be this cynical, this completely distrusting, and the outlaw had got the best of her in perhaps the one way a man could have done it, by playing on her feeling for animals.

Now, watching his grin, reading his mind with no difficulty, she felt a deep disillusionment mingled with a rising, blind will not to succumb to him regardless of what resisting him might involve.

He jerked his head again, more peremptory this time, the grin gone and the dark eyes brightening in a peculiar expression.

She waited another moment before starting along. The bay horse had stopped being curious about something, some sound or scent out behind the barn, and dropped his head back to the contents of his manger.

A little gust of frigid wind swept along out front. Part of it was diverted, adding to the coldness of the barn's interior. Neither she nor the outlaw noticed. She was almost abreast of him and turned her eyes so she would not have to see him, staring stonily dead ahead across in the direction of the yard.

Then she swung. Using both hands, gripping the shotgun fiercely and wrenching her upper body around with all the desperate force she could summon, she swung the long double barrels of the shotgun. He was cat-like but the surprise gave her a definite advantage. He had no more expected this savage sudden attack than he had expected her not to yield to him once he had the power to force her.

He already had a hand on the six-gun at his waist, but as he reflexed to draw, the double barrels caught him hard on that side. She was a powerful woman. Two years of having to do it all herself from sawing and splitting winter wood to snaking down logs to patch buildings had developed what had always been a normally muscular body.

He went sideways off balance, struck a manger low along the legs, and sprawled. He also made a sharp, short outcry when that shotgun struck him, but although she hauled around to strike again, wasting seconds by drawing the shotgun far back before swinging it, the outlaw drew. He drew slowly and with desperate effort because that arm had been the one she had struck. It did not particularly pain him, not yet, but he was sure she had fractured a bone, perhaps even broken something, although he was able to draw.

She had the shotgun coming around again, all her body straining for the blow, when he fired. The sound made the bay horse set back in abrupt fright, but the shank held, so he came up on it, turned, and rolled his eyes.

The woman's body seemed to break at the middle, seemed instantly to lose a lifetime ability to stand, but, as she fell, she went sideways and the second gunshot missed her because the slug had been aimed where she had been.

She felt an excruciating pain that was hot, searing hot and nauseating. Her shotgun fell, *clattering* to the

18

compacted earth floor, one way, the woman falling another way.

From the rear barn opening a man spoke past the final gunshot echo: "Garrett, you son-of-a-bitch!"

The outlaw, in the act of arising, his attention fully on the woman, hung there, head suddenly tipping up and turning. He saw the man in the shadows out there, dropped on his belly, swinging the ivory-butted Colt. The stranger fired first.

Again the bay horse set back, fighting to free himself of the tie rope, and again it proved stronger than he was.

The outlaw fired as his body slammed rearward under impact. The other man stepped ahead, poised himself, then fired again. This time the outlaw's entire body arched, hung rigidly for a moment, then turned loose all over and spilled flat out and stone still.

The stranger's two shots had filled the rear section of the barn with gunsmoke and an acrid, cordite odor. He stood in it, cocked gun hanging at his side, looking. For quite a while he did nothing, not until the woman moaned, then he remained where he was while plugging out spent brass casings and thumbing in fresh rounds from his shell belt. After he had leathered the gun, he finally walked forward.

The bay horse eyed him with terror in both eyes. The man ignored the horse, ignored the woman, too, for a moment, toed the outlaw over onto his back, looked, then turned his back on him to lean and more gently ease the woman over. He saw the blood, its location, saw the chalkiness of her face, and spoke quietly. She

19

did not seem to hear. He laid a hand on her, gently shaking. She was as limp as rag. He considered her for a moment longer, then leaned, roughly gathered her into both arms, and straightened up — with a grunt — she was a lot heavier than he had expected.

CHAPTER
THREE

The wind rose with dusk. The day died early and the scent of turbulence, which was compounded of many things — moisture, dry-dead undergrowth, cured grass, and somewhere very far away a burn in the mountains — signified a storm was on its way, probably with lightning, the kind that had fired a distant forest. Darkness fell at 4:00p.m. Dust scurried in the yard between the impregnable log house and barn. The man had to abandon his hunt for lamp fuel and light candles. There were three coal-oil lamps, all dry, and, even when he looked in the cupboards, the closets and woodbox, he found no coal-oil can.

He stoked the stove so the house was warm, and he heated water to scrub himself in, then pitched it out and heated fresh water which he took to the bedroom where Margaret Fulmer lay, still passing back and forth between filmy consciousness and unconsciousness. He removed her coat and hat, loosened the muffler, tipped back his hat in the weak light, and bared her legs.

The bullet that had broken her right leg had hit her dead center in the upper leg, between the thigh and kneecap. He had found half a bottle of rye whiskey; some of it he poured sparingly into the hot water; some of it he tipped back his head to swallow, then he mixed some with more hot water, lifted her head, and trickled it down her throat. She gagged and he growled, shook her gently, and poured again until he had half a glassful down her. She fell back limply again, of which he approved as he pulled out a clasp knife, opened it, then tossed it into the basin of hot water, set his jaw hard, and went to work.

She sweated copiously, from the whiskey, from the heat in the house, and from whirls of sickening pain, but she lay as inert as a corpse while he cut through, mopped off the blood, located the big flattened lead slug, and pried it out. Then he took two more swallows of the whiskey and began forcing the swelling flesh closed. She had strong legs, muscular and golden-tanned. He shook his head, watched her sweat-shiny face, and went back to squeezing the ragged gash closed until he could bind it properly in place. As the bleeding diminished, he straightened back, winced at a pain from bending over too long, looked at her face again, then muttered to himself, and went to work making the larger bandage from a torn clean bed sheet.

The bleeding stopped but discoloration began faintly to show as he draped what remained of the torn bed sheet over her exposed upper legs, then tossed aside his hat, pulled up a rickety cane-bottomed chair, and sank into it, tired to the bone.

The wind continued to rise. Once, he went out back to gaze in the direction of the barn, solemn-eyed, then he sniffed the air, rolled and lit a smoke, shook his head, and spat. There was something else to be done but he had no intention of doing it tonight. Something he did have to do, though; he left the porch to head forward into the icy wind to look after it.

His horse was tied, head down, rump raised, in the final row of uneven timber over against the foothills. He got the animal and returned with it, tied it in a stall beside the big bay that looked around at the strange horse with friendly interest, then the man off-saddled, climbed to the loft to pitch down another couple of baits of that bone-dry cured meadow hay, and afterward he only glanced at the dead outlaw as he leaned into the wind on his way back to the house.

The heat was very welcome. He stood a moment by the stove, flexing stiffening fingers, then went to take another swallow of the whiskey — and forgot it as he stepped into the bedroom doorway because in the steady, soft glow of candles he saw the woman looking steadily at him.

He walked over without smiling, eyed her for a moment, then spoke.

"Do you remember what happened?"

She showed nothing in her face as she looked steadily upward. "I remember . . . he shot me."

"Yeah. Now, I'm going to mix you some whiskey and hot water."

"I don't touch whiskey."

"You're going to drink this, lady."

"I am not!"

He paused to regard her with personal interest for the first time, then he reached, snagged the chair to bedside, and sank down. "You lost a mite of blood, you've got a fever, and by now the pain had ought to be pretty bad. You're going to take a couple of shots if I have to pour it down you. Lady . . . in this case it's medicine."

She only moved her eyes. Her face was flushed and damp; her full, heavy lips were pulled flat from pain. She watched him without saying another word, until he half smiled and said: "You're going to need it."

Then she said: "It's the devil's medicine."

His gaze narrowed perceptibly. The world was full of them, evidently; people disliked whiskey, disapproved of it, for a hundred reasons, and he would find no fault with that, but he was also of the firm opinion that everything in the world had a purpose, including whiskey, so he said: "Lady, I'm trying to help you. There's no coal oil for the lamps, and, while I was lookin' for that, I also saw nothing but horse liniment . . . no laudanum or anything else . . . so it'll have to be the whiskey. Lady, take my word for it, you're going to feel a lot worse before you feel any better." He waited, and, when no response came, he slowly arose and went to the kitchen to get a tin cup three-quarters full of hot water that he took back with him, poured in the whiskey, and turned. She was watching his every move from bright, dry-hot eyes.

As he approached the bed, she said: "Who are you?"

He half smiled again. "After you take the medicine." He leaned to cushion her head under one arm to lift her partially. "It's not going to taste good. Most medicine don't. Just close your eyes and swallow."

Their eyes met and held. His were completely uncompromising. She opened her mouth and swallowed, rapidly, and water came into her eyes. He laid her gently back as she gasped, feebly turning her face away.

He considered the last swallow in the cup, tossed it off, then resumed his position in the chair, watching her. Normally she would be a very handsome woman. He reached to push back gently a thick coil of taffy hair and to use a scrap of bed sheet to dry her forehead and cheeks. As she turned back toward him, he smiled at her.

"We'll keep you warm and fed and flat down for a few days. By then we'd ought to know."

"Know what?"

"If you've lost too much blood and if there's going to be an infection set in."

She was silent a long time, watching him, but eventually she asked her previous question: "Who are you? Why were you out there?"

"My name is Chad Greene. I was hunting for Frank Garrett. I saw him ride around that town off to the northwest and shadowed him up along the foothills and on around here. I watched him looking this place over, but by the time I could get around and down here on foot, he had taken you to the barn. I watched that, and tried to get down here quicker . . . I heard the gunshot just as I was sprinting to the back door of the barn." He paused to shrug. "He shot you . . . and I shot him. That's about the size of it."

"He's dead?"

"Yes'm. If it don't freeze tonight, I'll borrow a shovel in the morning and plant him."

"Why were . . . you following him?"

"He's wanted in Idaho. Robbed two banks over around Fort Hall and shot three people. One of them lived, the other two died."

"You've been after him all that . . . time?"

He nodded. "Close to seven hundred miles, by my guess, and I was close half a dozen times, but he never gave me a chance until last night."

"You're a lawman?"

"Deputy U.S. Marshal."

She continued to look at him. He was not a youth; he could be about thirty-five, and he had strong, weathered features with friendly eyes, a pleasant smile, and the look to him of a man who would normally be good-natured. Under her unwavering regard he said: "His name was Frank Garrett, but he went by the name of Frank Helner part of the time. He's got quite a history."

She closed her eyes and opened them again as though each eyelid were very heavy. "How bad am I hurt, Mister Greene?"

"Broken right leg, ma'am. Bullet flattened on one part of the bone. I dug it out. You bled like a stuck hog."

"Mister Greene . . . ?"

"Yes, ma'am."

Her eyes closed, her body settled, and he watched her drift away, hoping she was sleeping and not unconscious again.

When she did not rouse, he arose and tiptoed back to shove another chunk of wood into the stove, then to stand listening. The wind was still at it, moaning around rafter ends, tumbling across the rooftop, whirling dust and the first few snowflakes.

He returned to the bedroom doorway to look at her. She was sleeping. Her chest rose and fell with an even cadence. He sighed, and went back by the stove to start a search for food.

There were nowhere nearly enough bottled vegetables to fill the cupboards. He had to settle for beans and ham rind, but to a very hungry man it was adequate; what mattered more than the quality of the food was the quantity of it. He found enough to heat and fill up on. Afterward he went out to fetch in an arm load of wood, and noticed the depleted condition of the woodshed. He stood a moment listening to the icy wind, judging its direction, watched the snowflakes whipping past in their wind-driven frenzy, and returned to the house.

He was tired and worn down, so when he sat in an old rocker in the semidarkness, surrounded by pleasant heat, he slept.

Not until a heavy silence replaced the plunging wind did he awaken to listen again, but this time there was not a sound. He waited a moment, then arose to crack the rear door and glance out.

The snowflakes were as large as spur rowels. They were dropping straight down. The world was hushed and dark, but it had warmed up a few degrees and that was something he was thankful for.

He went back to the bedroom doorway, saw the condition of some of the candles, and went in to snuff out the stubs and trim tallow from the others. When he turned, the handsome woman said: "Water . . . please."

Her fever was higher, her eyes were glassy and dry again. He helped her drink and went after a wet rag for her forehead. Then he sat down and looked at her. This, he thought, would probably be her worst day. If she still had this rising fever tomorrow, and perhaps the next day, the only thing to do was try and get her over to that town he had passed the day before. If they had a doctor over there . . . if . . . Few cow towns had physicians residing in them.

He looked around at the whiskey bottle. It was still a quarter full. He turned back and leaned to reverse the damp rag. She opened her eyes. "Mister Greene?" He answered, but perhaps she had only said his name to be sure who he was because she did not respond and closed her eyes again.

He loosened the bandage. Her leg was purple and huge, but the bleeding had stopped completely. He rearranged the bandage, covered her again, and this time he gently pulled a thick old worn quilt up over her, turned the hot rag again, and sat back, feeling helpless. A doctor no doubt would have known more to do; he was a manhunter and only knew about bullet wounds from having seen them before, from having treated a few, but beyond logical and cursory care he did not know what else to do.

Restlessness drove him outside for another arm load of wood. The snow *crunched* under foot and was still floating down, big, ragged flakes of it, and the hush was deeper now.

Eventually he went out to water and feed the horses. He dragged the dead outlaw into a tie stall and draped an ancient horse blanket over him, took the ivory-handled six-gun, the Winchester in the saddle boot, everything from the corpse's pockets, and returned to the house.

He put the weapons and personal effects upon a table and went to shove another burl into the woodbox of the stove, rummaged through the cupboards again for something to make her a gruel out of, and made oat porridge that was as thick as paste and about as tasteless. There was no sugar. He found a tin of molasses, poured some of that atop the gruel, found a bowl and spoon, and took this to the bedroom. But she was sleeping again, so he tiptoed back to the kitchen and ate the gruel himself. It was not as bad as it should have been. At least it ameliorated the hunger in his belly.

He kept the pot warming, and, when he went to the doorway about midday to look in, she was awake and crying.

He went to the chair, sat down, and reached for one of her hands. It was hot against his palm. She kept her face turned away until he mentioned eating, then she feebly turned her face toward him, hastily swallowing to hold back the tears.

"I'm not hungry."

He hadn't thought she would be. Not yet, anyway. "But you've got to eat anyway, ma'am. You'll be down to skin and bones if you don't. And you got to keep your strength up."

"Mister Greene . . . I don't care."

He had heard despair before, but not as solid as this. "You've got to care or you're just not going to get well," he told her reprovingly. "I'll get some porridge. It's not very good, but it'll stick to your ribs."

She clutched his fingers, holding him there.

"Did you ever know a man named Tom Fulmer, Mister Greene?"

"No, ma'am. Not that I recall."

"He went away to work on the railroad . . . two years ago." The tears came slowly again.

"Your husband?"

"Yes. We came out here four years ago to take up this claim. Tom worked for the blacksmith over at Hidatsa until work slackened, then he found a job laying ties for the railroad . . ."

"Two years ago? And he hasn't come back since?"

"Yes."

That would account for the empty woodshed, for the meager store of food in the cupboards, for her candles instead of coal-oil lamps, for a lot of things he had noticed. He thought of reassuring her, and lamely said: "Well, maybe the railroad sent him down to Wyoming or out to Idaho."

"He would have sent me a letter up at Hidatsa."

There was nothing else he knew to tell her so he looked at the hand he was holding, work-roughened, strong, and calloused. "Tell you what, Missus Fulmer

. . . you eat the gruel, and, when I can, I'll go ask around for him. That sound like a fair trade?"

She nodded, fighting the tears, and he leaned to take the damp cloth and dry her eyes, her cheeks with it, then reverse it, and place it gently back upon her forehead. And he smiled down at her.

"This'll be the worst porridge you ever ate," he said, freed his fingers, and arose to go back to the kitchen.

The wind was rising again. He went once to look out, saw the high, sullen heavens showing soiled rims around its far edges, and sighed aloud; the storm was breaking up. He rebarred the door and returned to the stove.

He was right; after one mouthful she made a feeble grimace of distaste, but that did not deter him. He spooned the full bowl down her, then laughed at the look she gave him. "I never could cook, ma'am. I had a partner once . . . we rode together for three years down in Colorado. He quit the work and got married. He used to tell folks I was the best man he had ever run across to cook up a batch of wolf bait."

She seemed almost ready to smile up at him.

Their glances held for a moment before he arose, empty bowl in his hand, and turned to leave the room. At the door she stopped him.

"Mister Greene?"

"Yes'm."

"You've got work to do."

He looked back at her. He had done the work — the assignment — he had set out to accomplish. It was lying in her log barn under a smelly old stained horse blanket. But all he said was: "With a foot of snow outside, ma'am, I can't go very far anyway. When things let up a little . . ."

He left the room.

CHAPTER
FOUR

There was another skiff of snow just before daybreak the following morning. Altogether, when he went out again to the woodshed, he estimated the snow depth at fourteen inches, not prohibitively deep if there had been work that had to be done, but if there was not that kind of work, then fourteen inches was just enough to keep folks inside. But the sun appeared, rather miraculously he thought, just after noon, bringing with it a completely unexpected and agreeable warmth.

The snow melted, especially atop the house roof that was also getting heat from below. Water trickled in little piddling rivulets from the rafters as Chad Greene examined Margaret Fulmer's leg, shook his head over the swelling and the discoloration, but seemed to find the fever was localized, then made a clean bandage after gently cleansing the leg.

When he finished and replaced the covering, the torn bed sheet, and finally the quilt, she avoided his gaze until he went to the kitchen and returned later with another bowl of that sticky gruel with molasses in it.

She ate stoically, this time. He pitied her and admired the degree of courage she was demonstrating. When she had cleaned the bowl, he set it aside, sat down, and said: "It's downright awful, isn't it?"

Her reply was curt and forthright. "Yes."

"Well, it's about gone." He leaned to feel her forehead, her cheeks, and her throat.

As he leaned back, she said: "Fever, Mister Greene?"

He did not think so. "Cool to the touch. Even around the wound you're cool to the touch. I was keeping my fingers crossed about infection." He leaned forward. "Do you know anything about splinting broken bones?"

She didn't. "Not a thing. Don't you?"

He grinned. "The reason I asked was because, if you don't, why then I reckon the splinting job I did on you will look pretty fair. But if you do know, it might look pretty bad."

"I will be all right, Mister Greene. I have a lot of confidence in you . . . and trust, too, I think."

He left her and went outside, out behind the barn where sun heat was always warmest because it bounced off the big log wall. The ground was cloyingly soft for the first foot of digging, then it turned crumbly damp the way it should be, easy digging and without rocks the farther down he went. At three feet he paused to climb out, lean in afternoon warmth, and rest. At five feet he quit, wrapped the dead outlaw in his ancient horse blanket, put him down, and began the tiresome chore of filling in the hole.

It was not especially hard work; it was steady, monotonous, and repetitive work that he was unable to conclude until about sunset. He did not mound the grave with any thought in mind of making it a thing for folks to remember; he mounded it to allow for settling, so that come next spring the gravesite would look no different than any ground back there.

Then he returned to the house to scrub and then comb his hair, dig out two flat sardine tins from his saddlebags, and prepare a meal on two plates around them. He was grinning at himself at his efforts to make a pleasing arrangement on the two plates so that the greasy little fish would be palatable to her, when she softly called. He went to the door. She was very thirsty.

She did not reprove him for not appearing all afternoon, but she asked if he would fill a bottle with water and leave it at the bedside for her.

Later, when he had to light the candles, then went back for their two plates, he smiled as he brought one over to her, set the other on the chair where he would eat at the bedside, and watched her expression.

Her eyes considered his artistry blankly for a moment, then slowly humor showed. She did not allow her mouth to show amusement, though, and, when she spoke, it was as if she felt he might be serious in his attempt to create a tempting meal for her.

"It looks wonderful, Mister Greene."

He propped her up, looked straight into her eyes, and shook his head. "You're not going to hurt my feelings by laughing. I laughed out in the kitchen. It's really a kind of joke. Our joke."

She still did not laugh, but she smiled and her eyes twinkled at him.

He sat beside her eating, waiting for her also to eat. She did, eventually, but in the fashion of someone who had no desire whatsoever for food.

He would have given a silver cartwheel for a cup of coffee after supper. The nearest coffee was over at Hidatsa. He knew that without being told.

All afternoon she had been lying there, thinking. Now she asked him how men hunted down other men. He knew instantly why she had enquired. As he explained a little of his work, he said: "It's almost impossible for a man to really disappear. Unless he starts out about a year ahead to deliberately do it. Even then, if manhunters got a fair description, they can usually find him. As for your husband . . . let's worry about that later. In a month or so when you're up again on the leg."

"But two years, Mister Greene . . ."

He was not impressed. "Five years, ma'am, six or seven years . . . if he worked for the railroad very long, he can most likely be found."

"What would it cost, Mister Greene?"

He hadn't been thinking in those terms; he was thinking of how often a hunt ended in some cow town cemetery, the manhunter standing in front of a stone with a name and some dates on it. A man who would abandon this particular woman, handsome and capable and likable as she was, was lying under a stone somewhere. Or else he was crazy.

"Mister Greene . . . ?"

"Yes'm? Oh, the cost? Darned if I know. Let's figure it all out later. Would you down some watered whiskey if I mixed it for you?"

She shook her head, so he went out to the kitchen and mixed it for himself, returned to take her plate, to hand her a towel to wipe her hands and face, and filled a basin with warm water for her.

She was as weak as a kitten. Just raising both hands to comb her hair, or to soap and rinse her face, made her pant for breath and lie back momentarily with both eyes closed.

He sipped his whiskey and they talked, not about anything in particular, at first, but eventually she told him about the big cow outfit that adjoined their meadow, and rough, hard-as-iron Grant Shelby who owned it.

"We have the only decent spring over on the foothill side of the range, Mister Greene. I guess Mister Shelby's been using our meadow and our spring all his life. He just never filed on it, and, when we did, then he came out and claimed he didn't like it. I guess something like this has happened before."

Chad Greene nodded. It not only had happened before, it was still happening in a lot of places over an awful lot of unsettled frontier range country.

"Last summer he made the only offer he's ever made. He would buy me out, Mister Greene. But the price wouldn't have been enough for me to buy a wagon and team to move off with."

He sipped and listened. There was nothing new to any of this, so far. He had heard about it a hundred times just as he was now hearing about it.

"And he runs cattle over you, Missus Fulmer?"

She paused at her drying to gaze at him. "Yes. You've seen this before?"

He nodded without answering, drained the glass, and set it aside. "Mind if I smoke in here?"

She smiled. "No. Tom smoked. That was something else I missed terribly . . . the smell of tobacco smoke of an evening after supper." She gathered her strength together and started brushing her hair again.

She was feeling much better. He was enormously relieved because, frankly, although he had hid it very well, he'd had misgivings. Bullets were not only lead, which was poisonous, but they were never clean. He'd heard somewhere that the percentage of people who survived being shot, especially if the bullet, or lead fragments, remained inside the flesh, had a very low survival rate.

That she was healthy and strong as an ox he had never doubted. Two years of just staying alive out here meant she'd had to work as hard as a man.

He smoked and watched her. Once, she cast a sidelong look in his direction — and blushed furiously. He pretended not to notice. In fact, the first day when he had performed his crude but incisive surgery, he had scarcely been aware of her as a woman, but now he was. Not just a woman, but a very handsome one; not pretty in the sense that dance-hall girls were pretty; frothy with rouged cheeks and red mouths, but handsome in the bone structure of her face, round and lovely in the strength and perfection of her features.

He leaned to smash out the cigarette, then arose to take their plates back to the kitchen. As she commonly did, she waited until he was at the door, then she spoke.

"Mister Greene . . . there's not much wood."

He nodded. He had it in mind to go forth tomorrow and, using his saddle horse and lariat, snake some deadfalls down closer to the yard for cutting up. "We'll get some," he told her, and went out to wash the dishes.

Frank Garrett's guns were still on the table, along with the other things he had brought into the house. He considered where to put them, then let that slide because it was nothing that he thought had to be cared for right now.

He went down to the barn to feed the horses, and later returned with his bedroll, that he made up on the floor of the living room side of the kitchen area. Those candles were wearing down fast, which one objection to tallow candles over wax ones. But in range country people could manufacture tallow candles easily and wax candles were expensive. Townsfolk used them, when they had to, but country folk, especially homesteaders, rarely could afford them.

He had no intention of making candles although the tin moulds were hanging from pegs on the kitchen wall. When he got a little more time, he would ride to town and buy a can of coal oil.

It did not bother him in the least that he was killing time here, which was one advantage of being a manhunter. No one had ever devised a way to estimate correctly how long it might take to run down fugitives, and in his particular job no one expected it to be done swiftly. He had no family, no reason to want to be elsewhere particularly. He worked out of Idaho, kept a room at a boarding house near Fort Hall, but spent very little time there.

His guarded guess was that the woman would be unable to do much for maybe three weeks, until she could at least limp around on that mending leg. He was reconciled to remaining that long, although in the back of his mind he knew winter could arrive any time now, and, if early storms arrived, too, it might be several weeks before he would be able to plow his way through snowfall to a town.

In the morning he went forth with the axe from the woodshed, his coat and gloves and muffler, his lariat and his scant knowledge of the north slope, to hunt up some deadfall logs, preferably fir or cedar, which would be dry enough despite the recent moisture, to make firewood.

The morning was cold but clear, and, although the ground was spongy, downright slippery in many places, his stout sorrel horse had little difficulty.

Someone, her husband no doubt, had snaked a lot of house logs from the lower elevations. There were plenty of stumps and no dry wood, so he had to go higher. That was when he came across horse tracks, and sat a long while examining them, then forgot about the wood for an hour or so while he followed them.

Whoever it had been, had been over here since the snowfall. That recent warmth had melted all snow except in small drifts in protected places. He guessed the rider had been through the day before, and that made him thoughtful because it was possible someone had seen him, may even have watched him digging that grave out behind the barn. The tracks left the timber around the curve and went westward after that, arrow-straight in the direction of the distant stage road.

He turned back, scouted for logs, found a good dead fir that was not too leaden, snaked it down with his lariat all the way to the yard, and happened to glance toward the house where a full head of smoke was rising from the stovepipe. He stood a moment wondering about that, guessed what it probably augured, and instead of crossing to the house, coiled his rope, stepped up, and returned to the slope to find another deadfall. He brought down four of them before the sun turned tarnished on its way across in the direction of the high-country peaks.

After the last log he rubbed down his perspiring horse, fed both animals, made a close inspection of the dead outlaw's big bay, patted the animal, and climbed to the loft to pitch down more of that brittle, dry hay. There was a fair supply of it, which was fortunate.

The sun was departing by the time he beat snow and dirt off, using his gloves and hat for this, and trooped across to the house.

The signs were abundantly evident that what he had guessed hours earlier had been correct. The woman had somehow got out to the kitchen. She had used up all four buckets of water, which meant she had probably bathed. He went to the bedroom door and looked in. She was sleeping like a log, her color good, her hair shiny, and her face freshly scrubbed. He smiled to himself and tiptoed away, easing down the blanket to the doorway.

If that had been a man lying in there with a broken leg, he would simply have remained steadfastly in bed. Women had a powerful urge to keep clean. He did not know a lot about them but he knew that much.

He stoked up the stove, pondered over what to prepare for supper, and was still pondering when she called softly out to him.

He went to stand in the doorway. She studied him for a moment, then said: "There's a razor in the cupboard beside where the candle moulds are hanging, Mister Greene."

He nodded, conscious of how he must look, not having shaved for a week now.

"And my husband's shaving mug still has some soap in it."

He said: "If you put weight on that leg, you can bust the healing parts and we'll have it all to do over again, ma'am."

She reddened slightly but did not take her eyes off him. "I was very careful."

The only way he knew she could have been very careful was to slide a chair ahead of her and not let the splinted leg touch the ground. But he did not scold, or even pursue this except to say: "I'll fetch the tin tub in here along with the hot water from the stove. Just tell me when you want it." Then he told her he'd snaked down four fir logs, and she smiled at him.

"Mister Greene . . . I'm very grateful."

He felt uncomfortable. "Well . . . anyway it's done. Maybe tomorrow I can find us some meat up there." He did not mention the tracks, but later, when they were eating together by feeble candlelight, he asked about the Shelby cow outfit.

"They want me to leave, I know that, Mister Greene, and I know they prowl around watching to see if I'm still here." She met his steady gaze with a level look. "I can't leave. Well, I have nothing to move out with. Once we had a team and a wagon. We had to sell them one autumn." She paused, considered the food, then looked up at him again. "If they'd make a decent offer, I'd sell to them. Tom won't be back."

It was the first time she had ever allowed herself to think this out loud. He saw the pain it cost her to say it now, and looked down to concentrate on his meal.

"We were married a year before we came out here from Illinois. We worked very hard making this house, the barn, the corrals and all. It kept getting harder but Tom . . . wouldn't give up. He wasn't the giving-up kind, Mister Greene. Nor was he the kind to just ride off and never even write."

He leaned to put the plate aside, saw the hot tears forming, and quickly said: "Let's just take it one thing at a time. You get up again, to start with, and meanwhile I'll hunt us some meat and cut wood. Sort of keep busy until you're able again." He waited a moment before also saying: "That town I saw the other day . . ."

"Hidatsa."

He nodded. "You have any friends over there?"

"Mister Greene, that's a cow town."

She did not have to explain what that meant. He had grown up in cow country. The bane of townsmen as well as range men in cow country was settlers. They rarely increased the trade for storekeepers and they invariably homesteaded land cattlemen had used free.

He smiled at her. "Well, in a few days I figure to ride over and get us a tin of coal oil. Those candles aren't going to last much longer."

"I have no money, Mister Greene."

He arose, still smiling at her. "I don't have a lot, but I've got enough."

Again she allowed him to get to the doorway with their plates in his hands before stopping him. "Mister Greene . . . I can't pay you back. And I don't like the idea of being beholden."

He turned. "Missus Fulmer, this isn't anything either one of us asked for, but it happened, and we'll make the best of it. As for being beholden . . . once I lay sick as a dog for three months in a cow camp. They kept me alive, fed my horse, and, when I was able to ride, they filled my saddle pockets. It sort of goes with the country, I guess." He walked out to the kitchen and had to make three trips to the spring to refill the buckets before he could wash their dishes.

44

And he kept thinking about that skulker who had been up there spying yesterday. It worried him, not because the watcher might have seen him burying Garrett, but because he did not like the idea of skulkers, whatever their business was or what their intentions might be.

CHAPTER
FIVE

Even the old towns, which were not more than a generation old in the Montana high country, had started out with log walls because the only building material in abundance came off the slopes and out through the roaded cañons where it was possible to cut uphill timber and roll it onto stripped-down running gears. But the new towns such as Hidatsa had not as yet made any attempt to veneer over the logs with civilized planed lumber. In fact, Hidatsa had once been an Army cantonment, not a fort, just a big sprawl of hutments and stables and wash sheds and mess halls. But the Army had been gone for some years now, part of the buildings had been torn down and set up closer in, forming a very wide single roadway.

Hidatsa was headquarters for all the cow outfits, and it also served the more distant mines. It was a bustling place, for the size of it; strangers were commonplace even this time of year when seasonal range riders had been paid off and had headed down south to escape a Montana winter. No one paid the slightest attention to Chad Greene when he rode in, tied up, and went into the big rambling old general store — once a barracks for non-commissioned officers — to buy a tin of coal oil, some tinned peaches and pears, some salt pork, and a bag of rock candy. His last purchase was a bag of coffee.

He saw the town constable, a big, thick, graying man in conversation across the road, and wondered about him, but did not cross over. The only person he talked to was the saloon man. Because it was midday, the saloon was almost empty. Three old men sat like owls near the iron stove, two chewing, one smoking a pipe, as motionless and silent as carvings.

The barman was a paunchy individual, friendly, with shrewd, knowledgeable eyes and a knack of worming information from his customers. When he brought a bottle and set it up, unopened, then returned for a half full one and a shot glass, he said: "You must be figurin' on wintering it out." He nodded at the unopened bottle.

Chad nodded, dropped one neat shot straight down, and pushed back the glass as he said: "I've wintered it out before. In Montana and also in Idaho."

"Work hereabouts, do you?" asked the genial older man.

"Sort of," the deputy U.S. lawman replied. "It looks like fair trapping and hunting country."

He had deliberately let this fall between them so the barman would place him as one of those range riders who trapped and hunted through the winter months to make their living. It was not an uncommon thing for range riders to do, providing they did not mind the short winter days and the everlasting cold.

"Been pretty well trapped out, so they tell me," confided the barman. "When I first came in here as a soldier fifteen years ago, there was trappers all over the mountains. Indians, *voyageurs* from across the line in Canada, and even some of them old American Fur Company men, with lodges full of kids and a fat squaw or two. But the last five, six years I don't think trapping's been too good."

"How about hunting?"

"Now that," responded the older man, smiling, "is something different. Folks hereabouts buy meat off pot hunters all winter long. Providin' the price ain't too high." He had pegged Chad to his private satisfaction. "You go high enough . . . when the snow ain't too deep . . . and you'll get plenty wapiti, elk, sometimes even a moose or two. And bear meat sells . . . cheap though." He refilled the glass for Chad, even though when it had been pushed away that signified that the drinker did not want another drink.

He shoved it back.

"On the house," he said. "You can make it, but you got to be careful you don't get caught up there in a blizzard, or maybe camp out and freeze your butt off."

Chad considered the second shot. The first one had tasted — and had burned — the way only green liquor could. He pulled the glass over as he said — "Shelby's outfit ever hire anyone for winter work?" — and lifted the glass.

The barman shook his head with emphasis. "Not that I ever heard of. He's tighter'n the bark on a tree. Tough, hard as iron, and don't part with a red penny until he sees there's goin' to be four pennies come back to him."

Chad turned the glass upside down this time. "He's got plenty of land and cattle. Must be a rich man, so why not spend a little of it?"

The barman eyed his customer with a speculative glance. "Mister, this is a darned poor man to talk about, especially in this town. He does all his trade in Hidatsa. All I can tell you is . . . ride out and brace him, if you want to. It'll be a waste of time but try it anyway, if you need winter work."

The green whiskey created a pleasant warmth all over. Chad leaned on the bar and slowly manufactured a cigarette. "I might do that, for a fact," he informed the saloon man. "I came across the northwest range, down across all those timbered hills, without seeing a single animal. And there's feed over there . . . and a hell of a fine all-year big spring. Seems to me, if he'd hire someone to winter watch, he could run a lot of cattle off that grass until the snow gets too deep."

The barman studied his customer. "Northwest range? Well, there's a settler over there. If you'd rode on the south slope, you'd have seen a big meadow with a log shack over there."

Chad lit up and exhaled. "Settler?"

"Yeah. Feller named Fulmer. He's been gone couple of years now but his woman's still hanging on. Old Shelby used to autumn cattle over there, until those folks took out a claim on that meadow and that big spring you spoke of. Now, he's settin' back and waiting. But you know, by God, that woman's hangin' on out there like grim death and by law he das'n't run over her." The barman leaned his paunch against the worn

49

wood. "I give the devil his due ... her due. Old Shelby's been waitin' two years, and she's still over there. Between us, I been expectin' to hear she had a fire. Got burnt out." The barman dropped a wise wink. "It's happened before."

Chad smiled. "Often, mister."

A pair of rough men stamped in pulling off lined thick big gloves. They were range cattlemen. The barman grunted and softly said: "Speak of the devil ... that shorter, grayer one is Grant Shelby. The other one, the bigger dark feller, is his range boss, Galt Hays." He moved slowly up along his bar to meet the pair of coated newcomers and Chad turned slightly to study them. The cowman was wearing a bright red muffler. His range boss was graying over the ears and had an unsmiling, slightly predatory, Indian-looking face.

Chad left some coins atop the bar and strolled back out into the thin but warming morning sunlight. He was ready to head back.

The gunny sack containing his purchases flopped gently as he walked his sorrel horse down the wide roadway out of town. He wished he'd had another few minutes with that saloon man. He was interested in Tom Fulmer. The trail would be as cold as ice, no doubt about that, but the place to pick it up would be right there in that town where he had worked for a while.

It took until mid-afternoon to get back to the big meadow, and, because of the autumn position of the sun, there were long shadows forming by the time he rounded the timbered slope and saw smoke rising from the tin pipe above the Fulmer cabin.

The bay horse softly nickered when he heard the sorrel coming. He was a friendly, guileless big animal. Chad turned them both out in one of the large rear corrals for exercise and trudged over to the house with his sack.

Margaret Fulmer called the moment he entered. "Is that you, Mister Greene?" Her voice had fear in it, so he stepped to the bedroom doorway after putting aside the sack and looked in.

She had that old shotgun aimed squarely at him. The last he remembered seeing that thing it had been out in the barn.

She turned it aside and hastily said: "I'm sorry. It's just that living alone for so long . . ."

He leaned there looking at her. "How did you get that thing?"

She had to lean to put the shotgun aside, and spoke without meeting his gaze. "I had all morning to get out there and back. And I was very careful. The ground's soggy but not frozen."

He walked into the room, shaking his head. She was tougher, more resolute than most men he had known. "Keep it up," he told her severely, "and odds are that you'll bust it again, Missus Fulmer. Anything you want . . . all you have to do is ask."

She colored a little. He had seen her heavy lips flatten before and understood that when she did it now she was annoyed, but this time he did not favor her. He sat down and waited until she met his glance, then

51

smiled. He had a very nice, gentle smile. Her expression softened a little toward him.

"I didn't really think of it until you'd been gone half the morning. Then I heard a horse whinny. I think it was the big bay in the barn. Then I began to worry."

His interest quickened but he said nothing about the horse. He, instead, asked how she felt. She looked good. Her only complaint was that her leg ached from being outside in the cold. He could have said something about that, but he didn't. He turned and went out to make supper for them. He filled two coal-oil lamps, lighted one in the kitchen, and took one to her bedroom. She looked pleased and smiled a little at the friendly, warm brightness.

Later, he brought her hot coffee, salt pork, and tinned peaches, and she swallowed twice, her eyes getting brighter by the moment as though she were going to cry, so he sat down, arranged her plate on the quilt, propped her up, and said: "You know, a person can get fatter'n a hog lying in bed and all."

She stared at him, until he laughed, then she laughed, too. The tears would not come, which was what he had been trying to prevent.

She ate, drank the black coffee, then leaned back, looking at him. "Don't you have a wife?" she asked.

He blinked in surprise. "No."

Her boldness did not appear to bother her. "You should have, Mister Greene."

He did not like this conversation, so he said: "When that horse whinnied . . . ? Was it shortly after I'd ridden away, or a long time after?"

"I'd say about two hours after." She watched his brow crease. "I doubt if he was whinnying for your horse, Mister Greene."

He doubted it, too, but all he said was: "Some saddle tramp up the slope passing through, maybe."

"Maybe. And maybe it was Galt Hays or Grant Shelby."

He shook his head at her. "Not unless they got wings. They both came into the bar in town while I was there."

"There have been other range riders . . ."

Sitting in the warm lamp glow, looking at her, he decided there probably had been. In fact, he thought it would be a pretty sorry specimen of a range rider who, having seen her once and knowing she lived here alone, would not drift over once in a while just to look. She was something to see, even propped in bed with a broken leg.

He thought of the wound but hesitated about examining it. When she had been too ill to care, it hadn't bothered her, or him, but she was recovering fast and now she would be terribly embarrassed, which would make him feel the same way.

It would have to be looked at though. As he arose to take their plates to the kitchen, he said: "Have you looked at the bandaging?"

She had. "Before I hobbled out to the barn for the shotgun."

"It's not red anywhere but right around the wound, is it?"

"No," she answered, and did not falter when she also said: "I can show you, Mister Greene."

He colored and shook his head and went into the kitchen.

CHAPTER
SIX

He foraged the slope but did not find any fresh tracks. Spent two hours scouting around up there before deciding it hadn't been there, if it had been anywhere, that some rider had prowled, so he went off to the east a mile where those same bulky hills folded around the wide meadow, and within thirty minutes had found where a rider had sat for quite a while, judging from horse droppings and trampled earth.

The bay horse was exonerated. For a while Chad had suspected the big bay had simply whinnied because he missed his barn mate.

On the ride back to the barn to off-saddle and turn his horse out in the weak sunshine, he wondered, less about the identity of the prowler than why he had not come down at least as far as the barn. He had not been up there before yesterday. At least he had not been over along the eastward slope so he probably had not witnessed the burial.

It was possible Grant Shelby had sent one of his year-around range men over to spy yesterday while Shelby and his foreman were in town. It seemed logical, since those other tracks he had discerned a few days back had not come down. Someone may have instructed this rider to remain out of sight, too. If this were the case, then it was likely that the most recent spy was also a Shelby rider.

He removed his hat and jacket, hung his shell belt and gun on a post nearby, spat on his hands, and went to work with the bucksaw. When he had cut five rounds, he split them. This was the way he had always made firewood, saw for a while, then rest up splitting, and, if he had been preparing for winter, he would have stacked the Vs of fir inside the shed, two down, one up, in order to get all the wood possible stacked under that roof, but he was not that particular now, so he simply pitched the wedge-shaped splits inside. He worked hard most of the day, sawing and splitting, grinned at his oncoming aches and at the way he had to pause every hour and rest. He had done nothing like this in a long time; a man got out of shape when all he normally did was ride. Hunt a little, in the autumn, but mostly just rode.

For once the sun seemed warm. He sweated out there, thought of the whiskey bottle he'd brought back from Hidatsa, derived satisfaction from the pleasure a cup of it with hot water would give him this evening after supper. Thought, too, of the bag of candy he'd brought back. She would smile about that tonight. She was a very pretty woman. Her smile made her even prettier.

The bucksaw was a bow of light steel with the blade between the lower ends of the bow. Someone — her husband no doubt — had not only kept it sharp, but had also tallowed the blade after using it, which everyone knew a man should do, but which few men actually bothered to do. It made a rasping, steady sound as it slid back and forth, dragging out curly wood rakers that fell at his feet, something he could watch with satisfaction. It was a pleasure to work with a sharp saw and a frustration to work with one that simply chewed its way through.

He sweated, and, after he had cut the fourth round from a dry cedar deadfall and leaned to lift the saw, something, a noise, an instinctive warning, maybe just a hunch, made him look up and backward. Two horsemen were sitting there, less than twenty feet away watching, their faces red-bronzed and weathered, their eyes reptilian steady and unblinking. One wore a bright red muffler tucked inside his riding coat and the other man was lean and raw-boned with flat high cheek bones and a flaring, high-bridged nose.

He stood a second just looking. They had evidently come across from the direction he had finally located sign, over east of the barn, and for that reason he had detected nothing because they had kept the barn between themselves and him until they came around from out back.

He had no idea how long they had been sitting there, but probably not very long. The rasping sound of the saw had completely masked their walking horses. He knew who they were. This would be the second time in two days he had seen them. As he leaned to prop the saw, he said — "'Morning, gents." — and neither moved closer to offer a hand, nor smiled. "What can I do for you?"

The shorter, heavier, and older man with the red muffler spoke. "Get on your horse, pack your other horse, and head out. Don't ask no questions, just do it. Today. Right now."

There was no loudness, no overt menace in the command, but there was a threat in the dark blue eyes.

If they thought one of those horses was his pack animal, then clearly they had made an incorrect but plausible deduction based on what they had seen, and not on what they might have known. They did not know about the dead outlaw.

Chad's belt and gun were draped over the post fifty feet away. "The woman's had an accident," he started to explain. "I'm making a little wood for her and sort of looking after things until she can get around again."

He might just as well have recited the alphabet. Grant Shelby said: "Today, cowboy. Right damned now. Get your butt in the saddle while you're still able to ride."

He still did not raise his voice.

Chad studied them. There was no way to do other than he had been ordered to do. These two were a long way from being novices and the best way for him to prove that would be to try something. His irritation came slowly, not so much with them as with himself for foolishly leaving his handgun out of reach, a cardinal — and often fatal — sin in his business. But he had no intention of doing as they said.

The axe was handy, as was the saw. Poor substitutes and both his antagonists had the tie-down thongs on their six-guns pulled loose, their coats unbuttoned.

Shelby said: "Now!"

Chad turned to pick up his hat and jacket. They sat, watching. He knew they would follow him to the barn, watch him saddle up. They would then discover there was no pack outfit for the second horse.

He was caught between a rock and a hard place. He was going to lose this round no matter what he did, and to a great degree it was his own fault, but he turned and shuffled across the yard.

If the woman had been up and around, she would probably have appeared with her scatter-gun. But that was not going to happen. Nothing helpful was going to happen.

He walked across the yard, heard them turn, and ride along behind him. He decided to make some kind of effort, fatal as it might be, because otherwise he was simply going to get into deeper trouble than he was now in already. He picked up the gait a little, reached the barn opening about fifteen feet ahead of them, heard them urging their horses, reached the opening, and jumped swiftly around to his right into the shadows of the barn. Both men outside swore and sprang down. He looked frantically for a weapon, any weapon at all, saw the pitchfork he had leaned at the foot of the loft ladder, grabbed it, and, as Galt Hays jumped ahead, gun swinging, Chad hurled the fork.

It missed Hays by inches, stuck into the doorway balk, and quivered. Hays recoiled, bumping into Grant Shelby, and he fired. Chad did not know whether he had been shot at or whether the trigger pull had been instinctive, but he ducked low and sprinted for the protection of a horse stall. Shelby cursed and also fired. This time there was no doubt he had aimed; wood flew from a stall partition just ahead of the ducking, dodging lawman. Galt snarled and ran ahead. He had his gun cocked and ready, and he was safe in what he was doing because Chad had no weapon to use against him. Shelby stepped just inside the door and yelled: "Kill the bastard, Galt!"

Chad was trying to keep wood between himself and Galt Hays as he ran for the rear barn opening. He had no plan except to get out of handgun range.

Galt yelled something that Chad did not make out, but he ducked, expecting a gunshot. It did not come but Galt did, long legs rising, heavily booted feet coming down hard. Chad risked a rearward look, saw the range boss come charging around a horse stall, and jumped sideways as Galt saw him and fired. This time the bullet struck solidly into dry wood with a rending sound. Galt cocked his gun as he lunged, and this time Chad did not run; he turned on the balls of his feet, drove in hard with both heels, and dived directly at the charging man.

Where they collided, the packed earthen floor was as hard as stone, and, as Hays went backward, he gasped and tried to bring his gun hand around before he fell with Chad on top of him.

From the doorway Grant Shelby called savagely: "Get him! Get the son-of-a-bitch!"

Chad lunged with both hands for the foreman's gun wrist, caught it, and heaved all his weight to press the arm back and to the ground. Hays swung with his other hand, swung again and again until the pain began to register on Chad Greene. In a combination of fury and desperation he raised up, put all his weight upon the gun wrist, and wrenched backward as hard as possible. The gun fell. Hays yelled as his hand bent farther back than it had been intended to bend, and bone *snapped*.

Shelby was coming. Chad heard his heavier footfalls and aimed one blasting blow at the twisted face below him, felt dazzling pain shoot all the way to his shoulder when bone ground into bone, then he rolled, grabbed for the gun, and kept rolling, but Shelby did not rush around the partition as his range boss had done. He halted for a moment, which was the time Chad needed to roll up onto one knee, aim, and fire. Wood flew and Shelby yelped. Then Chad sprang up and fled out through the rear barn opening.

For ten seconds there was not a sound inside the barn.

Chad did not run blindly to gain distance. He went around the north side of the barn and waited, trying to keep his breathing from being noisy as he sucked down big gulps of air.

There was still no sound from inside the barn.

He worried for fear Shelby might be stalking him from around front. He was exposed if anyone came toward him from either front or back. He eased closer to the back, expecting the attack, if it came, to come from around there. He waited what seemed half a lifetime, then had to bend over slightly to ease the pain in his soft parts where Galt Hays had repeatedly struck him with great force.

The moments turned into minutes. No one came from out back or from around in front. He sidled closer to the corner, peered around, saw nothing, and stepped back along the rear wall close to the barn opening. Finally he picked up a sound; there were horses moving somewhere beyond the barn. His own horse and the big bay were standing motionlessly in the rear corral, poised as though for flight, watching him with the unique intensity horses show when they are fearful without understanding what they should be fearful of.

The sound of those other horses picked up a little. They were louder but they were also diminishing. He stepped inside the barn, listening, then eased ahead toward the front keeping as much wood in front of him as was possible all the way to the front doorway.

Movement across the yard made him crouch. Margaret Fulmer was coming painfully and awkwardly out of the cabin with her shotgun, but using it as a crutch so she would not have to lower her injured leg to the floor.

Shelby and his range boss were riding in an easy lope toward the southwestern end of the meadow, Shelby supporting Galt Hays.

Margaret leaned on a porch upright and raised her shotgun. It would never reach that far so Chad called to her: "Let them go! Don't shoot!"

He was not concerned with whether she could hit them or not. That old double-barrel had a kick to it like an Army mule. It would knock her off balance and probably knock her down. The splinted leg would never survive that kind of fall. He called twice more, with more insistence each time.

She slowly lowered the gun as he stepped out of the barn, starting across the yard. She turned, leaned, and watched. When he got close, she said: "You're hurt."

He looked down. There was blood on his hand and on the front of his jacket. It must have come from the range boss's face.

He walked up beside her, looked out where the cowmen were growing small, and let all his breath out, then very slowly drew in a fresh, shallow breath. His ribs pained him, as did the muscles along the side Galt Hays had pummeled, but there was not a cut anywhere.

He forced a smile. "It was my fault. I didn't hear them until they were right there behind me."

She turned toward the door. "Come inside." As she preceded him, she said: "I heard the gunshots."

He eased the door closed and reached up to remove the hat that was not there; it was somewhere in the barn. Then he stepped to the table where Frank Garrett's guns were and tossed down the gun of Galt Hays, and shook his head.

CHAPTER
SEVEN

He wanted her to go back to bed but she refused, eased carefully down into a rocker, and watched him as he drew water from the stove kettle to wash in, continued to watch as he examined sore knuckles, and, when he ruefully turned, she said: "Mister Greene, it's not worth it. They'll kill you. They'll burn me out. And for what? I've been hanging on because Tom might come back . . . He's never coming back, Mister Greene. God, I never wanted less to face something than that, but after two years . . ."

He watched her slump slightly in the chair, the splinted leg awkwardly and stiffly thrust forward. He wanted to say something cheerful, at least sympathetic, but nothing came. He knew how to scoff, to insist her husband was coming back, but he did not believe it, had not in fact believed it after she told him how long Tom Fulmer had been gone.

He went out to get his belt gun, his coat, and to go in search of his hat, and, so as not to waste anything, on the return he brought back an arm load of dry cedar for the woodbox, stoked the stove, shed his outer garments, and went to stand in the bedroom doorway. She was back in bed and had her face averted, pressing into the pillow. He turned soundlessly and went back to the stove. This time he stripped to the waist and washed again, examined the sore side where discoloration was setting in, and swore under his breath.

Until right now he'd had no time to be really angry. Now he could afford it. He redressed, combed his hair, felt a fresh start of beard stubble, and, while gazing at himself in the kitchen mirror, he decided what his course of action would be. He was a professional manhunter. He had been dispassionately at it for seven years. He'd never had another goal, and, while he had never felt like standing on a box to tell the world about his trade, as a lawman under oath he had never felt ashamed of it, either. He had learned a lot of things about men in those seven years. Not merchants and storekeepers and other orderly folk whose lives spun out within the small confines of their law-abiding existence, but of range men and mountaineers and outlaws. If there was a trick to his trade he did not know, then probably no one else knew it, either, because he was still in one piece, still successfully running them to earth, and bringing them in. If there had been some ruse or trick he had overlooked, something outlaws knew and he did not know, he probably would not still be above ground; he would be under it.

As he lighted the lamps and started to make supper, he also considered the things available to him, now that open hostility existed. The idea that Shelby's outfit wanted the Fulmer meadow for its water at this end of the range, and also — but no doubt to a lesser degree

— the protected large meadow for late feed, had interested him exactly as similar situations had interested him elsewhere. But he had not considered himself in danger. He had rather thought it possible, once they saw him around the yard, they would stay away. An armed man on a claim was a lot less likely to be bothered than a lone woman. Evidently Grant Shelby did not operate like that. Or else the intrusion of a stranger aroused in him a desire to stop playing cat-and-mouse, to move in and get it over with. That had been his attitude when he'd come up behind Chad today.

Well, if that was the way this game was to be played, Chad knew the rules as well as anyone. There wasn't much difference between facing an outlaw on the Wanted list and facing a cowman who used the same renegade tactics. He knew the next move.

When he had their supper ready, he dropped the little bag of rock candy into a pocket, took the plates to her room, propped her up as though unaware of the red swollen eyes and flushed cheeks, and pulled over his chair as he said: "Sure getting cold out. But there's not a cloud up there."

She was not hungry. He sat down and started to eat, still not looking in her direction. "I guess Mister Shelby won't be back right away, and we can get the wood cut and stored and maybe bring in some meat. This time of year it could hang in the barn for a long while, until I got around to cutting it up." He finally looked over and smiled. "You think I'll ever make a cook?"

She sniffled and smiled, kept her face profiled to
him, and started to eat. "Maybe, Mister Greene . . . as
long as they put peaches and pears in tins, I think so."
She raised swimming eyes in a smile, and he laughed.
Things got easier for them both.

She said: "What really happened?"

"The feller named Galt came charging around a
partition and I was waiting for him. We went down. I
got his gun, hit him in the face, and ran like hell."

The parts he omitted did not require resurrection in
his view. The bloody face and the broken wrist were
unimportant in relation to the end result, which had
been that Grant Shelby had got his range boss across
leather and had headed home with him.

"What did Mister Shelby say to you, Chad?"

"To get on my horse and get away from here.
Something like that."

She finished her meal, solemn as a judge. "You
should do it."

He nodded. "In time."

"Chad, Grant Shelby has a terrible reputation among
the settlers."

She had not had to tell him that. He hadn't heard it
before but that hadn't been necessary, either, not after
he had seen Shelby near the woodshed today, had seen
the look on his face.

He dug out the little paper bag and offered it to her.
She looked from it to him, took a piece of the rock
candy, and laughed. This was the first candy she'd had
in two years.

It was named appropriately. It was like granite, but then it was not made to chew, just to hold in one's mouth as it dissolved. His eyes twinkled at her. "Always had a hankering for this stuff," he confided. "Sometimes I'll take a sack with me to suck on while I'm on the trail. When I was a kid, we didn't get much candy. Maybe, around Christmas time, sugared squash or sugared plums. I've always had a strong likin' for candy. And that's sort of silly in a grown man, isn't it?"

She shook her head at him, one cheek pushed far out. "I'm a grown woman and I have the same hankering . . . Mister Greene?"

"Yes'm."

"Where are you from? I know it's none of my business and it's bad manners to ask but . . ."

"It's all right, Missus Fulmer. I grew up in northern Arizona. My father had a trading post down there. My mother died when I was about six or seven. A big fat Navajo woman raised me . . . and she had a hand like a canoe paddle. When she'd say something once, and you didn't mind . . . *wham!*" He laughed.

"They're dead, then?"

"Yes. She died first. Stomach fever they called it. My paw died two years later. His heart just upped one night and quit while he was sleeping." Chad put the little paper bag on the bed and leaned back to roll a smoke and light it from the mantle tip of the lamp. As he leaned back, he said: "I ran mustangs to keep alive for a few years." He considered the tip of his smoke. "Then got into law work, and been in it ever since."

"You never farmed?"

He blinked. "Farmed? No, ma'am, I never farmed. Never particularly wanted to."

"Oh," she said softly, looking at the little paper bag in her lap.

He knew instantly he had said the wrong thing. Being honest was good policy, but being tactful was better, so he started out to qualify it by saying: "Where I grew up, there wasn't much farming country. Well, anyway no one did much of it. The Indians raised squash and corn . . . maize . . . and the Mexicans raised melons and peppers . . . stuff like that . . . but only for their own use. No one really farmed."

"It's a decent profession, Mister Greene."

He met her grave look with an expression of absolute agreement. "Yes'm, it sure is. Why, folks wouldn't be able to live in towns if someone didn't raise stuff for them to eat."

Her eyes twinkled. "But you don't think much of it as an occupation."

"Well, Missus Fulmer . . . no, I guess not. I worked on cow outfits, though, and that's sort of farming."

She laughed. "You don't have to humor me, Mister Greene. I know exactly how range men look at farmers. Anyway, Tom wanted to start with cattle out here on the homestead. He farmed back East, with his father and his uncles, but he wanted to be a cowman out here."

"The meadow's big enough, ma'am, and the water's good. The place is sort of protected from bad winds by the hills. A man could do a lot worse than start out with cattle here, for a fact. Of course . . ."

"There's Grant Shelby."

He smiled, trickled smoke, met her look head-on, and said: "Some folks live and learn, and other folks just live. Mister Shelby's got a lesson coming."

He took their plates to the kitchen, and, after washing them, drying his hands, and pitching his cigarette butt into the stove, he went over and examined the guns on the table. Galt's weapon was standard. Good enough and cared for, but the best gun had belonged to Frank Garrett. It was a custom-made gun, perfectly balanced with an easy hammer and a feather-light trigger pull. Someone had spent a lot of money making this gun as perfect as it was possible to make it.

She called to him. He put down the ivory-butted six-gun and stepped to the doorway. She was still propped up with soft lamp glow on her face making her look closer to sixteen than her mid-twenties. With a solemn expression she said: "I just understood what you said, Mister Greene. Please . . . don't go over there . . . please."

He considered his answer carefully, and chose to appease her by saying: "I don't figure there'll be any more trouble for a while. All you have to think about is that busted leg."

She kept looking straight at him. He got the feeling she was not likely to be diverted. He was getting to understand her better as the days passed. One thing he was confident of was that aside from courage enough for three people, and a dogged, unwavering determination, she had a tough mind.

"Mister Greene, my leg is getting much better." She did not mention whether it pained her or not; that was something else he knew about her: she did not complain, and although she was all woman — emotion brought tears — she was strong.

"But if something happened to you . . . I guess I'd have to limp over to town. I couldn't stay here, could I?"

He thought he knew what she was doing — making it appear that unless he stayed close, she would have to rely upon herself even though she was crippled. He sighed and gently smiled. "You're a connivin' female, Missus Fulmer."

Her smile came, bright and contagious. "All women are. We have to be. Please . . . don't go over there."

He answered truthfully. "I didn't figure on it. Care for some coffee?"

"No, thanks. Is it clouding up again?"

"No, ma'am, clear as a bell, and it's going to be bitter cold by morning."

He returned to the kitchen, stood gazing at that ivory-stocked six-gun, went over to palm it, handle it, finally put his own worn Colt atop the table and holster Garrett's gun. He practiced with it from different positions, different stances, and finally put it back atop the table, took the stub of a candle, removed his shell belt, and worked meticulously at waxing the inside of the holster.

A wolf called from the north slope, its fluting, lonely cry ringing faintly across the cold, star-bright night. There was no answer. Chad leaned, expecting one more call. It came, more lonely the second time, then the old lobo gave up and trotted on. The age-old war between stockmen and wolves had taken a heavy toll. The packs that had formerly roamed were now reduced to single animals. Like this one, which had been seeking a companion, the high country had become a very lonesome place.

Chad stoked the firebox, massaged his sore side, blew out his lamp, and went to the bedroll to lie in sooty darkness, thinking. Nothing was going to happen to him, he was confident of that. But on the off chance that it might — she was right. Not as right as she had attempted to make out; she would not have to hobble up to Hidatsa. She'd said that to wring a promise from him that he had avoided giving. But the hardship would be severe if he, too, failed to return.

But he would come back. Grant Shelby's actions had given Chad Greene a fair insight into how the man operated. He had not once tried to close in on Chad, even though Chad had been unarmed. But he had shouted encouragement to his range boss. Chad thought about that, and some other things, then sank down and slept like a log until a whispering wind along the eaves awakened him just ahead of dawn.

Outside it was bitterly cold, and silent. The hush was as deep as it would have been if it had snowed during the night. Bad hunting weather. Every footstep would *snap* a frozen twig or *crunch* through a rind of thin frost. He washed, shaved, stoked the stove, and went outside to feed the horses.

His sorrel horse was gone.

The corral was still barred and the big bay horse was listening for his footfalls and nickered to be fed. He took care of that, then leaned on the corral, studying the ground. It had been too hard to take a footprint, but not hard enough not to show the imprint of a horse wearing steel shoes. Someone had led his sorrel toward the east, in the direction of the forested slope over there.

The puzzling thing was why they had taken just the sorrel. He rolled and lit a smoke, waited for the first brightness to arrive, then without moving followed the horse sign as far as it was visible.

Inside, his saddle, bridle, and blanket were still in place in front of Garrett's outfit. Over at the house smoke was rising straight into the still, cold air. He stepped on the cigarette, swore, and crossed the yard.

Margaret was washing. He could hear the water in the basin as he worked over breakfast. When he called, she answered almost gaily, so he took their meal in and sat down, showing nothing on his face. There was no need for her to know, nor was it probable that she could throw any light on this mystery.

He told her he'd take his carbine and hunt the foothills. She reasonably assumed he meant he would be pot hunting, not manhunting. There was nothing about him to make her suspect he was mad all the way through.

Even if it were just an itinerant horse thief, which he did not believe for one moment, otherwise both horses would be gone, he was going to get his horse back. Not only was he fond of the sorrel, but he had a particular

73

aversion to thieves, horse thieves, cattle thieves, or any other kind of thieves.

The sun was up by the time he left the house, wearing his hat and coat and carrying the carbine. He knew everything that he now did would be visible if there were watchers, so he did exactly what he thought someone might expect him to do, he rigged out Garrett's big gentle bay horse, and rode out the back of the barn following the sorrel's tracks.

The air was like glass. Each time he looked dead ahead he could make out the separate limbs of trees along the upper slope, against the pale blue, flawless sky. The tracks went directly to the timber, something no horse would head for, especially at night, in a country where the smell of wolves, bears, and panthers lingered, unless he had been led over there. But there were no boot tracks. Even after he got in past the first ranks of tall trees where the ground was spongier, he found no human tracks.

He was confident someone had led his horse away, but until he was also in the timber his actions remained those of someone looking for a stray horse. Once he was able to utilize the shelter, though, he dismounted, tied the big bay, took his Winchester, removed his spurs, and hiked directly up the hill.

The tracks were not up there. They had turned southward about where he had tied the big bay. Nor did he turn southward to parallel them.

It was dingy in the forest despite bright sunshine elsewhere. It was also much colder than it had been out in the open after the sun had arrived. He blew on his

74

hands, selected a particularly shadowy place, and waited with all the patience of someone who knew exactly what he was doing.

There was no proof that he had been watched, and possibly his suspicion was incorrect, but the possibility of being incorrect in this suspicion was a lot less likely to provide difficulties than taking no precautions and suddenly finding out that he had made another mistake. One thing he knew now was that Grant Shelby was not the kind of a man to overlook what Chad had done to him the day before.

CHAPTER
EIGHT

It was a long wait and only the gregarious nature of the bay horse made him believe he was not wasting his time. The bay nickered. It did not whinny the way a horse might because it was lonely; it nickered the way a horse does when it scents another horse.

He stood motionlessly beside an old pine tree, covered in layered gloom. For a while he detected nothing, then came the measured cadence of a ridden horse crossing around from the north, below him perhaps thirty yards, each hoof fall snapping brittle, frozen pine needles and twigs. Except for two things, the frozen ground and the big bay horse, he might not have been warned.

The rider was a long time moving into sight. Evidently that nickering horse had stopped him for a moment or two. But eventually he came on cautiously, a carbine balanced across his lap, his head up as he peered down where the nickering sound had emanated.

Chad watched him with strong interest. He was not Galt Hays or Grant Shelby; the man was a complete stranger, but he was clearly not new to this area because, from time to time, he craned westward down the slope in the direction of the meadow. He knew the house and outbuildings, that were no longer visible up here, were out there, and he was stalking the big bay horse as surely as he was riding with a Winchester across his legs.

Chad had an idea who he might be. When the range rider began to angle downslope a little, probably because he had seen the bay horse, he was within carbine range. Chad utilized the slight interval when the man was looking in the opposite direction to slip downhill a little.

He was certain this man was not alone, or, if he was alone right this moment, there were others within shouting — or gunshot — distance. They, not the stranger on ahead, were Chad's worry.

Finally the cowboy was close enough to see the big bay clearly, to see he was tethered and alone. It was this moment Chad had been aiming toward. He was close enough to see the man's features when he swung in the saddle to look back, realizing when it was too late he had been trapped.

Chad lifted the carbine and aimed it. The rider saw movement, traced it out to a saddle gun barrel, traced it beyond to the man aiming at him, and froze where he was.

Chad did not raise his voice. "Where are the others?"

The cowboy seemed torn between trying a bluff and being truthful.

Chad cocked the carbine.

"Hold it, mister, I was going to tell you. They're on southward, waiting."

"Who's waiting, cowboy?"

"Mister Shelby. Them fellers with him."

"Galt Hays?"

"No. He didn't come along."

Chad lowered the carbine a little. "Shuck your Winchester. Good. Now your six-gun." When the cowboy was unarmed, Chad gestured to him. "Climb off. I guess shootin' you'd make too much noise."

"Hey!" exclaimed the cowboy. "Mister, I'm the only one can get you out of this."

Chad shook his head while shaking his hand with the saddle gun in it. "This is what'll get me out of it, buckaroo."

The rider did not relent. "The hell it will. They got your sorrel horse down south, around the hillside where Mister Shelby's waiting. They left the bay so's you'd do exactly what you did . . . ride up here. Only you smelled a trap, I reckon. Anyway . . . five minutes after you rode out, down there, a big feller named Shandon come up on the blind side of the house."

Chad lowered the Winchester as he listened. Shelby had indeed planned well, which should have been no surprise. Commonly men like Grant Shelby were good planners, and very careful supervisors of their plots and schemes. "This Shandon," he said to the cowboy. "He's to wait inside the house and nail me if I happen to come back?"

"Naw. You ain't comin' back, not if Mister Shelby sees you. Shandon's to get the woman out of there, bundle her into some blankets, and fire the place. Both house and barn."

Chad smiled. "You sure do work for a fine, upstandin' man. What's your name?"

"Ed Scaggs."

"Ed, turn downhill and lead your horse and don't make any more noise than you can help. And tell me . . . who else was supposed to get in behind me to make sure I followed those horse tracks down to Mister Shelby?"

"Just me. There were three other riders farther along, though, to make sure you don't turn back once you're close to where Mister Shelby's waiting."

Chad gestured. "Quietly now."

After the disarmed range rider turned to obey and lead off downhill, Chad yanked loose the shank restricting his own animal and followed. They made noise, it was unavoidable since the ground up in here was still frozen, and they also moved in and out among the trees, something else that was noticeable. The best Chad could do was keep the bay horse between his body and the southward slope, where an attack would evidently arrive from, if one came at all.

At the fringe of trees his captive halted to turn and look quizzically back. Chad said: "Where's Shandon?"

"He'll be over there, you can bet on it. Maybe he hid his horse around front or maybe in the barn, but he'll be over there."

Evidently Shandon was someone who inspired respect. In this particular cowboy anyway, but then anyone with a gun in his hand could probably have done that; Ed Scaggs had the open, guileless face and the bovine eyes of a man who took orders, did his work, and because of an otherwise uninspired spirit could readily admire men with more strength and resolve.

Chad said: "Show me where Shelby is. Point out the place."

Scaggs faintly frowned, confounded by this order that he could not obey. "I can't point it out. He's on around the side hill, a mile or a little more. On around to the southeast."

"You can't see the place from here?"

"Hell, no. It's better'n a mile on around . . ."

"Get on your horse, Ed, and ride at a walk down out of here across to the cabin. When you reach the yard, call Shandon out. Tell him to get his horse and follow you because old Shelby says for him to. Tell him you think there's been a change in plans. When he asks if Shelby caught me . . . tell him yes. You got that?"

Ed Scaggs understood it; he was just a long way from being happy over having to do it. He shifted from one booted foot to the other. "Listen, mister, why'n't you just climb on that big bay horse and poke on around through the trees in the other direction and just keep on goin' because sure as hell Mister Shelby's goin' to nail your topknot to the barn if you don't."

It was said quietly, in a tone that had not been either tough or antagonistic. Ed Scaggs thought he was giving very sound advice, and in fact maybe he was, but it was not advice Chad Greene wanted right now; it was movement. He pointed to the house. "Ride over there, Ed, and do like I told you. Sit out in the yard, don't dismount, and don't go inside the house. Sit out where

I can pick you off like a crow on the fence, and get Shandon to follow you back over here . . . Ed?"

"All right," the cowboy mumbled, and swung up. He looked down. "You want to know something, mister? You're makin' the god-damnedest mistake of your whole life." He lifted his reins and turned.

The sun was climbing, the ground was thawing, had in fact already softened out where Ed Scaggs rode, and there was a pleasant, golden quality to the day as Chad leaned aside his saddle gun, rolled and lit a smoke, then hooked the saddle gun through the bend of his arm, and wondered just how much of what Scaggs had been directed to do he would remember.

He remembered to halt in plain sight in the yard between house and barn evidently, because, as he called over to the house, he reined to a halt.

Chad could not see Shandon very well, but he saw enough. The man who stepped out of the house to take a wide-legged stance was better than six feet tall and as broad as a mature oak. He had a tied-down gun but it did not seem to Chad Greene that he needed it. He was one of those powerful, big, heavy men made of pure bone and gristle and muscle. Chad understood Ed Scaggs's feeling about Shandon.

As he smoked and watched, Scaggs and the big man on the porch spoke back and forth, then Shandon swore, and this time the words carried. Something had angered the big man. Chad could guess about that as he dumped his smoke and stamped it out.

Shandon started across the yard, slamming his feet hard down in obvious rage. But he did obey, and that was what had worried Chad right from the start. If he hadn't, if he'd retreated back into the house . . . But it hadn't happened. Evidently when Grant Shelby hired them, he did so according to their ability and willingness to do exactly as they were told.

Chad considered the rear porch, the long, gray, log back wall of the house. He could guess about Margaret Fulmer's reaction when someone she had no doubt thought would be Chad stepped to the bedroom doorway — and took away her scatter-gun.

But a more pressing concern was just how long Grant Shelby was going to wait around there, out of sight, before he got suspicious and sent someone to investigate.

Two men appeared, riding slowly across the meadow. Chad shook his head. Sometimes a man was lucky. Chad's luck had been to encounter Ed Scaggs, an unimaginative man of loyalty whose actual inherent feelings did not go very deep, nor were they rooted in the yeastiness of most range men. If, for example, he had encountered Shandon coming along to keep track of him, as he went tracking his sorrel horse, things undoubtedly would not have progressed as they were now doing. Some people called it cleverness or shrewdness; Chad had been hunting men long enough to know it was more than that, and it rarely happened the same way twice.

He picked up the carbine and eased to his right a couple of yards where he could watch the slow progress of the horsemen better. Shelby was going to get impatient soon now. The question was whether he might send someone back who would see Shandon and Scaggs crossing the meadow. It was a chance that could not be avoided.

Ed Scaggs came up close to the trees and looked dead ahead where he had last seen Chad Greene, then he walked his horse on up as Chad came in from their right, holding the Winchester low across his body in both hands. Shandon saw him first and pulled back to a dead halt. He was a man of quick perception. He turned toward Scaggs.

"Ed, you son-of-a-bitch!"

Chad snarled: "Keep your hands atop that saddle horn and shut your damned mouth!"

Shandon turned slowly to study the man with the saddle gun aimed at him. He was not a person who yielded easily. His face reddened. He was a bear of a man who, undoubtedly, had faced few things he had feared in his lifetime. The Winchester kept him from moving, but the moment it was not pointed in his direction . . .

"Reach back and toss down that Colt," Chad ordered, cocking the Winchester.

Shandon sat like stone, skeptically eyeing his captor. Chad was using up time with this confrontation. Time was all he had, really, and he did not mean to see it dissipated to his personal peril.

"I'll blow you out of that saddle, Shandon!"

The big range man reached down slowly and tossed away his Colt, but his expression was deadly and his gaze never once left Chad.

"Ed, get down!"

Scaggs obeyed easily, also watching Chad, but with a more detached, accommodating expression.

"Get out of the way, Ed. Shandon, swing off and keep facing me."

They both dismounted, Ed first, then the big man. Shandon's cold fury was lessening as the fact of his betrayal was replaced by a crafty, calculating expression. He finally spoke to Chad.

"You ain't goin' to make it, cowboy. You bought yourself a headboard yesterday when you hurt Galt Hays."

Chad gestured. "Take his horse, Ed, and lead it out of the way." For a moment Scaggs stared, then in a rising tone he said: "You aren't goin' to shoot him, for Christ's sake! That'd be murder."

"Get the god-damned horse out of the way!" snarled Greene, and, as Ed moved to obey, his face turning gray as he moved to take the reins from Shandon, the big man began to change, to look steadily at Chad Greene with an expression that was changing. It did not show fear; it showed something akin to incredulity. He said: "By God, mister, now wait a minute . . ."

Chad told him to turn, to face the meadow. Shandon acted as though he might not obey. Chad swore at him. Shandon turned. Chad stepped soundlessly over the soggy pine needles and swung hard.

Shandon's hat was driven down over his ears, his knees turned loose, and he fell in a big mound of inert human being.

Ed's breath whistled out.

"Tie him," Chad ordered. "Ed, use his belt and your belt. Arms behind his back and ankles belted tight. And use his bandanna to muzzle him. Move, damn it!"

CHAPTER
NINE

Shandon resembled a bear in man's clothing as he lay limply on his side. He badly needed a haircut and his upper body was massively thick.

Chad watched Ed truss the large man, made sure it was well done, then he pointed to Shandon's horse. "Dump the saddle and bridle."

Ed looked up. "Turn him loose?"

"Yeah, and damn you, move!"

Scaggs freed the big horse and waved his hat. The horse did not turn and charge; he turned, but he only trotted a few yards, then settled to a walk out where the grass was tallest. There, he stopped to browse.

Ed turned and saw the speculative look on his captor's face. He swallowed and said: "Listen, mister, I take a man's pay, I do his work, but that don't include gettin' shot, nor shootin' other folks."

"How about burning them out, Ed?"

"Mister, he never told me to do that. He sent Shandon." Scaggs worked up a feeble smile. "Tell you what, mister . . . you just let me ride off and I'll step right out of this mess and keep right on riding."

Chad motioned with the Winchester. They were wasting more time. "Get up there, keep your mouth closed, and walk ahead of me on around the slope like you were supposed to do . . . like you were shaggin' me."

Ed swung up but looked troubled. "We're going to meet the other fellers. And you ain't out front. What do I say about that?"

Chad ignored the question. "Walk the horse, Ed, and keep him on the trail because I'll be directly behind you on foot. You're going to cover me. Now walk out."

Ed wanted to say something; judging from his expression, he wanted to protest. Chad swore, Ed settled forward, and resignedly poked along.

The frozen ground was turning punky. The sun reached down through in some places, and, where heat reached, there was mud with rivulets of running frost turned to water. Elsewhere, although the thaw had set in, sunlight did not reach lower than thick pine tops.

Ed's horse was a quiet, tractable, fatalistic brown horse with a snip. He had no idea where he was going but had all the faith in the world in the judgment of the rider on his back. When he heard something up ahead, he raised his head only a little to gaze from liquid-soft brown eyes. Chad missed this at first. Ed may have guessed as much because suddenly Scaggs called ahead. His voice was high, slightly shrill, and insistent, as though having incompatible armed men this close, one behind, one ahead, he wanted to do all possible to protect himself.

"Curly? That you, Curly?"

Chad got closer to the back of Ed's horse.

A gruff voice said: "Naw. It's me, Ed. It's Erwin . . . Hey, where's that son-of-a-bitch who's supposed to be in front of you?"

Ed was desperate. "Where's Mister Shelby? I thought he'd be right hereabouts somewhere."

"He's a piece on back around the slope. Where's that feller hurt Galt yesterday?"

Chad stepped away from the horse. "Here, mister." He angled up the saddle gun barrel.

Erwin was an old range man, graying and lined, sparse and warped. He considered Chad and the saddle gun without so much as a grunt. Then he looked over at Scaggs. Ed made a little gesture of helplessness. "Couldn't do nothin' else, Erwin."

The cowboy sighed and fixed his attention upon Chad. "Mister," he said in the most matter-of-fact voice imaginable, "if you got one lick of sense, you'll shag-butt out of here as fast as you can."

Chad's answer was soft, but curt. "I'm fresh out of a mood for advice. Get off the horse. Get . . . off!"

Erwin dismounted, ignoring Scaggs. "It's your play, mister. From now."

"Shuck the six-gun and the saddle gun."

Erwin dutifully obeyed, but being careful to place his weapons where the ground was at least fairly dry.

"Now turn and lead the way back to where Shelby is."

Erwin blinked. "You crazy? There's three of them around there. Mister Shelby and . . ."

"Just step ahead of your horse, and walk. Don't get cute and don't try to signal them when we get around there."

Erwin and Ed exchanged a look. Ed shrugged and Erwin turned, clearly of the opinion that shortly now it was all going to be over; the maniac back yonder would be dead in the damned mud.

But they had scarcely begun to move when three riders came around through the pines, uphill a short distance. They were moving, which helped Chad locate them, but by now the soggy ground muffled rather than accentuated most sounds so he did not really hear them until someone whistled. He thought it was Erwin, up ahead, but who whistled was not as important as what the whistle seemed to signify, because at once one of those uphill riders yelled and swung off on the far side of his horse.

Chad jumped to the big bole of a bull pine at about the same time Ed Scaggs yelled up the hill: "Fer Christ's sake be careful, it's me 'n' Erwin!"

But Erwin had dived, headfirst, down the hill to roll up behind some small trees as he yelled to the men up the hill. Chad had five men against him now, with two of them being unarmed. He saw someone up the hill drop flat with a six-gun in hand. He fired, levered up, and fired again over where that first man had jumped off on the uphill side of his horse.

He did not allow any of the armed ones to get set. He could fire a Winchester as though it were a Gatling gun. He had only the bullets in the magazine with no way to reload, but what he was doing was making them root into the mud and press belly down. They did it; none of them fired back. When he had one bullet left, he sought a fair target, squeezed off that last round, then hurled his saddle gun at the broad rump of Ed Scaggs's horse. The animal, already fidgeting, gave a tremendous spring into the air and lit, head bogged, four legs as stiff as steel. Scaggs sailed over the beast's head.

Chad was moving before the horse started to buck, ducking and bobbing back and forth among the trees on a retreating course.

He gained time. Enough, he hoped, and kept moving as swiftly and as indirectly as an Indian, back the way he had come. Someone up ahead was spurring a horse to get parallel up the hill. Chad heard the cursing and the scrabbling of shod hoofs, turned straight down the hill until he was within the final few rows of trees, and the man up the hill dashed past, offering Chad just one scant glimpse. The man was too distant for Colt fire.

Chad now had one of them to the north, the others still southward. He smiled and worked his way soundlessly almost back to the bay horse whose head was up, little thoroughbred-type ears moving, brown eyes looking and showing full interest, along with a good measure of uneasiness. Chad crouched, scooped a stone, and pitched it over upon the far side of the horse. Immediately the bay swung to look over there. Chad systematically blocked in square yards of uphill forest shadow. He was as sure that man was up there waiting for him to reach the bay horse as he was sure of his own name.

But the man did not respond to the stone falling. Only the bay horse was duped by that.

The man up there was waiting for just one thing — movement. Otherwise, in the shadowy, mottled gloom a man could not detect even another human being thirty feet away.

Chad had also to await movement, but in his situation he could not wait long. He may have completely upset the other riders but that condition was no more than very temporary. He studied the trees nearest him, selected those which were very close to one another, and crawled between them through cold mud, and slowly, not swiftly, until he had Shandon in sight. He spat and crawled closer, saw Shandon's mighty back arching in a powerful attempt to break his leather bonds. No man could have broken those two belts without leverage and Shandon could get none.

Chad kept crawling, concentrating on Shandon. When he could reach him, he rapped the big cowboy on the temple, and, when Shandon briefly wilted, Chad freed his ankles from the leather belt, then he crawled backward in more mud until he was near the big bay horse.

Shandon flopped, threshed, worked his legs, and slowly recovered from being stunned. Then he groaned and, kicking around, managed to get into a sitting position. It was this movement that brought the gunshot. Shandon came half up off the ground, twisting his body.

Chad saw only this much from the corner of his eye. He'd been waiting for the uphill gun flash, the smoke, and maybe movement. All he had to fire at was the muzzle blast. He squeezed a shot, hauled back, and squeezed off a second one.

There was no return shot. In fact, for as long as the echo lasted, there was not a sound anywhere at all.

He leathered the Colt, yanked his tie down snug, sprang up, and hurled himself at the bay horse. The animal was only half able to see in that direction. Chad called at the horse and lunged for the tied reins as the horse swung in surprise, then pulled back. He jerked Chad off his feet. He swore at the horse, staggering sideways and waited for the animal to rush past. When it happened, he aimed with both hands for the horn and let the rush of the horse, the momentum as the beast broke past, to hurl him into the saddle.

He was nearly brained twice by low limbs. As they broke clear, he went down the off side of the horse, praying the cinch would not allow the saddle to turn, and with one boot behind the cantle emulated an old-time bronco side rider. He expected gunfire as the big bay flattened in his race toward the only familiar place of safety in sight, Fulmer's long barn.

A gunshot did eventually break the hush back along the forested lower slope, but it was too late. That bay horse had been bred to run. He was the best life insurance his former outlaw owner could buy or steal. He was very fast and very powerful. By the time someone got into position to see Chad out there speeding across the meadow, to determine that it was not just a free-running saddle animal, and to fire, the bay and his side-riding companion were within 100 yards of the barn.

Chad looked ahead, decided the horse was not going to stop, was probably going to charge blindly right into the barn and probably out the front opening, eased up a little, freed himself, and, when he was close enough, he let go. The ground was already close, so striking it was not likely to cause damage, but the momentum sent him rolling end over end, flopping like a rag doll, and once he hit his left shoulder against something that did not yield, probably a half-buried rock, because the contact was jolting. He felt as though he had been unmercifully kicked by a mule by the time he finally halted. He was within thirty feet of the barn.

The bay horse did not do as Chad had expected. He set back on his hunches, slid into the barn, and halted in there. Chad was crawling toward the rear wall when he heard the horse snort. Whatever that signified, Chad had no interest in finding out, but something had halted the horse in a flinging stop.

He got inside, turned away from the sunshine, felt log wall on his right, and eased over to lean upon it.

Margaret Fulmer was standing there. She had Chad's discarded six-gun from the kitchen table shoved into her shirt front, and she was holding a carbine in both hands. She had watched his race from the side hill, and, although he did not know it, she had been seeking a target when that man back yonder had fired one round, then had not fired again.

Chad leaned to pull loose his tie down. His shoulder hurt and some of the breath had been knocked out of him. She came over and stood, leaning with her injured leg off the ground, looking anxiously downward.

He wanted to smile but had first to suck back big lungs full of air, to clear the fogginess from his vision and the murkiness from his mind.

She sounded as though she were a quarter mile distant when she said: "Chad, you're hurt. Your shoulder is bleeding!"

He nodded, unaware that both his shirt and skin had been torn. With fresh breath in his body he gathered himself to lean and peer around the rear opening.

She said: "They're not coming. There's no one out there. What . . . did you do?"

"Caught a couple, then got caught," he told her, minimizing words to save strength and breath. "You're all right?"

"Yes. Well . . . yes, I'm all right. I thought it was you out on the porch and . . ."

"Shandon," he interrupted to say. "Shelby is out there. Five or six of them I think."

She turned a flinty face toward the yonder empty, sun-lighted meadow. "I'm going to get the constable. I'm going to sign a complaint against Grant Shelby, and, cowman or not, the constable's got to serve it."

Chad was feeling less dazed. He was also very aware of the pain in his shoulder along with the resurgent pain in his side, which had been bothering him before, the result of that fight he'd had with Galt Hays. He turned to reach with his right hand for leverage along the wall, and straightened. The bay horse, now that the excitement was all over, had marched into his stall and was picking through the chaff left from earlier meals. He was sweaty and still saddled and bridled, but he was not at all concerned with other things inside the log barn.

Chad hobbled over to pull off the bridle and saddle. Margaret swung herself expertly along, using the Winchester as a short crutch or a long walking stick. When Chad finished, he said: "We'd better try for the house. Keep the barn between us and the side hill." He looked at her. "Can you make it?"

She could, she said, and hobbled past to demonstrate how adept she was using the Winchester as a substitute for her injured leg.

He finally smiled.

They got to the edge of the front wall. With a cleared mind he speculated about the cowmen. They would either gather up their men, their horses, and leave, or they would try to get along the northerly slope and watch the yard for someone to try and cross it.

The bad part was that Chad could run but his companion could not even limp very fast. He took a position on her right, the side that would be exposed to the north slope, and said: "Let's see how far we get."

He had been inside the barn too long, he thought. It had taken too much time for him to recover enough to get back on his feet. If those cattlemen out back had got reorganized, they would surely by now be rushing around through the hills to get up where they could watch the yard.

The alternative was to stay in the barn where they would eventually have to come out. He offered her his hand and she shook her head, looked up briefly to meet his glance, then started hitching along. She moved as fast as was possible; it was slower than a child would have moved.

He had his holstered Colt but the range was far too great. She had a loaded Winchester, but without it she could not hobble along. He swore under his breath, turned to rake the north slope for any kind of movement, any kind of sun-bright reflection off gun-barrel steel, and had to force himself not to move faster than she was moving. It seemed to take hours. The heat was pleasant, for a change. If he would have had time to think about it, or had been in the mood for thinking of it, he might have recognized that the weather had changed, was no longer so bitterly cold with occasional threatening clouds. That most magnificent of all seasons was arriving. Indian summer.

He had both sweat and blood running under his torn shirt by the time they reached the porch, and he turned to help her whether she liked it or not up the wide, low steps.

The door was ajar. He let her step past him and enter, then he turned for a final look, feeling sweat and pain and enormous relief all mix together, as the land up yonder where trees stood along the north side hill remained silent, still, and evidently empty because Shelby and his range men had not got around there yet.

CHAPTER
TEN

She eased down and looked over at him. He was filthy with mud the full length of his clothing, his shirt was torn, and there was blood from the injured shoulder. His hat was gone, his face was streaked, and he was grinning crookedly.

She smiled back.

"Nice day," he said. "Looks like we might be in for some decent weather."

She could not quite come up to his mood so she simply nodded her head as he arose and went over to see if the firebox had a decent fire in it. It didn't, so he stoked it, and went over to set a pan of water to heat, then he stripped off his soggy, mud-encrusted shirt, and she watched him examine the bruised shoulder.

He was a muscular man with a tone of light tan to his body. She watched his awkward movements for a moment, then said: "Bring a cloth and some water over here."

He had to kneel, and, until the water on the stove got warm, she worked with cold water and a clean rag to cleanse gently his scratched shoulder. It had looked much worse than it really was. She used warm water, later, and would have bandaged the wound, but he told her a few bloody little scratches weren't worth it, and arose, also saying: "You know Shelby better than I do. Will he skulk around here tonight?"

She had no idea, but as he went back to sit down opposite her, she said: "We've got to get away from here, Chad. Maybe he won't come back tonight, but I'm sure he will tomorrow."

He sat gazing at her. After a while he said: "It's a good idea. I just don't think we'd make it. Shelby got shellacked today. Seems to me our best bet is to stay right here inside the house . . . but keep close watch. Shandon was supposed to burn you out."

She already knew that. Shandon had taunted her about it. "He terrified me," she confided.

For a moment Chad felt impelled to say what he thought had happened to the big range rider, but he was not sure, had not actually seen the bullet strike Shandon, and had not afterward lingered to make sure, so he said nothing.

He made her go to her bed and lie down. Later, with the outside warmth beginning, finally, to seep through into the house, he washed his muddy trousers and shirt, found an old pair of trousers that had belonged to her husband, and used a bit of twine to make a clothes line near the stove.

He also had a drink of watered whiskey, and after a look around from the rear door he sat down to clean the ivory-stocked six-gun, and finally, the last thing he did, cleaned and oiled his boots that had also been soggy with mud.

It should have been much later than it was. By the time his clothes were dry enough to put back on, the whiskey, the warmth, all the desperate physical exertion, and finally the day-long warmth made him drowsy. He made a light meal for them and took it to her bedroom doorway. She was sound asleep, so he took it back to the kitchen and ate a little himself, then slipped out the front door to stand where shadows partially shielded him to make a long study of the hills to the north.

He saw nothing until about an hour later, when he went for another look and saw a horseman riding boldly across the open country from the northwest. The man had no booted saddle gun and he was riding slowly, the way a man might who wanted to take full advantage of the magnificent, unseasonable warmth. It was not Shelby, and, if it were one of his men, he certainly was making no effort to conceal his approach.

Chad went inside, belted the shell belt back around his waist, considered awakening Margaret, decided against it, and returned to the front porch. The rider was close enough now for Chad to make out everything but his features. He was still too distant for that.

None of the horses Chad had seen today had been black. This man was astride a black horse. Also, all the riders he had formerly encountered had been carrying saddle-booted Winchesters. This man had only a belt gun.

Then the rider got close enough to be recognized and Chad pursed his lips. It was the town constable from Hidatsa.

The man walked his horse down into the yard, and, when Chad stepped to the edge of the porch, the constable reined in that direction, studied Chad with interest, and, when he reined down to a halt, he said: "'Mornin' mister. My name's Ralph Harris. I'm lawman over at Hidatsa." He smiled but not very strongly, and settled two big, gloved hands atop the saddle horn, waiting.

Chad gave his name and that was all, then he invited the peace officer to alight, and, as Ralph Harris got down and walked on up to loop reins at the tie rack, Chad pulled a slat-bottomed chair forward and motioned for the lawman to sit in it.

Constable Harris had his badge on his vest front and the tie down was hanging loosely on his holstered Colt. He was a large man, graying slightly around the ears and temples, and, as he climbed the two broad porch steps, drawing off his gloves, he said: "Some packers was comin' through, mister, and heard a reg'lar war bein' fought out here." Constable Harris sat, pushed out thick legs, and raised hard, appraising gray eyes to Chad Greene. "You hear a lot of gunfire this morning?"

Maybe Constable Harris was telling the truth and maybe he was easing into his topic prudently, feeling his way, but in either case he was here, and that meant there were no longer going to be just Chad and Margaret, and Shelby's cow outfit, involved.

"There was a little trouble," he admitted to the lawman. "I think a feller named Shandon got shot, and maybe another feller or two up in the timber east of the barn, out back."

Constable Harris did not even blink. "Shot. That'd be Grant Shelby's man, Shandon?"

"Yeah." Chad studied the heavy, coarse features trying to make an accurate judgment of the big, older man in front of him.

"What happened?" asked the peace officer, without raising his voice, and looking steadily at Greene.

"I guess it goes back a ways," explained Chad, and told Constable Harris all he knew, including his first day on the Fulmer claim. The only thing he omitted was the outlaw named Garrett. When he had finished, Constable Harris sighed, considered scuffed boot toes for a moment, then said: "And you, friend . . . what about you?"

"I just told you," Chad replied. "I was riding through."

"I see. And Miz Fulmer . . . you said she broke her leg. Is she inside?"

Chad nodded. "Right now she's sleeping."

Harris continued to study his boot toes. "Well, maybe Grant shouldn't have come over onto her land," he said rather quietly. "On the other hand, friend, we got open range in this territory and a cowman's entitled to go where he figures his cattle might be."

Chad was shaking his head before the lawman finished. "There are no cattle over here. There's no sign any have been over here for a hell of a long while, Constable."

Harris slowly looked up. "I guess I better get Shelby's version, hadn't I?" he said quietly. "About your fight with Galt Hays, Shelby's foreman . . . you picked a bad one to tussle with."

Chad smiled without a shred of humor. "Sometimes, Constable, that's a two-way road."

Harris continued to appraise the stocky, strong man sitting on the porch rail. "We don't tolerate trouble around here, Mister Greene."

"But you tolerate folks defending themselves."

"If that's what it was."

Chad's humorless smile lingered. "And you figure you'll get truth about that from Grant Shelby?"

"I'll get something," replied the lawman, shoving up to his feet and reaching unconsciously to settle his shell belt. "I've been at this business a long while, Mister Greene. I get lied to, I expect, more'n anyone else for a hunnert miles in all directions. And I didn't come down in the last rain." Harris made a wry smile. "Now then . . . apart from my position as lawman, I'll give you some good advice. Think about this, Mister Greene. Grant Shelby is just about our biggest cowman around. He can hire men to do just about anything he's willin' to pay 'em to do." Harris walked to the steps and down them before finishing. "You tangled with a bad man to begin with." He looked up where Chad was still sitting on the railing.

"So you figure I'd ought to saddle up and ride." Chad shook his head slightly. "Mister Shelby's still got my sorrel horse, Constable. That amounts to horse theft."

"*Pshaw*, Mister Greene. Grant's got a couple hunnert head of horses. If he's got your horse, it's some kind of accident, that's all. He's no common horse thief."

"When you go over there, Constable, look up a rider named Scaggs. Ask him about that sorrel horse. How they got it and why they took it. To bait me into their gun sights, just exactly as I told you."

Ralph Harris tugged gloves from under his shell belt and slowly pulled them on. "I'll do that," he agreed. "I know Scaggs. He's been workin' for Mister Shelby for couple years now." Having finished with the gloves, Harris glanced out and around. "Sure looks like we're goin' to get an Injun summer, after all, don't it?" He turned and smiled at Chad. "The feller at the saloon said he talked to you the other day, said you was figurin' on trappin' or pot huntin' through the winter."

Chad wondered how Constable Harris had matched him to the man the saloon man had talked to, since neither of them had even known his name at that time. Evidently the lawman was less dense and lax than he pretended to be.

"Well, Mister Greene, you could probably make it through, huntin' and trappin' but not around here. You shoot a man who works for Grant Shelby, and cripple up another one, an' come the spring thaws someone'll maybe find your carcass in a snowdrift. Now, all I'm sayin' is . . ."

"I know what you're saying, Constable. Thanks for the advice."

They looked at each other for another moment, then the lawman nodded, walked on, turned his horse, swung up, and rode out of the yard on a diagonal southwesterly course. In the direction of Shelby's cow outfit.

For a while Chad sat watching the constable grow small, then he rolled and lit a smoke, looked up along the hillside, felt the unseasonable warmth, and eventually went back inside.

Later, after he had lit the lamps and made supper, and took it in to set a tray on Margaret's lap, he calmly related his discussion with the town constable and Margaret, who had slept through it, looked at him with large eyes.

"He's a former range man," she said. "He's a friend of Grant Shelby."

Chad sat down and started to eat. His body ached and where cloth touched his scratched shoulder there was a sensitive area. "I guess," he told her, "we'll have to wait and see about that peace officer. He knows what his job calls for him to do. So do I. We'll just sort of wait and see what he does."

"Did you tell him about Garrett?"

"Nope."

"Did you tell him who you are . . . a U.S. marshal?"

"Nope." He grinned at her. "Eat your supper. For now anyway, we can rest a little, and for a darned fact I could sure use a little rest."

She watched him eat, seemed ready to say more, then did as he had said, started to eat. She was half through before she spoke again. "I wish we had a team and a wagon."

He looked up. "You're not going to run. Why should you?"

"Because . . . they'll kill you and burn me out. We'll lose anyway, Chad."

"We didn't lose today. Shelby did."

"Next time he won't try to bait you up into the hills away from the yard. He'll have a bushwhacker lie up there and when you . . ."

"I think I'd like a little water with whiskey in it," he said, arising. "Can I fix you one?"

She shook her head, then, as he reached the door, she said: "Yes, please. But a very weak one."

He went to the kitchen, filled two tin cups, weakened hers, and stood a moment, gazing at the table where the guns were lying. He had guessed right this morning. There had been a spy along the hills; his sorrel horse had been taken to draw him away from the homestead into a bushwhack. Being right once made him speculate further.

Grant Shelby had tangled with a puma today, had tangled with one the day before. So far, Grant Shelby had got the worst of it, and, since he was not the kind of man who reacted with blind fury, Chad guessed he would do nothing tomorrow. Maybe for the next few days he would do nothing. But as that lawman had said, he was a bad man to make an enemy of, and he could hire men to do whatever he wanted done. What it amounted to, then, Chad told himself, was that he probably could make out for the next day or two, but after that he was going to have more trouble. The best way for someone to act under those circumstances was exactly as Chad had acted today: not wait for trouble, go out, take the initiative, and make trouble first.

He took her drink back with him, sat down, and said: "How's the leg coming?"

"It hurts." She sampled the drink, found it weak enough, and swallowed a little of it. "It bled a little today."

That came as no surprise. "I'm grateful to you for being in the barn," he told her, and smiled. "We make a pretty fair team of wildcats."

She smiled, reddened a little, and drank the rest of her watered whiskey. "At least Grant Shelby wasn't able to walk over you or burn me out." She gazed at him, the heightened color very becoming. "But I have to look at it another way, too. What happens when you leave?"

He had no answer to that except the weak one he offered her. "I guess we could say that'll be up to Constable Harris."

"Then I might as well pack as soon as I can walk again." She leaned to hand him back the empty cup. Their eyes met and held. He cleared his throat and turned to set the cups aside. "Mind if I smoke?"

"Please do." She watched him roll the cigarette, studied him, and, while he was lighting up, she said: "There are some work shirts behind the old blanket in that storeroom off the kitchen. They're worn, but at least they're not as torn as the one you're wearing."

He trickled smoke. "Thanks." He met her gaze. He'd thought, briefly, of asking Constable Harris about her husband this afternoon, but it had not seemed the thing to do, so he'd refrained. But now he thought the next time they met he would ask.

One thing was clear. Even without harassing cattlemen, she could not stay out here alone much longer. Maybe it was her only home, as she'd told him once, but if a really bad Montana winter arrived — and one would eventually, they always had — she'd be snowed in without the means to survive.

She jolted him free of his private thoughts when she said: "What are you thinking?"

For no real reason, he blushed, so he turned to pick up the cups and arise from the chair. "Just sort of pondering about things," he told her, paused to look into her tilted face, then said: "This just isn't the country for a woman alone, Margaret. You've been lucky so far. Sure, you can put up vegetables, but that empty woodshed can finish you if we get ten-foot drifts between here and Hidatsa."

"One time you say no one can run me off, Chad, and the next time you say I can't make it alone out here."

"No one's going to run you off, but Mother Nature could freeze you to death in your blankets," he told her. "It's not folks that worry me, it's the winters. We've got Indian summer now. Maybe it'll last a week or two, but winter's coming."

"You snaked in some logs, Chad."

He gazed at her. She was tough. He had to smile a little. "All right. We'll get the wood split and stored and maybe we'll get in a little meat." He turned to leave, then turned back. "You should've been a man, Margaret."

She did not return his smile as she said: "Would that have been better?"

He felt the sudden change between them. It may have been in the atmosphere before but he had never felt it as he did now. He blushed and said — "No, ma'am." — and ducked out of the room, hurrying to the kitchen.

CHAPTER
ELEVEN

He split wood in the morning with a carbine leaning close by and with his belted Colt lying always within reach, and even then he worried about a bushwhacker being up in the northward timber. But he'd have to have a rifle; no carbine or six-gun could reach all the way to the yard, and to add a little protection the woodshed was partially in the way of a sniper. But it did not make him feel relaxed at all, so when he had finished with one log, had split the wood, and had pitched it inside the shed, he went down to the barn to turn the bay out back, and did not hear her call from the house until she had called three times.

He went to the front doorway. She was using a chair to lean on over there in the porch shadows as she called again: "There's a rider coming!"

He went back for the carbine, then walked to the house. She was waiting just inside the door, with Galt Hays's six-gun hanging at her side. He shook his head. If that leg ever healed properly, it would be a miracle. "Go back and lie down," he told her, but the look on her face told him he might just as well have asked her to fly to the moon. She hitched over to the front door.

The horseman was riding a big black horse. This time he had a booted saddle gun. Chad leaned his Winchester just inside the door, pulled loose his tie down, and stepped outside. Margaret closed the door — almost closed it — and stood motionlessly behind it as Constable Harris rode up, nodded, and swung off without waiting to be invited to alight.

He did not smile and his gaze at the man on the porch had no warmth in it at all. "I found your sorrel horse," he said. "Shelby didn't have him. He was wanderin' loose between here and Shelby's home place. Wandered off, I expect."

"Sure he did. Opened and closed the corral, too," Chad said, motioning for Ralph Harris to take the same chair again, but this time the lawman walked up onto the porch facing Chad without even looking in the direction of the chair.

"Shandon's dead," he announced, and waited for some kind of reaction. All he got was a close look as Chad eased down upon the railing.

"Did you get the man who shot him?"

Constable Harris avoided a direct answer. "Shelby's got another man over there hurt. He was up the hill and someone laid his cheek open as neat as though they'd done it with a knife."

"Too bad," stated Chad. "Did you talk to Scaggs?"

"No. He drew his time and rode south."

They looked steadily at one another for a moment before the town constable spoke again. "And you never told me about no grave, Mister Greene."

"Who said there was one, Mister Harris?"

"Feller rides for Mister Shelby was lookin' for cattle along the east hillsides and saw it out back of the barn, plumb fresh and mounded."

"Hell. In the first place there were no cattle along the hillside and haven't been. In the second place, that man couldn't see a grave from there . . . but he sure as hell could if he skulked down here in the night and stole my sorrel horse out of the corral . . . and closed the corral gate after himself."

"Just answer me flat out . . . is there a grave?"

"Yes."

Constable Harris may not have been expecting that answer. He pushed out his cheeks with a big breath of air, then let it all out. "Who'd you bury back yonder?"

"Man calling himself Frank Helner. His real name was Frank Garrett."

"Garrett? Frank Garrett? I got a dodger for a man by that name."

Chad made a decision, slowly, reached inside a pocket, and palmed his deputy U.S. marshal's badge. Ralph Harris stared at it a long time, then looked up. "You . . . ?"

"Yeah, I've been after Garrett since midsummer. He's wanted in Idaho for murder, attempted murder, and bank robbery." Chad dropped the badge back into its pocket and continued to sit on the railing.

Finally Constable Harris went to the slat-bottomed chair. "Why'n hell didn't you tell me you was a U.S. lawman yesterday?"

"Because it didn't have anything to do with what we talked about yesterday."

111

"The hell it didn't. Grant Shelby said you were some kind of fugitive and he was goin' over to town today and make up a cowman posse and come down here and get you."

"When did he tell you that?"

"Yesterday. Late yesterday afternoon, just before I left his place to head for home."

They exchanged a knowing look. Chad said: "That means today."

The lawman looked unhappy, and no doubt felt unhappy. He fidgeted from time to time. Finally he said — "You should have told me." — and got up out of the chair, running a narrowed gaze out in the direction of his town. "God damn," he muttered, and went down to the yard and over to his black horse. He said it again, out there, swung up, and without another look toward the house eared his animal over into a long lope.

Margaret opened the door. "He was upset," she said, leaning to look out where Constable Harris was covering ground.

Chad sat in thought for a while. It was past noon, getting along toward mid-afternoon. If Grant Shelby had been in Hidatsa this morning, he should have been over here by now. But if he'd had to go over the countryside to make up his cowman posse, it might take longer. He might, in fact, not even be able to get back to the Fulmer place until perhaps this evening or in the morning.

Chad turned from gazing across the empty land and said: "I guess Mister Harris is going to try and find Shelby and stop him."

Margaret was sanguine about that. "He'll tell him you are a federal marshal, but I wouldn't care to wager money he can stop Grant Shelby."

They went inside. Chad went after several arm loads of wood, filled the box, and shoved a couple of knotty burls into the firebox of the stove, then he went down to the barn to feed the bay horse. His sorrel was out back, standing in reflected heat, head down, drowsing.

Chad stood a long while just looking at his horse. The animal might have come around here by himself. Horses occasionally came back. They just did not very often do it, and, if Constable Harris had brought the horse back, he would have said so. Maybe Harris hadn't returned the horse. Chad walked out, opened the corral, and let the sorrel walk past before closing the gate and turning again to study tracks. This time, as before, there were no boot tracks, but this time, because the ground was spongy, there should have been — if a two-legged critter had led the horse over here.

He shook his head and went inside to climb aloft and pitch down another bait of dry hay.

The sun sank. It might have provided the world of upper Montana with heat this day, but it was still bound by ancient rules, and at this time of year it dropped like a plummet once it got low enough. It was still autumn whether the days were warm or not.

Darkness followed swiftly. Unlike midsummer and late springtime, when the sun sank now, there was a brief interlude that hardly qualified as dusk, then nightfall came.

Chad had not done what he had planned last night. Instead, he had made firewood, and had wasted the afternoon with Constable Harris.

He returned to the house to find Margaret working at the stove, her splinted leg hitched so that she could lean without putting her weight on it on the floor. He shook his head but said nothing. He was beginning to understand more and more about her.

She turned, flashing him a little, questioning look. He said: "Nothing. Quiet out there. Except that my sorrel horse was behind the barn. I corralled him and fed them both."

She kept gazing questioningly at him. "He returned by himself?"

Chad went over to watch her work at making their supper. "I guess he did." He smiled into her tipped-up face. "Anyway, there's no sign Shelby sent him back."

She went back to work. She was making some kind of stew using one of her few remaining bottles of put-up deer meat.

She was a remarkable cook. When they sat to eat, the stew was as good as any stew Chad had ever eaten, yet she had lacked most of the real essentials for making a good stew.

He smiled across the table at her. No man in his right mind would ever leave this woman, let alone leave and remain away two years.

He sighed. He'd had another chance to ask the Hidatsa lawman about her husband, and had not asked.

She produced the little bedraggled paper sack of rock candy. He had not thought about it again after leaving it in her lap. She had only eaten two or three pieces. She said — "Dessert." — and kept her head lowered.

Afterward, he helped with the dishes and admonished her about being on her feet too soon and too long. She turned to look at him. "You look a little used up."

He'd had no reason to guess how he looked to her, but in fact he felt almost normal by this time, a full day after his adventures with the Shelby outfit. Even those ribs he had favored after Galt Hays had pummeled them so unmercifully were only slightly sore now. The scratched shoulder was discolored and there was swelling, but he had been able to use a saw and axe today. He said: "I think we're getting along fairly well for a couple of cripples." And laughed.

She smiled up at him. Her hair shone in the lamplight. She must have brushed and brushed it. She had also scrubbed; her cheeks shone and her rounded, strong chin looked soft enough to touch. She let both hands rest on the edge of the dented old wash pan and kept looking straight up at him. She did not have to work very hard at this; he was about average height and she was tall and sturdy.

"You have no idea how much I owe you, Chad, and I have no idea how I'll ever be able to repay you."

He was vigorously drying a tin cup on a clean flour sack dishtowel, thinking of Grant Shelby. He stopped rubbing and looked up.

There was not a sound inside the house or outside it. Even the customary little vagrant breeze that scrabbled along the eaves was not around. He could feel the

115

change in himself, the strange sensation of warmth and difficulty, of delightful confusion and growing anxiety.

"You don't owe me anything, Margaret. Those bullheads weren't after you as much as they were after me. They wanted to run me off. It was a personal thing."

She kept looking at him, taffy hair showing a dull shine in the light, full mouth loose and gentle, liquid soft eyes steady as stone.

"I'm going to miss you, Chad."

He pulled in a silent big lung full of air and returned to vigorously drying the tin cup, which had been thoroughly dry for a minute. He looked at it, set it upon the shelf, and leaned to take the next one from the drain board.

He knew what he wanted to say, knew exactly how he wanted to say it, too, but until she said — "I'm sorry." — and half turned back to the dishpan he held it back. Then, watching her solemn-sad round profile, he said: "Well, I guess it hasn't really been just a man's resentment about being punched a little that's kept me here. Maybe in a while we'll be able to find out about your husband. Margaret, it's not seemly for me to say anything until then. Is it?"

She did not look up again but she shook her head when she answered. "I expect it's not."

They finished the dishes. She went to lie down and rest her leg. He went outside to smoke and look at the vaulted vast sweep of a star-filled night, and, regardless of how their difficulties turned out, he knew their personal relationship could not be the same again.

He had to sort that out. He had known his share of women and he had never felt the least inclination to settle down — with or without a woman — although last year he'd felt a little excluded, a little lonely and out of place when he'd visited his old riding partner down in Colorado, had met his wife and seen their child, and listened to his old partner talk about the beef herd he was building up.

There was another thing. Something he had only admitted to himself. He was tiring. It took longer now to roll out on icy mornings and longer to leave warm saloons and cafés. It seemed the days and the trails were longer and harder.

He dropped the smoke, grinned ruefully at the picture of himself he was painting in his imagination, cast a final look at the magnificent, serene night, and went indoors.

CHAPTER
TWELVE

He half-expected Grant Shelby to appear in the evening, or afterward, in the stillness of late night, but nothing happened that night. When he finally bedded down, he had rationalized Shelby's latest dilemma. Undoubtedly, after having been hurt twice by Chad, Shelby would gladly have overrun the Fulmer place with torch and guns. But he could not enlist very many responsible stockmen for something like that regardless of how they also felt about settlers. Not and do what Shelby no doubt had in mind — plain murder.

Some, of course, would ride with him. To various cattlemen, settlers meant different things; it depended upon their principles and their ethics whether they would deliberately burn a woman out and murder the man who was protecting her. But Shelby's biggest mistake was to let Constable Harris know what he intended to do. No lawman, regardless of his sympathies, could responsibly stand by and watch murder and arson being committed. If there were such a lawman, he would not be able to stay long in one location. Townsmen would be angry over a murder if not entirely incensed about arson.

Shelby, it was beginning to dawn on Chad Greene, was a fool. Maybe he was a very successful range stockman, but all that guaranteed was that in this one line of endeavor he was capable. It did not mean he was particularly clever at anything else. The world was full of half-smart people. Chad had noticed years earlier that big landholders and other successful people were overly compensated in an ability to do just one thing successfully. Invariably they were unequipped to succeed at something else. Shelby was a big range cowman. As a heroic leader of gun-handy range riders, he was not very good.

Chad was still turning all this over in his mind when he fell asleep and did not open his eyes again until just before first light. A little wind had awakened him. He listened to it for a moment, then sighed. Without being conscious of it, he had been balancing upon the thinnest edge of wakefulness during his night-long rest.

He arose and fired up the stove, went out back to clean up, shave, and prepare for the new day, and saw a horseman sitting in plain sight halfway between the house and the northward foothills.

He put down Tom Fulmer's razor, set aside the towel and chunk of brown soap, exchanged a look with that motionless figure, then shook his head, raised an arm in salute, and beckoned the horseman on over.

It was that young range rider named Scaggs who had left the Shelby place. At least that was what Constable Harris had reported.

Chad, shirtless and naked from the waist up, leaned and nodded gravely as the young cowboy rode up. "'Mornin', Mister Scaggs."

The rider grinned. "'Mornin', Mister Greene. Goin' to be another fine day. Seems like this time of year ever' once in a while . . ."

"Mister Scaggs, when I see a man sitting like you were doing, I usually think of Indian scouts. And the constable from over at Hidatsa said you'd pulled out."

"Well, yeah, I sort of pulled out. I wasn't going to let no one get me killed because they hated someone else . . . someone I never seen and didn't even know. And, Mister Greene, you sure gave Mister Shelby a real lot of trouble, and he's not the kind of a man to let someone do . . ."

"Why were you just sitting out there, Mister Scaggs?"

The cowboy smiled, which he seemed to do easily, maybe even unconsciously. "Well, I got to thinkin' and figured . . . hell, I ain't no coward, Mister Greene, and . . . hell, it just didn't look seemly, Mister Shelby with all the fellers he's got, an' as many more hangin' around town he can hire, makin' war against one hurt feller and a woman."

They looked steadily at one another. Chad pointed. "Put up your horse in the barn, Mister Scaggs, if you're figurin' on staying. There's some old dust-dry hay in the loft. Feed him and come on back."

He watched the lanky young cowboy turn and ride across the yard. A ruse? Some trick of Grant Shelby's? No. Scaggs wasn't the type. He wasn't devious by

120

nature, and he wasn't mean or overbearing, things it would take to become part of Shelby's schemes. Chad sighed, filled the basin, rubbed brown soap over his face, tested the razor blade on the hair of his forearm, and went to work.

Later, when Scaggs ambled back from the barn, he said he had pitched feed to the sorrel and the bay, too, then he leaned his booted saddle gun against the railing, shoved back his hat, and watched Chad finish up. He methodically rolled a smoke, lit it, and turned to study the north slope. "Colder'n hell up there in the early morning," he said casually. "A man hires out to ride, and first thing he knows he's skulkin' around like a lousy Indian." He turned back, trickling smoke. "You sure come on as one hell of a surprise to old Shelby."

Chad toweled off and looked at the younger man. "You figure to hang around?"

Scaggs considered the ash tip of his cigarette. "Well, the weather's turned out nice, ain't it?" he said, and raised guileless eyes. "You got objections?"

"No, I guess not. But maybe you'd ought to know Shelby's rounding up a herd of range cattlemen to come over."

Scaggs blinked. "When?"

"Maybe today. That town constable from Hidatsa told me that yesterday." Chad laid the towel aside.

Scaggs went back to examining the ash, and flicked it before taking down another drag of smoke and exhaling it as he regarded Chad. "Likely too late for me to hitch up now, anyway," he said. "But you know, Mister Greene, I'm just a range man. I hire on, do what I'm

121

supposed to do, give a man his money's worth, and that's all. I'm not even a very good shot with a gun, but I'm fair at ropin' and doctorin' cattle and shoein' horses and such like."

"Then you'd better saddle up," responded Chad, believing all this had been some kind of prelude to Scaggs's deciding he had changed his mind about remaining.

"Oh," said the cowboy, "it's more'n likely too late. If Mister Shelby's on the way with his friends . . . it's likely too late for me to get clear. And, anyway, I ain't had any breakfast yet."

They looked at one another for a while before Chad shook his head slightly. Scaggs smiled, and got up off the railing, stamped out his cigarette, and waited.

"A man's got to eat," Chad said, and caught a faint smile on the younger man's face.

"Yeah, for a fact, Mister Greene. And there's something else a man's got to do. I got three married sisters. I wouldn't take it kindly if some son-of-a-bitch took to ridin' roughshod over them, neither."

Margaret opened the door and looked out. She had heard masculine voices and had a six-gun in her fist held behind her. She did not know Ed Scaggs. All Chad said was: "This is Mister Scaggs. This here is Missus Fulmer."

She nodded, unsmiling and still gripping the hidden Colt.

"Mister Scaggs might be around for a few days. He used to ride for Grant Shelby."

This time her gaze was as hard as flint. Ed Scaggs smiled. "I quit. Got to thinkin' about what Mister Shelby's tryin' to do, ma'am. Just came by for a spell."

Chad saw the heightened expression of suspicion on Margaret's face and wondered aloud if they could talk a little more over coffee.

She stepped aside for them to enter, hitching her injured leg. Chad caught a glimpse of the six-gun behind her as he motioned for Scaggs to precede him into the kitchen.

The morning was cold but the sky was clear, the sun was coming, and there was not a breath of wind. As they sat around the oilcloth-covered table, Scaggs dropped his hat on the floor, looked self-conscious, and, when Chad brought over tin cups of coffee, Scaggs looked at the handsome woman with a little smile.

"I don't mean you any harm, ma'am. In fact, I've been gettin' a little fed up with what Mister Shelby's been tryin' to do over here."

She was not convinced and she had reason not to be. She did not know Scaggs but she knew Shelby and how his riders had helped him harass her for the past two years. She could guess that Ed Scaggs had been part of Shelby's schemes, so she said: "Mister Scaggs, I wouldn't expect you to sit at my table and tell me anything different."

Scaggs accepted this. "I don't blame you one bit, ma'am."

Chad brought the fried meat and beans she had been preparing. Margaret had to sit sideways on her chair, splinted leg rigidly to one side. As Chad seated himself to start eating, she said: "How much would Mister Shelby pay someone to burn me out, Mister Scaggs?"

The range rider answered without any pause. "Twelve dollars. That's what he offered Shandon."

Chad said: "He'll never collect it. Shandon's dead."

They both stared at him.

Chad reached and lifted his tin cup, half drained it, and spoke again. "Whoever was up the slope trying to nail me, shot Shandon. I didn't see the feller, just the flash of his gun. I fired back . . . that's all I know about it."

"Constable Harris told you Shandon was dead?" asked Scaggs, and, when Chad nodded, Margaret stared at him. "You didn't tell me that."

Chad had his fork poised when she spoke. Their eyes met across the table. "You've got enough worries. Anyway, it won't make any difference, except that Shandon won't come around to scare hell out of you again." He completed his movement with the fork.

For a while none of them spoke. The two men ate steadily and Margaret Fulmer watched for a while, then let her gaze drift elsewhere. Her thoughts were sober and despairing. "What is the use of it," she eventually said. "Men act like wolves . . . and for what? My homestead isn't worth that much to Grant Shelby or anyone else."

Scaggs answered her thoughtfully: "I guess maybe it stopped bein' your land some time back, ma'am. It started out that way . . . him pickin' at you, troublin' and pesterin' you. Then you stood up to him, and Mister Shelby ain't a man who can stand anything like that. From then on it become personal with him. He had to fight you and he wanted to."

Chad listened, agreed, and eyed Scaggs from under his lashes. Maybe the cowboy was young and detached-acting, but he was no fool.

Margaret Fulmer arose and hobbled to her bedroom. The pair of men exchanged a glance, then went on eating. Outside, the sun rose, climbed, brought more pleasant, unseasonable warmth, and later it would also cause that hazy smoke-like mistiness over the far mountains from which the unique season got its name of Indian summer. It was said, but no longer believed, that the Indians were curing meat, smoking it for winter. Once people had believed that was what brought the smokiness. Indian summer meant they were up there in their camps and *rancherías* preparing for winter. Indian summer it remained, even though the old legend had been disproved long ago.

But it would not last long. It never did. Then winter would arrive. As Ed Scaggs said, leaning back to savor his coffee, time was against folks this time of year. No matter what they figured to do out of doors, time was against them and would remain that way for maybe six months.

Chad fleetingly thought of this job, of his superiors in the U.S. Marshal's office over at Fort Hall, and also down in Denver. They were not only remote; they seemed remote. He rolled a smoke and tossed the sack and papers to Scaggs, who also rolled and lit up. He eyed Chad a while, then said: "You ever work for the Wyoming Stock Grower's Association?"

Chad understood what he meant. The Wyoming Stock Grower's Association was notorious for hiring small armies of gunfighters for their wars against settlers. They only hired men willing to gunfight. Yesterday, and earlier, Chad had demonstrated a capability the average range man did not have, and in fact was never eager to develop.

"Never did," he replied.

Scaggs was a forthright man. "You sure give me the impression you did, Mister Greene, the way you've taken on Shelby's whole crew."

Chad sat a moment thinking and smoking, then he palmed his deputy U.S. marshal's badge, and watched. Scaggs looked, stiffened slightly, and leaned to look closer, then he took down a deep drag of his smoke and twisted to pitch the stub into the firebox of the stove. When he faced back, he was paler in the face and Chad smiled. Scaggs's reaction had been swift and deep and bad. Chad had seen the identical reaction in a lot of men. He was experienced enough to know the look when he saw it.

But all he said was: "I was lookin' for someone and came onto Missus Fulmer . . . and Shelby. Maybe, if he'd just hung back to spy I wouldn't have bought in." Chad returned the badge to his pocket. "Not the Wyoming Cattle Grower's Association, but another outfit just about as tough in a different way."

"Yeah, Lord," mumbled Ed Scaggs, and pushed back to arise. "I'll help with the dishes an' all."

Chad was no longer smiling. He studied Ed Scaggs, trying to remember his face. It was one of Greene's attributes that he could memorize faces from Wanted posters. He had not seen Ed Scaggs's face yet. But that did not mean much; the West had plenty of fugitives whose crimes had not reached Fort Hall or Denver. In time they might, unless the outlaws were apprehended or killed — or disappeared.

CHAPTER
THIRTEEN

The wait was over when Margaret called to Chad from her room. When he stopped in the doorway, she turned from her front-wall window, splinted leg stiffly before her as she leaned upon a chair back. She said just one word — "Riders!" — then pointed.

He crossed to lean at the window. At first he saw nothing but endless miles of sun-bright grassland, then faint movement showed for him to concentrate on. They were bunched up, at first, but gradually as they came half a mile closer, they spread out a little. He could not make an accurate count but he guessed them to be at least ten in number, maybe three or four more, but it made no difference; ten would be enough.

He straightened up, still looking out the window. From one side she said: "I've heard how they do it, Chad."

He nodded. He also knew. "They'll know they've been in a horse race," he told her, and looked around. She was white to the eyes.

From the other room Scaggs called, with an insistent sound to his voice. He had also seen them coming. Chad ignored the call. "Shelby's doin' a damn' fool thing," he said to her. "Even if he wins, it's a damn' fool thing."

Her direct grasp of circumstances prompted a dry answer. "Who will be around to see it?"

He smiled. She was tough enough for any ten females. "We will. Now you stay in here."

"What are you going to do?"

"I had an uncle who went to sea. He used to tell me stories about pirates and such like. He used to say they'd fire a shot across their bows. That's what we're going to do, just as soon as they get close enough."

He lingered, then went over and lightly placed a hand on her shoulder. He was thinking of her absent husband when he wagged his head. If Tom Fulmer was alive, he was a damned fool.

Out in the kitchen Ed Scaggs had his carbine in the bend of an arm. "That feller in the middle is Mister Shelby." He pointed. Then he said: "If he catches me, I'm a goner."

Chad did not bother to look out; he picked up his saddle gun, opened the front door, eased into overhang shadows, and cocked the weapon. Then he waited. He knew just how close they would have to be, so he measured the distance with practiced eyes, and stood there.

The cattlemen slackened to a plodding walk, but if their horses were poking along, the riders were erect in their saddles, eyes fixed on the log house dead ahead.

Scaggs crept to the door. "You better get inside. They'll be able to see you in a minute or two."

Chad did not speak. The cattlemen were almost close enough. He knelt with slow care, raised the Winchester, took a thumb rest on a porch upright, and Ed Scaggs said: "It's too far."

Chad fired with his gun barrel elevated a degree or two. He and Scaggs watched. A horse suddenly shied violently, nearly unseating its rider. The cattlemen stopped out there. Chad levered up a fresh load and lowered the carbine to watch.

Scaggs shook his head. "One good thing . . . it's open all around the house and barn." Something else occurred to him. "But we sure better keep them from gettin' around behind that damned barn."

Chad turned. "You always talk a lot when you're nervous, Mister Scaggs?"

The range man colored, but he answered truthfully. "Yeah. And when I'm really scairt, like I'm goin' to be directly, I babble like a shoat caught in a gate."

Chad grinned in spite of himself.

The cattlemen were moving, dividing up, and starting off on an angling course. Scaggs said they were going to get around behind, and Chad had already arrived at this conclusion, so he eased down the hammer of his carbine and stepped back inside.

Margaret Fulmer was in the middle of the room with Hays's six-gun hanging at her side, looking straight at Chad. He met her eyes with a sober but unworried look. "You and Mister Scaggs stay here. I'm going out to the barn. We've got a weak advantage. They don't know we're not still alone." Her gaze swept past to Ed

Scaggs, then back to Chad. "I don't trust him, and I don't think you should."

Scaggs stepped close as he replied to that. "Ma'am, if I'd still been working for Mister Shelby, I sure wouldn't be inside this house right now with you folks."

"Why not?" she shot back at him. "As soon as Chad walks out, you can shoot me in the back . . . Chad, let him go down to the barn."

Chad got no opportunity to answer. "All right," Scaggs said. "All right, ma'am. I'll take the barn." He started toward the rear door and Chad watched him go. They exchanged a look, then Scaggs walked out onto the rear porch, shot a swift look north and south, and ran.

Chad watched in silence as the range man reached the barn. Behind him Margaret said: "You're too trusting."

He eased the door closed without replying. Maybe, and maybe after manhunting as long as he'd been at it, he was a far better judge of men than she was. But all he said, as he turned toward her, was: "I don't know what to do about you. Sure as hell you're going to hurt that leg."

She did not yield an inch, and he had not expected her to. "I'll be very careful. I set out an extra box of handgun bullets on the table."

He grinned at her. "I'll tell you something. You're one hell of a woman, Missus Fulmer."

He returned to the front of the house and looked out there. The cattlemen were beyond gun range as they rode without haste to flank the house. "In broad daylight," he mused aloud. He had indeed enraged Grant Shelby, but his appraisal of the man remained the same. Shelby was not a fighter, he was a schemer, and, if that did not seem likely to help much now, with those other cattlemen out there, who probably were fighters, it remained in the back of Chad's mind as he watched. What he particularly wanted was one clean shot at Shelby. But from this distance he could not tell which group the rancher was riding with. Nor did it appear, for the time being, to make much difference.

He shook his head and stepped away from the window. Margaret was watching him. For all her toughness she seemed to rely entirely upon his movement and his decisions. He smiled but she did not seem very reassured as she said: "That man in the barn . . . suppose he helps them get inside?"

"Then I guess it'll be up to you and me to keep them there."

She nodded, able to appreciate his logic, probably because it was succinct and directly to the point the way her logic was, also.

He watched her hitch her body toward the rear of the house, knew it would be useless to add any more warnings to the ones he had already given her, and wished also there were windows in the side walls. But it was a genuine indication of extravagance that there were any windows at all in a homesteader's house.

He knew that if they remained inside, they could be attacked along both the north and south sides of the house. If they could not see stalkers approaching from those directions — with firebrands no doubt — they could be smoked out or burned up. He reached past her to open the door and she caught his arm. "No! By now they're in range of the house!"

She had scarcely got the words out when a Winchester gunshot made its high, snarling sound from the barn. There was another shot, then for a long while there was silence, until two other carbines opened up, but from the sound they were a fair distance off.

Chad looked at Margaret to see if she had interpreted those shots as he had. One from inside the barn, two more from out back, some distance from the barn. She said: "It could be for our benefit, Chad."

"Margaret, you never give up, do you?"

"I learned about cowmen, and not giving up, Chad."

He faced the door, cracked it a little to peer out. The yard was empty and what little he could see of the area north and south of the house was also lacking in movement or horsemen. They had ridden completely around the house evidently, to come up in strength behind the barn where they would not be visible from the house. Ed Scaggs must be feeling terribly alone by now.

"If you can keep watch in here," he said without looking around, "I could lend Scaggs a hand."

"You'd never make it across the yard." She reached and lightly restrained him with a hand on his arm again. "Please . . . don't go out there."

Another gunshot sounded from inside the barn. This time someone answered with a Colt. If anyone was close enough to the rear of the barn to use a handgun, Scaggs was in real danger.

But a moment later a man's hard footfalls sounded up along the north end of the rear porch. He must have leaped up from the yard. It was a thoughtless thing to do, and, since he did not make another sound, he had perhaps realized his dangerous error, but now the pattern was beginning to make sense to Chad. They thought that it was he in the barn, thought they had only an injured woman inside the house. They could afford to be bold as they closed in, even though they knew she would be armed.

Chad lifted out the dead outlaw's finely balanced and ivory-butted Colt, eased the door back another few inches, strained to hear movement, then wrenched the door back, stepped out, body twisting, six-gun cocked and rising. He saw the bearded, burly range man at the same time the stranger saw Chad, but the man was holding a Winchester in both hands, poised to move, not aimed yet. Chad fired from the hip. The man was punched backward, tripped, and fell off the porch. Chad was back inside with the door closed as someone off to the right, over on the north side of the cabin, let out a yell.

Chad pulled Margaret away from the door, made her flatten along the logs well away at his side, holding her there. His hunch was right; someone outside slammed two heavy slugs into the door. It buckled on its hinges because the drawbar would not allow it to burst inward, but it would be unable to stand many more shots like that.

Then the silence settled, more ominous and deeper than ever. Margaret's fingers crept into his palm and held tightly. He slowly loosened as he waited, turned his head, and saw the way she was looking up at him.

"Chad . . . ?"

"Hold on, Margaret. We're still able to kick a little."

"Chad . . . ? You're . . . one hell of a man."

He smiled. "Care to know something, Margaret? If we get out of this, I expect I'll up and marry you."

She could not return the smile but she almost repeated it word for word. "Know something, Chad. I think if we get out of this . . . I'll want you to marry me."

Scaggs fired again and Chad wondered if he had any extra slugs for that Winchester. Someone called loudly from the south. Chad went over to the front door, opened it a crack, and listened. He could see nothing more than the porch, the front of the house, and some sunshine out where the land showed, wedge-shaped, from his point of vantage.

The call came again, indistinguishable except as sound, as noise made by a man shouting; if there were words, Chad was unable to discern them, but the voice sounded full of alarm. Chad opened the door a crack wider, saw nothing on his right, which was across open range land, eased out to look northward, saw nothing, and was going to risk a forward step when Margaret grabbed his arm.

"They want you to do that!"

He hesitated, and a six-gun slug ripped into the log wall ten inches from his head. He recoiled, spun to seek the gunman, saw nothing, and finally yielded to Margaret's insistent, strong pull. As they retreated, she

135

barred the door, then turned and said: "Men! Strong as oak . . . and twice as thick!"

There came a long interlude of silence that made Chad nervous. He knew cowmen; they did not do as soldiers, did not fall back to regroup. They fought more as Indians fought, individually, relying less upon numbers than upon personal assessments. Those cowmen out there were leery, had no doubt by now realized that forcing the woman inside the house to yield was not going to be easy, and were waiting, like vultures, for the chance they were sure would come if they waited long enough. Chad understood the rules of this game even though he had never before been under siege inside a residence. What had to be done now was to take pressure off Scaggs and further to upset the cattlemen, to shock and surprise them.

He motioned for Margaret to hitch over to the back wall. There, he cracked the door a few inches, peered around, saw nothing, then leaned and said: "Wait until I'm in position by the front door. When I nod, blaze away."

"There's nothing to aim at."

"Yeah, I know." He touched her cheek, did not explain, and returned to the front door to open it and get set. When he nodded, she eased the door open a little more, pushed out her six-gun, and began firing. Chad did the same over along the front of the house. For ten seconds the thunderous explosions were deafening, then Chad stopped, barred the door, and stepped widely away from it. Margaret, taking her cue from him, did the same. They met over by the table to reload, and from the barn Scaggs emptied his Winchester.

It was altogether an impressive array of gunfire, but Margaret looked despairingly at Chad as they pushed out spent casings and plugged in fresh loads. "What did that accomplish?" she asked him.

"Now they know there is more than a woman in the house and a man in the barn."

His tactic seemed to have proved something because there was no more gunfire for a long time. Maybe the range men Shelby had brought over were becoming chary. Maybe they were willing to question Shelby about his promise of an easy triumph over an injured woman and one man. At any rate, time passed without additional gunfire and Chad used it to move from the front of the house to the back, peeking out, trying to find something to fire at.

Finally, too preoccupied with the search for targets, he was unaware of something deadly until Margaret came over, leaned, and said: "Smoke!"

He smelled it, then guessed they had probably fired either the north or south wall, cursed the lack of windows in those areas, and told her to cover him. He yanked open the rear door before she had a chance to grab his arm, and jumped forth, racing to the north end of the porch, out there where he had met that stranger he had shot. There was no sign of the stranger; maybe he had not been killed. Maybe someone had dragged the body away. Chad did not look for the downed man; he leaned, gun up, poised and cocked, to see who was up along the north wall.

A carbine made its high, sharp sound. Lead struck the wall as Chad leaned, peeling out splinters where his head had been. He saw a crouching form — two of them — he fired at one, hauled back the hammer, and fired again. Both crouching men sprang up and ran hard for the front of the house, got around the corner as he fired his third shot, whirled, ducked down as that gunman with the carbine fired at him again, and made it back inside the house in five lunging jumps.

Whether he had wounded anyone or not, he had no idea, but one thing he could report to Margaret Fulmer was that the smell of smoke was not coming from along the north wall.

Winchesters sprayed the rear of the house. Chad pulled Margaret clear of the door, which was splintering under repeated gunshots. He released her and crossed to the front door. The fire had to be along the south wall. She tried to hitch her way over there to restrain him but did not cross the room before he had the door open and had jumped forth toward the south corner.

This time, no one fired at him. Evidently the cattlemen were out back where they could see the barn, the yard, and the rear of the house. He leaned, saw the man working his way along with a firebrand that he was trying to hold in one place long enough to get the old logs to burn, and fired directly at him. The man dropped the torch, turned and stared, then collapsed.

Margaret had the door wide as Chad ran back. She slammed the bar into place and leaned away, but still no gunfire came from around front.

CHAPTER
FOURTEEN

The range men seemed to have learned extreme caution, and in fact with three or four exceptions they had not been outstandingly reckless from the beginning, but their siege showed no signs of slackening off, either, and that more than anything else worried Chad.

The man who had been trying to get the south wall to burn was dead. Chad was sure of it. He had seen the odd, disbelieving look in the man's eyes one second before he collapsed across his firebrand. He had been unable to get the wall to burn, thanks probably to the bad weather a few days earlier.

Scaggs had been silent for a long time. That prompted Chad to utilize the moments of quiet to peer out the splintered rear-wall door. But there was nothing to be seen. The barn, too, was wreathed in a hushed depth of ominous silence. He had no way of knowing whether they had been able to get in there and kill Ed Scaggs.

Margaret had to sit down. Her good leg, which had been supporting all her weight, ached with tiredness, and, when Chad looked at her, she smiled for the first time, but probably not from any sense of well-being, but because she and he had shared something in which they had both learned great respect and admiration for the other. He smiled back, checking any impulse to tell her of his anxiety about Ed Scaggs.

A moment later his worry was banished. From inside the barn someone fired three times, very fast, with a Colt. There was no immediate reply, but it eventually came, from carbines some distance off.

Scaggs had prevented them from getting inside the barn where they could have shot away the door of the house. He had also taught them respect because none of them came close to the yard. Chad shook his head in tough approval. Maybe, as Ed Scaggs had said, he was not a good shot and did not possess much individual bravery, but he was demonstrating that he had enough of both for the time being.

Then silence resettled, and this time it ran on and on until Chad wondered if perhaps the cattlemen had given up. It was difficult to believe. On the other hand, so far they had not gained a single objective and they had lost one man he was sure of, another one he may not have killed but who he had certainly shot off the porch, and, if Scaggs had even winged one out beyond the barn, it would mean the cattlemen, for all their numbers, were losing. The improbability of an hour before was turning now into a distinct possibility. The besieged people just might win after all.

The silence was a little unsettling. There was no way to be certain what Shelby was up to, and that was cause for anxiety. Chad had him figured as a sly, devious, scheming individual, the kind of person who would perhaps be even more dangerous in silence than in active fighting.

Margaret watched Chad draw off two cups of coffee. Her house smelled of burned gunpowder, the rear door was a wreck, but oddly her prized possessions, those three windows in the front wall, were intact. Probably because the attackers had made no attempt from the front.

She accepted the coffee, tasted it, made a face, and Chad laughed. "I never made a decent cup of coffee in my life. In fact, I never cooked a decent meal."

She defended him. "You've done very well. I think I've put on weight while you've been here." She blushed for some reason. He noticed this and teased her: "You know, taking care of that bullet wound gave me some idea that you're strongly hung together ... Missus Fulmer."

She averted her face.

"My paw used to say when a man went out to pick a woman he should bear in mind that the horses with the shortest back and crested necks an' strong legs lasted the longest and stood up to work best."

She turned back. "Thank you ... Mister Greene. I'm delighted to be compared with a horse!" He laughed. She watched him a moment, then also laughed. "You're good for me, Chad."

Their eyes held in humor, until something else crept in, then he went over to the back door to look out.

"Too darned quiet," he muttered. She did not reply. She sat sipping her coffee and watching him. Only

141

when he opened the splintered door a little did she call a soft caution.

There was nothing to be seen anywhere he could watch: beyond the house, across the yard, northward toward the forested hillside, or down around the barn.

"Maybe they pulled out," he said to her without looking around. "But if they did . . ." He shook his head to indicate doubt and skepticism. The front opening of the barn showed nothing but shadowy gloom as far as he could see. He considered calling to Scaggs, but decided not to.

The sun was still climbing. What had seemed like ten hours had actually been a short space of time. There was warmth in the air even though, far off, he could see the yellow-russet of hardwood trees and the very pale green of slim willows where frost had been. The evergreens were exactly as they always were, forming a somber background for the smaller trees with the riotous autumn colors.

A man's high call sounded distantly, catching Chad's attention. It had come from south of the barn and far back. He could not see the caller nor could he imagine what had occasioned the cry, but it meant the cattlemen had not departed and that settled the doubt in his mind. They were still out there.

He grew restless, knowing Shelby was close by and was using this interlude of silence to hatch more schemes. As he eased the broken door closed and reset the bar, Margaret said: "Would they just sit out there and wait for nightfall?"

It did not seem plausible. On the other hand, they certainly seemed unwilling to start the fight again. As for the wasted time, maybe the cowmen had that also in their favor. There were no other homesteaders close by, and, if there had been, it was doubtful that they would have bought into a battle against that many armed cowmen.

He shrugged wide shoulders without answering except to say: "Anything would be better than not knowing."

She disagreed. "Every minute that passes means we're still able to be here, Chad."

Again that man cried out from a long distance, and this time Chad took the carbine back to the door with him. But as before he could see nothing to aim at.

Unexpectedly Ed Scaggs appeared in the barn doorway to wigwag with his hat. As soon as Chad parted the door a little more, Scaggs called across to him.

"Something's got them roiled up. It's out front. I can see them back yonder signaling to one another. Look out there."

Chad closed the door, crossed the room in long strides, half expecting to see the cowmen sneaking up from the front. Instead, a long way off but moving fast there was a band of horsemen. He said — "Hell." — believing it was more range men, and, when Margaret heaved herself unsteadily up to balance upon her good leg to come over to see, Chad eased aside for her also to look out. He reached a supporting arm for her to lean on. She looked a long while before pulling back.

143

"It's the constable."

He leaned for a second look, but all he could be certain of was that there were a lot of them and they were riding in a swift lope, all bunched up.

She saw his frown of doubt. "Look for the big black horse. He's in the middle. I'm sure that's Constable Harris."

He was about tell her that her eyesight was better than his, when he saw two riders spurring in a belly-down run from around to the south. They were riding bent over, spurring their horses every jump. These two, he felt sure, were some of Shelby's range men. As he watched, the oncoming riders began to spread out, to fan southward in a quick run to head off the fleeing pair. Someone fired a six-gun but it was so far away the echo came back as a little *popping* sound.

Only that one shot was fired. The oncoming men suddenly spurred harder as more of their crew spun away after that gunshot to help bar the way of the fleeing men. Within moments there was a mêlée of horses and riders, a big swirling crowd of men engulfing the two fleeing men. The excitement did not last more than a moment. Everyone out there settled down. Whatever had happened was over.

Finally Chad could make out the big man on the black horse. It did indeed resemble the lawman from Hidatsa. He was not sure even yet, but one thing was abundantly clear, those oncoming riders now had the pair of fleeing cowmen in their midst as they turned back in the direction of the buildings.

Chad detected crafty movement to the north, over closer to the hills. Someone was trying to sneak around the oncoming horsemen and he was doing it cleverly by utilizing the rough dark backdrop of the hills to conceal his movement. He was also utilizing the log house, pacing his progress so that the riders to the south of the house would not be able to see him as he worked his way craftily along.

Chad thought he knew this one, went over to the front door, stepped out onto the porch, and sank to one knee to take a rest on the porch railing. The distant man was evidently watching that oncoming crew. He possibly could not have detected anyone on the front porch anyway because of the shade provided to Chad by the overhanging roof.

Chad estimated the distance at just about the limit of a saddle gun's range. He tilted his barrel for maximum distance and fired. Instantly those oncoming men stopped, sat perfectly still out there, looking ahead. Chad levered up, corrected the elevation, and fired again. This time the skulking rider twisted suddenly in the saddle. Chad was ready when the man paused, probably instinctively reining his horse almost to a halt. The third bullet was between Chad's earlier shot and his last one, not as high as the last but higher than the first shot.

The distant horseman suddenly had to ride for his life. The horse under him yanked slack in the reins, bogged his head, and bucked as hard as he could. His rider, not expecting this, was nearly flung off after the first jump, but managed to get squarely across leather again, and lost all interest in everything around him except his immediate peril. He rode well, straight up and leaning back. He was no novice on the hurricane deck of a maddened animal, but as the horse bucked, he jumped ahead until, finally, the man was carried out where those watching strangers could detect him. Four of them, including the big man on the black horse, peeled off in a swift rush.

The bucking horse was finally outmaneuvered by his rider. As long as the horse could get his head down and keep it down, he could not be satisfactorily controlled by his rider, but the moment he sunfished and turned his head to do it, the man got enough leverage on the reins to pull the horse's head up and farther around. It did not stop the horse's frantic fighting, but it threw him far off balance and he crashed to earth in a wild surge of threshing legs.

Chad was still on one knee, watching, when the four strangers got over there and surrounded the fallen man. As the horse fought back upright and turned to flee, the riders closing in opened up just enough for him to speed past, reins flying, saddle off to one side, head and tail up as he raced in blind panic out across the western countryside.

Suddenly Chad heard horsemen rushing past the house on the south side and turned to crane in that direction. They were riding hard in a bid to escape, strung out and widening their front as they fled. Several of the strangers turned to give chase, but a man's deep-down angry voice swore at them, calling them back. Whoever he was, he had a voice like distant thunder. Chad could even hear the swear words over by the house.

The fleeing cattlemen got away, and kept riding hard. That bull-bass individual growled another thunderous order. The riders with him turned their backs on the fleeing horsemen and jogged stiffly up where the other four were on the ground around that man who had fallen with the bucking horse.

Margaret came tiredly to the porch door, leaned a moment, watching the fleeing cowmen, then limped over to where Chad was. He stood up and leaned aside the Winchester, watching the drama up yonder where all the strangers were now swinging to the ground by that fallen man.

She said: "Chad, what happened up there?"

His answer was soft. "I don't know. I tried to knock him off, but I must have stung the horse over the rump. He started to buck, then he fell with the man."

"Could you tell who he was?"

Chad shook his head. He didn't know any of them. Well, he knew Grant Shelby, but that was the only one he knew, and at that distance he had been unable to make out much more than that it was a man in a heavy coat with a red muffler on.

CHAPTER
FIFTEEN

Two men rode away from the crowd up along the northerly slope below the timber, riding slowly in the direction of the house.

Margaret was sure, this time, when she pointed. "That's the constable. That other man . . . that's Harry Beacon. He owns the livery barn and trading corrals in Hidatsa. He also owns the stage-company franchise."

Chad watched the horsemen as a feeling of tiredness settled throughout his body. He thought of Scaggs out in the barn, thought of the man he was sure he had killed around the south side of the house, waited until he could be sure it was Ralph Harris, the law from Hidatsa, then eased down upon the porch railing to wait.

The constable had a drawn look on his face when he rode up, gravely nodded at them, and swung from the saddle as though his body weighed a ton.

"You folks all right?" he asked, looking longest at Margaret Fulmer. "This here is Harry Beacon," he stated, indicating the bull-necked barrel-shaped man who was dismounting. Beacon turned and said: "Howdy." That was all, but the depth and timbre of the voice clarified in Chad's mind who this was; he had

148

heard that same voice growl thunderously a few minutes earlier.

Margaret said: "I'm glad you came, Constable."

Harris did not look as though he were glad. "Shelby just got too big for his britches this time," he muttered, and twisted to gaze up where the other men who had ridden out with him were standing. "But it's his last mistake."

Chad stared. "I hit him?"

"No, Mister Greene. You creased his horse. When Grant went down . . . he broke his neck."

They stared at Constable Harris. "He's dead?"

Harry Beacon answered. "Deader'n a damned stone." Beacon looked around. "How long they been at you folks?"

Margaret spoke again as Chad reflected upon the way Grant Shelby had died. "They showed up shortly after sunup, Mister Beacon. Look at the back of the house. They tried to attack from behind the barn, but Mister Scaggs back there kept them away."

Beacon cocked thick eyebrows. "Mister Scaggs . . . ?"

"He used to ride for Mister Shelby. He came over this morning. He helped out."

The lawman still had that hang-dog expression on his face when Chad said: "Who'd you bring with you, Constable?"

"Six or seven fellers from town, Mister Greene, and there was a crew of five drovers came into town last night. They heard about you folks and volunteered to ride along." Harris looked up. "We caught two makin' a run for it. The others got clear but it don't make much difference. The fellers we caught can name all the

149

others." He looked from Chad to Margaret Fulmer. "Well, I'm sorry, ma'am. That's little enough, but that's about all I can say."

He sounded contrite enough, but Chad's impression was that Ralph Harris's sorrow was about equal parts divided between Margaret Fulmer and his friends, the cowmen who had got themselves into this situation.

"What do you figure to do?" Chad asked.

The burly, bull-bass-voiced man answered bleakly: "We had enough of this sort of thing. I side with range men most of the time, Mister Greene, but I don't side with no one who tries what Shelby tried, and I don't care if it's against settlers or Indians . . . we're not goin' to put up with no more of it." He looked at Constable Harris. "We got a circuit rider due in town in about a week to hold court. Ralph's goin' to swear out and sign the complaints. The rest of us . . . and you folks . . . will be witnesses."

Constable Harris nodded his head without saying a word. Chad arose off the railing, excused himself, and went through the house and across the yard.

Ed Scaggs was saddling his horse inside the barn. He turned quickly, saw who was standing in the doorway, and sagged a little. "Just figured it was time for me to ride on, Marshal. These winters up here . . ."

"I was wondering, Mister Scaggs . . . I got a notion to stay and fix the place up, get in some wood and game, and sort of get ready in the spring to get some cattle, but a man can't do it all himself."

Scaggs leaned across the saddle seat, studying Chad. Finally he said: "I never been so scairt in my life."

Chad grinned. "Me, too."

"Well, I figure these cowmen, especially Mister Shelby, will make life awful hard for . . ."

"Mister Shelby's horse fell with him and he broke his neck."

Scaggs considered that for a moment. "He's dead?"

"Yes. Like I was saying, to start this meadow off with cattle, I'll need a little help. We won't have a lot to do until springtime."

"You offerin' me a job, Mister Greene?"

"Yes."

Scaggs let his gaze drift around the barn before saying: "They sure shot up this damned barn. You'd ought to see that back wall. Looks like a whole darned army of woodpeckers been at work out there."

"The job, Mister Scaggs . . . ?"

"Well, I do appreciate the offer . . . I guess I can tell you something, we havin' risked our necks together."

Chad was shaking his head so Scaggs stopped speaking. "I don't especially want to hear it, Mister Scaggs. We're startin' fresh here, commencin' today, and next summer we'll have about all two fellers can handle. There are no working corrals, no squeeze chute for doctorin', no shoeing shed, or anything else. Then we'll have the cattle to mind. I'll pay rider's wages, Mister Scaggs." Chad grinned again. "And between the pair of us I guess we can put up a decent bunkhouse if this Indian summer'll hang on for another couple weeks."

Ed Scaggs studied Chad a long time. "You goin' to give up law riding?"

"Yeah. I've done it long enough. And my name is Chad, not Mister Greene."

Scaggs leaned to stroke absently the neck of his patiently standing horse. "No questions asked . . . Chad?"

"Not a damned one . . . It wasn't murder, was it?"

They both laughed. "Naw, it was stealin' a real flashy sorrel horse with a white mane and tail. Ten years ago when I was sixteen. But if you never ask, I'll never have to tell you, will I?"

"You sure never will. Care to hire on?"

Ed Scaggs stroked his horse a moment longer, then hoisted the stirrup leather to start pulling loose his latigo before removing the saddle. Chad watched briefly, then said: "We'll have something to eat over at the house in about an hour. By the way, do you know anything about carpentering?"

"Yeah, a little."

"That's good because I don't and Margaret's going to want us to fix that back door first thing."

From the far side of his horse Scaggs said: "My name's Ed. I'll finish up down here, put out a little feed, then I'll be over." He raised up, the two men looked at one another, then they smiled.

Chad started across the yard, paused in the warm, winy air to breathe deeply, then went as far as the rear porch where he stopped to roll and light a smoke. It tasted fine. He pulled up a battered chair and sat down. There were a dozen loose ends to be taken care of, but right now, for this brief moment, he wanted simply to sit alone and turn his nerves and muscles loose all over.

Margaret came to the open door and leaned, looking out at him. "Are you all right, Chad?"

He nodded without looking around. "I'm fine. Just hired Ed Scaggs to ride for us."

She stepped forward and went over to lean upon the railing. "Ride for us?"

He still did not look at her. "We got to have a decent bunkhouse, first off, then we got to start snaking down poles for working corrals, and put up winter wood, and fetch down some meat . . ." He turned slowly to meet her steady gaze. "In the spring we'll start up with some cattle. Maybe just fifty, sixty head to start with. Sort of feel our way along. Margaret?"

She sat back, gazing at him for a moment before answering. "People will talk."

"Do you care about that?"

"No. Well, I'm a woman. I guess I really would care."

"But about the rest of it?"

She nodded her head slowly. "It sounds wonderful." He killed the smoke and straightened up as though to arise. "Where's the constable?"

"He and Mister Beacon went back to have the posse men tie Mister Shelby to his horse. They also found a dead man around the south side of the house. And two of those men who escaped were wounded." She waited a moment before continuing. "I still have a problem, Chad."

He pushed up out of the chair. "That's what I want to talk to the constable about. We've got to start the search over there in Hidatsa."

Her eyes were round and solemn. "And if . . . Tom is still alive?"

He returned her gaze. "Then I'll ride on."

For a while they regarded one another before Chad turned and walked through the house and out front on his way up to where the posse men were working.

By the time he got over there, he did not have to look at Grant Shelby. Three posse men were already on their way in the direction of Hidatsa with the dead cattleman lashed across a saddle. Several other townsmen were preparing to ride away and paused out of curiosity as the stranger they had heard was a deputy U.S. marshal walked up. They found things to do such as loosening rigs to resettle saddles, and adjust headstalls as they waited.

Constable Harris had also watched Chad's approach, but Harry Beacon was on his way back to town behind the dead cowman.

Chad took the constable to one side. "I'd like to know as much as you can tell me about Margaret Fulmer's husband," he said, and the day-long look of disenchantment that Ralph Harris had been wearing seemed to deepen as he hung fire over a reply.

"To tell you the truth, Mister Greene, I was goin' to mention him to her when I rode down to the house with Mister Beacon. Only she'd been through so much, and her bein' hurt and all . . . well, I just didn't have the heart."

"You didn't look very happy," Chad retorted. "I thought it was because your friend, Shelby, was in trouble, or because he'd been killed."

154

"Yeah, I guess it was partly that, although to be right truthful with you, Grant and me haven't seen to an eye much lately. He's been getting meaner and more overbearing. But, yes, I was sorry for what happened to the darned fool. Only there was something else." Constable Harris reached into a shirt pocket, slowly withdrew a limp piece of folded paper, and held it without opening it as he said: "This here didn't come directly to me. It come to Mister Beacon. He's manager of the local way station for the stage company, you see." He offered the folded slip of paper to Chad. "That poor darned woman's had her share of grief for the past couple years, for a fact . . . That there is a death notice from the railroad company. Tom Fulmer was killed when a flat car loaded with ties run off the track and upset the load on top of Mister Fulmer and three other men."

Chad read the terse announcement, looked at the date — four months earlier — and raised his eyes. "That long ago?"

Constable Harris shrugged. "It come through the railroad office and was finally handed over to the stage company. It was sent to Mister Beacon because Miz Fulmer didn't have any mailbox address in Hidatsa." Harris did not seem to feel there had been unnecessary delay. "Anyway, I just didn't have the heart to hand her that thing when I rode up to the house an hour back."

Chad refolded the paper, pocketed it, and said: "I'll give it to her."

Harris showed immediate relief. "I'd sure be obliged, Mister Greene. I was hopin' maybe you would do that.

155

I'm downright obliged to you." The constable showed a brighter look now as he said: "And I expect you'll be movin' on. I want to tell you . . . it's been decent of you to take an interest."

Chad looked straight back as he said: "Someone had to."

Harris winced. "Well, I was going to. But until there was something done . . ."

Chad nodded curtly. "Yeah," he said, turned on his heel, and started back to the house. It was a long way and he had time to organize his thoughts.

Margaret was waiting on the porch with Ed Scaggs. She had washed and changed her dress, had brushed her hair, and they were drinking coffee while they watched him approach. As he came up the two wide low porch steps, he said: "That coffee sure smells good."

Scaggs arose at once. "I'll fetch you some."

The moment Ed went indoors, Chad handed the worn little folded slip of paper to Margaret. "He's dead. They just got word of it over in Hidatsa, Margaret. Maybe you'd ought to take the paper into your bedroom to read it."

She didn't take his advice, but opened the paper, read it very slowly, twice, then methodically folded it without raising her eyes, and then she got up and went inside to her room.

Ed came back with the coffee, did not comment on Margaret's absence, but eased down upon the porch railing and looked at Chad with a sardonic smile. "I'll likely be white-headed in the morning. I never been scairt so hard nor so long in my whole life."

The coffee was excellent. Chad sat in a chair and looked out where the posse men were finally drifting off in the direction of town. "You did a hell of a job out there, Ed," he told the cowboy without looking at him. "I guess two fellers who damn' near got killed together had ought to be able to build a cow outfit together."

Scaggs drained his cup and continued to sit a moment before speaking. "We can do that, all right. I don't know much about guns and never cared to know much about them, but cattle an' horses I do know about."

Margaret called Chad. He arose and went indoors, expecting to see the marks of tears. She was dry-eyed when she said: "I knew it. I've known it a long time. Women sense things like that."

He returned her look. "I'm awfully sorry, Margaret."

She smiled a little. "Thank you. I know you are. You're an honest man, Chad. Can we walk out back in the yard?"

He had to lift the splintered rear door for her. The sun was directly overhead, and that seemed strange. He would have wagered money it was late afternoon, close to evening.

Down in front of the barn she said: "Where would you put the bunkhouse and the corrals?" She avoided his gaze as he turned to look over the yard.

"I guess we'd ought to talk about it, Margaret. It's not where I'd put it, it's where we'd put it."

Now she turned. "Can I have a little time, Chad?"

157

He knew exactly what she meant and it had nothing to do with bunkhouses or working corrals. "All the time you want, Margaret."

She did not drop her eyes. "I know my answer to any question you might want to ask. I guess I already admitted that to you this morning. But . . ."

"I understand." He offered his hand. She took it and clung to it, then she stepped closer, and put her cheek against his chest. He encircled her shoulders with both arms. "There is no hurry, Margaret. Ed and I'll be busy filling the woodshed, then getting in some meat for winter."

"Just hold me, Chad."

He did, feeling the soft gentle way she relaxed against him full length while that high warm Indian summer sun seemed to remain utterly still in one place.

The Quiet Gun

CHAPTER
ONE

Frank Girard sat at his desk, staring out at the new day with his black hat on the back of his head, level gray eyes pensive, and his booted feet with their silver overlaid spurs draped indifferently on the bottom drawer of his desk. He heard Buelton coming to life around him without noticing. There was a blue-tailed fly *buzzing* frantically in a cobweb behind him somewhere, in the gloomy corners of his sheriff's office, and this went on unheeded as well. Strands of blond, sunburned hair showed above the broad, low forehead and the cant of his jaw was square below a humorous mouth that had an unspecified, haunting sort of sardonic humor to it.

Frank was aware of Clarence Black across the desk from him, sitting there like a wiry parrot, keen-eyed and slash-mouthed, watching the sheriff with all the intentness of what Clarence was — an attorney-at-law in the cow country. He was aware of Black's scrutiny because it annoyed him. He was wearing a mask. The necessity for it was in Clarence's known shrewdness when it came to reading people. Frank was mildly indignant at having to keep his guard up so long, then

Clarence started talking again, and, strangely, considering his build and disposition, the voice was low, melodious, and with a rich timbre.

"It's a matter of common decency, Frank. Besides . . . Buelton's quiet, and we want it to stay that way. Don't we?"

The sheriff's head came back around slowly. His indignation was increasing with the seconds. He dumped his hat on the desk, ran a hand through the jungle of his hair, and grunted. "Clarence . . . I can't think of a law that's being broken."

"You don't have to," Black said quickly. "It's the morality of the thing. The effect it'll have."

Frank looked steadily at this newcomer to the Buelton country, framing the correct reply. What he would like to say was out of the question — even to a fool like Clarence Black. "Well, Clarence, listen to me. In the first place our job . . . mine, anyway . . . has to do with keeping the peace only. I'm no preacher. Violations are one thing, moral mistakes are another. In the second place, Clarence, it's no one's business what George Carpenter or anyone else does in the privacy of their own damned ranch. Listen, enough trouble comes my way without inviting any. You" — the sheriff nodded his head curtly — "are new here. Don't rush out and blunder into things that don't concern you. This isn't the East, Clarence. Men'll fight here quicker'n they'll talk something out. In this case, I'd say just look the other way. It's nothing to you what George Carpenter does . . . so long as he doesn't run afoul of the law . . .

then, of course, you're supposed to prosecute him after I bring him in, that's all."

Black stayed silent for a moment, then he arose with an irate look in his blue eyes. "Sheriff, it's a good thing this isn't the East. Where I come from we'd've run George Carpenter out of the country overnight."

Frank's patience was slipping a little. "All right, but this isn't where you came from." He arose, too, all six foot of him, hard and lean and thoroughly capable-looking with the tied-down gun and thick chest. "Clarence, you keep horsing around, butting your nose into other folks' business like you're doing here, and you'll wind up shot all to hell. People won't stand for it out here, and you'd better get it straight in your head."

"Dammit, Frank . . . they tell me that girl's only sixteen years old." The city attorney's color was coming up. His zeal was falling back to make way for the indignation now.

"Sixteen or sixty, it's no one else's business," the sheriff said with an effort. "She's Indian, Clarence. Sometimes they look sixteen and have five kids at home. Anyway, even if she is sixteen, there's still no violation that I know of."

"What I'm trying to get across to you," Black said heatedly, seeing the sheriff's wrath and allowing his own to show now, "is that it's creating one hell of a furor in the bars. Young girls on the roads won't be . . ."

"Good Lord Almighty!" Frank interrupted explosively. "This isn't the first time a man took a squaw into his house . . . and it won't be the last. Besides, how about the Whitsett House?" The gray eyes were deeper by shades suddenly. "You can get more than liquor there and you know it. Clarence, if you're going to reform Buelton, you'd better start there, not out at George Carpenter's place."

The attorney went stiffly to the door, opened it, held it that way, and looked up at Girard. "I'm not going to reform anything. I'm an attorney, not a preacher . . ."

"That's a point cleared up," the sheriff said dryly.

Black went on as though unaware of the interruption. "But I'll be darned if I don't think the frontier should mature . . . grow up . . . start acting like it's a civilized place, not a . . . a . . ."

"A wilderness, or something," Frank said, letting himself down into his chair again and regarding his hat stonily. "Well, maybe it will, in time, Clarence, but until it does, you won't be the first casualty that tried to force it to age."

"You won't even speak to Carpenter, Frank? After all, dog-gone it, you two are on speaking terms, I know. Used to be old friends, they tell me, before Carpenter got married. It would be easy for you to sort of . . . well . . . discuss this thing with him, wouldn't it?"

Girard's gray eyes swung up slowly, pityingly, and held the attorney for a long moment before the sheriff spoke. "I wonder, Clarence, how in hell you ever survived to grow up. There isn't any man on earth so close to another man . . . a married man, in fact, who thinks he's getting away with something on the side . . . that would dare bring up the subject within gunshot of him." He shook his head slowly back and forth, still staring at the attorney. "If you can do that back East,

Clarence, then, by God, I don't know what kind of men you have there."

"All right, Frank. You're settled in your mind on this, I take it?"

Girard looked back quickly, saw no humor on the thin, pinched face, and let his head rock back when he laughed and shook it again. "What do I have to do, Clarence? Hit you on the head? No! I won't go near George Carpenter over this mess he's in, and I'd advise you to stay even farther away, too."

Black nodded slowly, his eyes showing a dull triumph in them. He waited until the office was as still as a tomb before he dropped his bomb. "Well, Frank . . . did you know Carrie's due in on the three o'clock stage this afternoon from Wagon Mound?" He knew the sheriff didn't know it when he asked the question. It just seemed the best, most shocking way to phrase a statement.

Frank's eyes widened a little. Aside from that there wasn't a move at all. Just that small, startled widening of the eyes. Finally, feeling his face getting tight from wearing the mask he'd forced on it when Black had entered the office, he waved an abrupt hand at the door. "Adiós, Clarence, come again."

There was no mistaking the strain behind the voice. Clarence Black was untutored in many frontier customs and usages, but he knew fury when he saw it, and it was just behind those words, and not far behind, either. One more remark from him and a whirlwind would erupt in his face. He nodded brusquely and went out into the early heat of the day, closing the weathered, checked, and scarred old oaken door behind him.

The sheriff regarded the door balefully for a full minute before he even moved, then he sighed, letting the air escape through clenched teeth with an unpleasant, sharp sound. Clarence Black was obnoxious, a fool, contemptible in his nosiness, but more than anything else — he was dangerous with the blind malevolence of a man ignorant of what he was about to unleash, if he wasn't stopped. Frank's face told the story of his inner feelings a little, too, after Black was gone. If George Carpenter, his old riding partner from days gone when both had drifted into the country, foot-loose and rubbing two coins together between them, wanted to take an Indian girl into his house in his wife's absence, it was no one's business really. What folks thought, Frank Girard included, was something else, but what they said or did in this land of hair tempers and hair-triggers, was bound to be altogether different.

Frank turned back to contemplation of Buelton and the open land beyond, from his single, stingy little window with its inartistic kaleidoscopic arrangements in flyspecks. What he saw was any trail town that had lived long enough to mature into a staid cow town in a solidly cow country. Weathered-looking, not ugly but not attractive, either, just functional, smoothed and rubbed round from the bars to the plank walk with the passing of cowmen, freighters, gunmen, and laborers of all kinds. Settling around the middle with comfortable prosperity that paid the town and surrounding ranches off in the good years, and allowed them leeway to coast and wait out the droughts, slumps, and seasonal prices in the poor years. Beyond the town lay the land itself, turning brown and drab now with late spring boiling over into the blistering summers of the range country where the sun dredged out its tribute of water from the earth and the men and animals that had to pay in sweat for the privilege of walking or riding under the scorching, relentless light.

Frank wondered how Clarence had known Carrie was returning. He pulled his mouth down and rolled a cigarette, lit it, and exhaled slowly. Some men have an ear or nose — for hearing things. The attorney was one of them. Arriving in Buelton two years before with a gleam in his eye and a degree in law, Clarence Black had settled down with the apparent intention of bringing Eastern law to a country that had heretofore relied on every man's discretion and gun to settle serious disputes — knuckles, boot heels, spurs, and gouging fingers to arbitrate lesser transgressions.

This wasn't Clarence's first attempt at tight-rope walking, either. He had come perilously close to being killed before, and hadn't really thought he was anywhere near the Great Divide. Frank shook his head. Some men live and learn, some just live. In two years Black hadn't accurately gauged the country yet. Maybe he never would; if not, there was reason to believe he'd die wondering why someone had shot him. Frank knew George Carpenter would shoot Clarence down like a rabid coyote. You don't drift with a man for a year without getting to know him pretty well. George was a

167

man who loved a joke, within bounds, and would give a stranger his last dollar or his spare horse. But Carpenter was also a bad man to cross in anything like this Indian girl affair. It was the custom of the frontier. Every man's mistakes were his own; if he found salvation, he did it alone, or, needing advice, he sought it. You never took it to him. George was no exception.

Just once, since Frank had known Carpenter, and as close as they had been, sharing the same bedroll and the same dismal luck on the trail, had George ever come to him for — not advice, actually — but a sort of discussion between partners, and that was when he was thinking of marrying Carrie Belleau. The discussion had been all one-sided then, too. Frank Girard had been too stunned, too completely overcome, to offer more than a few grunts. After the wedding — which Frank purposely avoided by taking off after a seedy horse thief like he'd been the most notorious outlaw on the frontier — their paths had parted. In the year since George and Carrie had been married, Frank hadn't seen either of them more than five times. He wanted it that way, too.

Now Black had had it, some way, that Carrie was due in Buelton on the 3:00p.m. stage. Frank dropped the cigarette, slashed it mercilessly with a spur rowel, and swore to himself. It didn't matter how Clarence knew, actually. What mattered was that Carrie was returning.

He got up and walked around the office once and came to a stand beside the desk again. If Carrie went out to her husband's ranch, she'd walk in on this —

well, this mess of George's. He winced. The picture was plain enough. He could see it, imagine it, just as it would be, exactly. Carrie was a big girl, not a girl really, because she was twenty-eight, but she was a wholesome, handsome woman with a sturdy, strong body that made your breath catch in your throat. She had blue eyes and ash-blonde hair and a mouth that was tender, firm, luscious, and patient, all at once. The kind of a mouth every man who saw it wanted to kiss, not just once, but for always. She was a woman who accepted adversity like it was a heavy cloak to be worn through a storm, then discarded graciously and heroically. There was an awesome capableness about her that was felt, seen, and appreciated instantly. But Carrie Carpenter was a one-man woman. She would help George get his ranch, guide and mother and sponsor him in everything, never complaining, but her full measure of payment was expected to be his loyalty and faithfulness. Now she was coming home to find it betrayed.

Frank perched on the edge of the desk and pictured the scene. Carrie wouldn't say anything; she wasn't the hysterical, wildly sobbing kind. She would see it all in their faces; her eyes wouldn't condemn the girl, but they'd rake George once, then she'd tell the driver to wait for her. She'd pack and walk out of George's life just like that. If there was a scene, George would have to make it, she wouldn't.

Frank went over to the little wood stove in the southwest corner of the office, picked up the graniteware coffee pot, shook it, listened critically to the sloshing, got his cup from the nail on the wall, and poured himself a cup of the lukewarm stuff and drank it slowly. Someone should at least warn George. He didn't deserve it, in a way, but, hell, for old time's sake Frank ought to let him know she was coming home so he could make an effort at redeeming himself — if he wanted to.

He hung the cup back up, worked the grounds around with his tongue, perched them expertly on the end, and fired them against the wall before he headed for the front door, went out and around the office to the lean-to barn behind, and saddled up.

Buelton was bustling with activity. It was still forenoon and the heat, while increasing, wasn't as unbearable as it would be shortly. Frank rode through the traffic with a nod where one was required, here and there, then he was on the north road leading over the distant land swell to Potter's Valley. He scowled to himself as he rode. At best, the subject would be a delicate one for a man who had never heard the word tact, or had more than a passing acquaintance with what it meant, still George Carpenter would surely give him an opening somewhere in the conversation. After all, it wasn't as though he intended to mention the Indian girl at all, but George, so damned touchy about things like his women, would understand what he was driving at right away. The sheriff shrugged. Well, all he could do was warn George. After that — hell — it was in the rancher's hands.

On the top of the ridge Frank reined westward and rode along the swell, thinking back to the times he had ridden the trail to Carpenter's Boxed C when the north wind was scourging the ridge like it was going to tear the ground apart. Today, though, it was the opposite. The heat was up with a full head of fire. It went through his faded cotton shirt and leeched the perspiration out of his flesh before it got well out of the pores.

He held the ridge for half an hour, then swung off it, following wagon tracks down the incline toward a breath-taking valley with a live creek at the bottom lined with great, bent cottonwoods. George's house, barn, and corrals all nestled in a shade that was almost purple. It was a sight that invariably made a summer rider's throat dry for some of the cool creek water. Frank lashed at his cracking lips with a moist tongue and shook his head. The Boxed C was as pretty a ranch as a man could find. No one in his right mind would risk losing it — or the female part of it — over a piney-woods Indian girl.

He rode through the gap, saw the gate lying in the grass, and looked up again as he came into the shade and felt its protection over his back before he swung down and tied his horse to a stud ring imbedded in an ancient cottonwood.

He hadn't gone ten feet from the horse when the cabin door opened and George Carpenter was standing there, wooden-faced, watching him cross the yard.

"Long way from home, Frank." Carpenter's voice had a tinge of antagonism underlying the curiosity.

Frank grinned mirthlessly and didn't speak until he was on the porch. He didn't move, either, after he was

171

opposite George, until it was obvious his old partner wasn't going to ask him inside, then he sighed, went over by the steps, and sat down, ignoring Carpenter, who was watching him balefully, his mouth sucked flat over his teeth.

"Sure hot this time of year." No answer came back. Frank's annoyance was turning to something more tangible and unpleasant. His eyes narrowed as they swept the yard, the sturdy barn, and the spidery network of corrals off to one side of it.

"Doing much riding, George?"

Carpenter evidently knew this interview wouldn't be over quickly. He crossed the porch and leaned against an upright, letting his own eyes, violet-colored and handsome, lift to the sheriff's eyes.

"Not much. Too early to start gathering yet."

"Thought you might come into town of an evening for supper. You never could cook worth a damn. With Carrie gone . . . and all . . . I've been looking for you. Figured we might get up a little two-handed trail poker."

There was an uncomfortable silence. Carpenter said nothing. Frank could tell, the way his feet shuffled against the porch planking, that he was uneasy. He turned a little so he could see the rancher and leaned back against a post, thumbing his hat back.

"Heard from Carrie, George?"

"No. She's not much to write . . . me, neither."

"Well, you knew she was coming in on the three o'clock stage today, didn't you?"

Frank was watching Carpenter's bronzed, square-jawed face. He saw the surprise spread out from the eyes downward, until the man's face was covered with it. He shrugged and looked away, uncomfortable under the revealed look of consternation that showed.

"I just heard it myself a couple hours ago. Thought I'd ride out and . . ."

"Warn me, Frank?" The words were silky soft.

Frank shrugged, feeling his irritation coming up again. "Call it what you like, George. Anyway, you'd want to drive your rig in and pick her up . . . save her having to use a buckboard from town, I reckon."

"Would I?"

Frank looked up quickly but didn't see Carpenter's eyes. The rancher's head was lowered while he twisted a cigarette into existence. Only the tight, reddish auburn curls of his head showed, the way he was bent over the tobacco workings. When the weed was going, George raised his eyes thoughtfully and looked straight into the sheriff's face. There was an ugly light moving in the background of his violet eyes. It might have been resentment, plain anger, or defiance, or a mixture of all three, Frank didn't know, but he did know it wasn't a friendly look. He waited.

"Frank . . . the news gets around, doesn't it?" There was no answer due and both men knew it. "I've known what folks are saying. No one's said anything to my face yet, and I don't expect they will, either. Now, it's you. Just guessing, I'd say someone put you up to coming out here to warn me that my wife's coming home. I don't think you'd do it on your own. You're not the

173

type, Frank." There was a long, pregnant silence, then: "Well, Sheriff, I'm not going in to pick Carrie up . . . but you coming out here so helpful like and all . . . that gives me a chance to send her a message." The violet eyes dropped to Frank's face again and hung there. "You can meet her at the stage and tell her I'm sending her clothes and stuff in to the hotel. She and I are through!"

Frank's gray eyes gave stare for stare with the violet eyes of George Carpenter. His heart was beating a thunderous tattoo inside, irregularly and lurchingly. Slowly he got to his feet, reached around in back automatically, and dusted off his seat.

"George . . . what in the name of God's gotten into you?" It was said more in pained surprise than anger.

Carpenter regarded him for a moment, then shoved off the upright. "You really want to see, Frank?" He didn't wait for an answer, just turned away, threw his cigarette down, stomped on it, and flung open the cabin door. "Come on in, Frank . . . and see!"

Frank Girard went in, not because he really wanted to see George's treasure at all, but because, in his shock and astonishment, he wanted to follow the conversation further. Inside, the cabin was as it had always been, with bear rugs and cat pelts on the floors and walls. Indian gewgaws hung disconsolately here and there and the big stone fireplace gaped at him with its smoky, black maw. The place wasn't as neat as Carrie always kept it, but it was the same in all other ways, except one. There was a woman standing by the fireplace, her arms behind her, looking directly at him with no expression at all.

There was no mistaking the sarcasm in Carpenter's voice when he went toward the kitchen and waved a hand toward a chair. "Have a seat, Frank . . . I'll make some coffee."

Frank didn't sit down, but he did take off his hat. Maybe she was sixteen, like Clarence Black had said, but he'd guess her closer to twenty, maybe a shade over — but, regardless of her age, there was one thing Clarence had said that was obviously, painfully, true: she was a woman!

The term Indian was used on the frontier to describe anyone partly Indian in blood. Sometimes, even, the term was applied to anyone of darker than ordinary skin coloring. But this girl was only an Indian by euphemism. Some subtle humor may have inspired calling her one, or, more likely, she was accorded the description instead of a less complimentary term, half-breed. Her hair and eyes were black but her skin was a luscious golden color with none of the dumpiness of Indians about her, or the unclean sallowness. She was tall, possibly five feet five or six inches.

Frank saw the compelling beauty of her face. True, she lacked any indication of spirituality, but so did all white women in this land. Her mouth protruded with a fullness that made his blood respond in spite of himself, and her nose was aquiline, straight and beautiful. He finally let his eyes drop in embarrassment, but the picture of her stayed vividly in his mind. Because of the inexpressive look she wore in her study of him, it was hard to say whether she had a personality at all. Frank had to fall back on his own acute ability to sense an atmosphere where she was concerned. He got the impression then, too, that, whatever else she was — or might be — she was an exquisite animal, strong-willed, passionate, blindly loving, violently possessive, and — cruel. These things were in the room with them, like phantoms, felt, sensed, and accepted, but with no basis solid enough to identify. Then she spoke and he looked up again.

"You're Sheriff Girard from Buelton, aren't you?"

Frank nodded, looking up to see what expression her face would show now. There was interest on the features, and something else that Frank thought uneasily was, possibly, a quickening of female design.

"Has George done something wrong . . . Sheriff?"

Frank's mouth pulled down ironically a little. He shook his head. "Well, I'm not the judge, ma'am. He is."

"My name's Irene Cobalt." She didn't sound the letter "t" at all. Frank understood. A lot of the upland hunters and trappers were French-Canadians. They usually dropped the "t" in everything unless there were two of them. It gave him more than a clue about her, too. She had got that inspiring coloring apparently from one of those old voyageurs, the size and proportions, and possibly even the regal, handsome carriage as well. He wondered if her mother was a typical companion, one of those myriad Indian women who went from bivouac to bivouac with her French-Canadian lord and master, fleshing his hides, cooking his meals, and

176

bearing his children between scouring traps and kneading buckskin for clothing. It didn't matter, though. All that mattered now was that Carrie was coming home to the dissolution of her marriage to George Carpenter — and standing in front of him was the most formidable reason for a broken home he had ever seen. A truly breath-taking girl, he even understood a little of George's violent decision.

"Is George's wife coming back? Is that why you are here now?"

Frank shifted his feet. The spurs rang with a melodious complaint. "His wife's coming back, all right," the sheriff said non-committally. "She'll be in Buelton at three o'clock today."

The wonderful face went blank again. It irritated Frank. This was the Indian, the ability to drop back into a secret world of aloofness where she would take council with herself. No one would know the outcome until she spoke it, if she did.

George came back into the room with three steaming mugs of black coffee. Frank took his, avoided the searching look on George's face, watched Carpenter offer the girl a cup, and saw the look in her eyes when they looked at one another, and his heart sank. Carrie had lost George as surely as night follows day. It was a crazy, inexplicable thing — and yet, to Frank Girard, it wasn't altogether strange or unbelievable, either. He had gotten to know Carpenter pretty well. He knew the spontaneity of the man, his nervous drive, and unbounded animal spirits. It would have been possible, even, to plot the course of George Carpenter and this

177

half-breed girl, Irene Cobalt, for Frank, if he'd ever seen them together before they had become so intimate. It would have been easy because Frank knew they shared a common passion of spirit and unruly independence that would admit no fealty as lasting, marriage or anything else.

He drank his coffee and set the cup down, took up his hat, and dumped it on the back of his head, ignoring Irene and fixing George with a calm stare.

"George, if you want that message taken to Carrie, take it yourself."

Carpenter looked up from where he sat perched on the arm of a leather chair. There was irony, hard and unrelenting, in his eyes. "Not even for old time's sake, Frank?"

"Not for that or anything else, George."

"Well," the rancher said slowly, looking into his coffee cup. "I don't give a copper colored damn what folks think . . . you know that . . . but with you it's different. We're old friends."

Frank shook his head emphatically. "Not any more, George. Listen, I'm no angel, but I . . . well, I don't know how to say it, but you understand, I think."

"Yeah," the rancher said dryly. "Morality. Isn't that it?"

Again the sheriff wagged his head. "No, not at all. Like I said, I'm no angel. If you want to do this, that's your business. It's something else. Loyalty, sort of, George, and I'll be dog-goned if I'm going to be the one who tries to explain it to your wife."

The Indian girl hadn't moved since Frank Girard had entered the house. Now she did. She walked over by George's chair and leaned forward to put down her empty cup, then she straightened up and smiled at him. It was a stunning smile, full of vigor and youth and — desire. "Sheriff, have you ever been in love?"

Frank was startled and showed it. He turned abruptly and went to the door before he turned back, saw them both watching him, and made a slight gesture with one hand. "No, not like this. Not like you two, not so that I don't give a damn who gets hurt, or how, by being so."

George Carpenter nodded slightly, his face unpleasant. "Thanks for coming out, Frank. One more thing. Will you do me a favor?"

"Like what?"

"Send out one of those rummies from Eaton's livery barn. I'll pay him a day's wages if he'll ride out here, get a message from me, and tote it back to Buelton and deliver it by the time the afternoon stage gets in. Will you do that?"

"I reckon." Frank opened the door, stood there thinking, then glanced in shock at George again. "You want this man to take the message to Carrie, when she comes in?"

"Yeah."

Frank's face was pale in the soft light, his gray eyes large and round. There was a savage anger showing in the bunched muscles along the ridge of his jaw when he spoke. "You'd do this . . . to Carrie? Have a damned rummy come up sudden-like and tell her you're

179

through with her . . . just like that? She doesn't get any more consideration from you than that, George?"

"One way's as good as another, Frank, I figure."

The sheriff's mouth opened. The lips moved, but no words came out. The gray eyes swung to the girl again, dropped to George Carpenter, then he went out and slammed the door behind himself.

On the ride back to town Frank was slumped in thought. Naturally he wouldn't send one of the filthy, rum-soaked drifters that hung around Eaton's livery barn out to George. Naturally, too, someone would now have to intercept Carrie Carpenter when she stepped off the stage and whisk her away before the malicious gossips of Buelton got to her first. And — naturally — she would have to be told, and spared the anguish and shock of discovering that her world had caved-in first hand.

Who was going to do all this? Frank writhed in the saddle and swore viciously into the stillness as he rode. His horse's ears flicked back and forth, then grew indifferent. Naturally! Frank Girard was going to have this chore to do — and that was new salt in an old wound, because Frank hadn't avoided George's marriage to Carrie Belleau because he cared a hang about the horse thief he'd used as an excuse to escape the affair. He had stayed away because he had himself been hopelessly in love with her for close to three years. Ever since the first time he had seen her, statuesque, magnificently poised, and so abundantly female and handsome.

CHAPTER
TWO

He was back in the office, sitting like a half-filled sack of grain, slouched and tucked up in the middle, when the grotesque humor of the thing struck him. In the first place, he had flatly refused to go to the Boxed C and talk to George. He had almost been mad enough to throw Clarence Black out of the office when the attorney had suggested it. And yet — he had done exactly that. He had gone. Again, he had resolutely refused to have any part in delivering the message to Carrie of George's infidelity and betrayal of her, and had even refused to send out a messenger who would tell her, then he had found himself in the unenviable position of being the most logical person to tell her, after all.

He made a cigarette and lit it with a savage slash of the match beneath his desk. Some way, for some reason, fate was forcing him into this thing up to the hilt, and he resented it every inch of the way.

There was an abrupt, curt knock on the door and before Frank could remove the cigarette from his mouth, the panel swung inward and Clarence Black was back in the room again, staring at him. The silence grew. Both men nodded and Black went over to the long bench against the wall and sat down. He mopped at his forehead and prominent nose with a grayish handkerchief.

"Well . . . you went out there, I see."

"How did you see?" Frank's rancor was showing in his face. His dislike of the attorney was getting more intense as the day went along.

Black shrugged. "I saw you ride out toward Potter's Valley shortly after I left you, Frank."

"Well . . . dammit all . . . there's more than the Boxed C out there, you know."

The sarcasm wasn't convincing and Clarence shook his head slightly. "Sure, but what's the use in fencing?"

"Fencing?" the sheriff said, startled. "What's this got to do with fencing?"

Clarence flagged the air with a small hand. His face was creased ruefully in an impatient grin. "I'm talking about a different kind of fencing . . . not building fences, Frank."

"Well." The sheriff's anger was in his throat now. The hint of condescension in the attorney's voice kept it there, too. "If you've got anything to say, Clarence, say it . . . then get to hell out of here. I've had about all the bull I expect to take today."

Black regarded Girard thoughtfully, remaining quiet for a while. He could see the wrath plainly enough and wondered just how far he dared go. He knew, moreover, that Frank Girard would do exactly what he said. Throw him out of the office. He knew it because he'd seen the sheriff do it to men before, even if he

182

didn't rely on the lawman's reputation, which was convincing enough without demonstration.

His voice was low and soothing. "Frank . . . let's act like grown men about this."

Girard swung in his chair and fixed a close stare on Black's face. "Clarence, dog-gone it, I'm sick and tired of the whole thing. There's no broken laws here." He saw the attorney's face light up and made a helpless gesture with one hand. "Oh, hell! I know what you're thinking. That damned morality stuff again. Well, it's not in the Buelton ordinances, so it's out of my line. Now you listen to me. Sure, I went out there. I talked to George and . . . met this girl."

"How old is she?" Clarence asked quickly, eyes kindling.

"To the devil with that," Frank said, annoyed. "Besides, I don't know. Listen, I don't want to hear another damned word about this mess . . . at all. From you or anyone else. Not a single damned word. Now, if you don't have anything better to do . . . or something else on your mind . . . get out!"

Clarence got up, but his face had lost its pensive look. His eyes were alive with animosity and antagonism. "All right, Sheriff. You won't take a hand in the thing, but I will."

Frank stared. "On what grounds?"

"On the grounds that the *thing* is detrimental to Buelton's standards of conduct. In fact . . ."

"Buelton's standards of conduct!" Frank arose in one lithe movement and glared, then he laughed. "Clarence, I told you this morning to start your house cleaning at the Whitsett House. There's enough work there . . . reforming . . . to keep you off George's back for a year."

"That, too, in due time. Frank, there was a meeting of the Ladies' Progressive Society in town this morning. Reverend Murphy led the . . ."

"Get to the point."

"Action was authorized against George Carpenter as a definite threat to the community's morals."

"Action!" Frank spat out. "Clarence, you're a darned poor lawyer if you don't know you can't do anything like this without the authorization of the town council."

"That," Black said with his customary canniness, the law-trained ability to drop bombs at the crucial time in a discussion, "has also been approved. We called a meeting and . . ."

"You mean to stand there and tell me, Clarence Black," the sheriff said, dumbfounded, "that Hugo Lesser and the others said it was all right for you to get out a paper against George Carpenter?"

"That's exactly what I'm telling you, Frank. Furthermore, as soon as I can pick it up, I'm going to take action, too."

Frank stood motionlessly for a full fifteen seconds, looking at the smaller man. He was stunned. The city fathers were lenient men; there wasn't a single one of them who didn't patronize the Whitsett House, Buelton's largest, most extravagant, and wide-open saloon and hotel combined. He sat down again, still looking at Black.

"Clarence, if you bring me a paper to serve on George Carpenter, so help me you'll have my badge in your hand the second you lay the thing down here."

"He's an old friend of yours, isn't he?"

"No, not any more. But that's not the point." Frank grew thoughtful. "Tell me something. Just how in hell did this all come about?"

Black shifted his weight and shrugged. "The ladies' society went *en masse* to the council rooms. They made such a scene Hugo called a special meeting. That's all there was to it."

Frank nodded somberly. He could see it as plain as day. Hugo, with his great blacksmith's arms and shoulders and ferocious heart, hadn't quite known what to do when the place had filled up with women. He couldn't throw them out, club them down, or shoot them — so he'd called the meeting.

Frank nodded at Clarence. "On your way, attorney. One last warning . . . you're making something that'll cause more trouble here than a range war. You'll see."

"With ample cause, Frank."

"With no damned cause at all . . . that's your affair anyway. Get out!"

Clarence went for the second time in the same morning. The sheriff fished for his watch, touched the top, and peered beyond the gold covering that dropped back. It was still early. He snapped the watch closed and pocketed it.

Clarence had an obsession. It was pretty plain. The lawyer's zeal had found another outlet, only this time it was like throwing matches into a dynamite barrel.

Evidently he had addressed the Buelton ladies' society and had whipped the suffragettes into militant action. All these women would need would be something like George's affair with the Indian girl. It was right down their alley. The fact that few of them had ever bothered to know Carrie didn't matter. They were fanatical now, unquestionably inspired by Clarence's persuasive, glib tongue. Result? Concerted action that had forced their perspiring fathers and brothers to take a step that was frenzied, ridiculous, and actually beyond the scope of the power of any city council.

He donned his hat and went out into the murderous sunlight again. Traffic was dwindling now. Most of the commerce of Buelton was attended to in the early hours. By noon even the little urchins and their eternally scratching dogs that dodged along the rim of the plank walks, perilously near horse's hoofs, with an acumen for dodging near injury with agility and rare perception found in no one else but their own kind were gone. The town lay under a siege of heat and had retired beyond its defensive walls to escape the fiery assault.

Frank went across the road where little dust devils jerked to life under the impact of his booted feet and settled a furry edge of brown along the welt of his foot gear. He stepped up on the opposite duckboards, turned slightly south, and shoved in past the louvered doors of the Whitsett House.

The big saloon was cool and shadowy inside with the comfortable, masculine smells of all saloons in the stuffy atmosphere. Frank went across to the bar, nodded to the swarthy bartender named Silva, and ordered an ale. When it came, he nursed it along, savoring the pleasantness of the place during the hot morning when it was deserted except for card players in a rear room. The bartender came over dangling a sour bar rag in one hand. He was a tolerant man with resignation written plainly in every line of his harassed face.

"Sheriff . . . you missed the fireworks."

"Yeah," Frank said dryly, "but I heard about them. Who started the thing, anyway?"

"Clarence Black." For a moment neither man said anything, then the barman's face twisted into a weary grimace. "What in hell ails some men? You sort of expect it from women . . . married ones anyway. They got to be meddling, sort of. 'Pears when a woman begins losing her . . . whatever in hell it is they got when they're single . . . they got to start meddling. A man," Silva said sagely, "thinks before he shoots off his mouth. Not a woman, no, sir."

"You saw it?" Frank asked, mildly interested although his head was full of more important things — like the hours going by and Carrie's coming home.

"Yeah," the bartender said slowly. "First, it sounded like a herd of Texas cattle coming along the duckboards outside." He raised and lowered his shoulders in mute eloquence. "You know how it is . . . what with this woman back East going around with a damned fool hatchet chopping up bars and all. Well, I run over to the door in time to see 'em nail old Hugo in his shop and herd him across the road to the council office. There wasn't no secret about it, the way they howled and yowled." Silva's face looked a little worried. "What'll they do? What can they do?"

Frank shrugged. "Darned if I know. But Clarence's getting almighty big, stirring up something like this."

"Yeah," the barman agreed. "What's your part in it? You got to arrest George?"

"No. Buelton's pretty quiet now. No rustling, shooting, not even any good fights. That sort of thing is my line. This other . . . well, it's no one's damned business but Carpenter's. I don't have any reason to arrest him."

"I know" — Silva nodded — "but if Clarence gets out a paper, you'll have to act on it, won't you?"

Frank drank the last of his ale and clasped and unclasped both his hands around the cool glass, looking down at the bar as he answered. "I look at it this way. I'm a lawman. I draw my pay to maintain order hereabouts. I interpret order to mean disturbances . . . fights, rustling, and the like. This other . . . well, I don't figure anyone's got a right to police a man's ranch or butt into his home life. Anyway, I'm not going to. I told Clarence that."

Silva said no more. He had his answer and more. He had found a man who regarded the entire affair much as he did. There was a certain masculine alliance between them. The fact that their thinking was purely male, and not at all in keeping with established conventions, didn't occur to them, and, if it had, they would have rejected the ideas as quickly as they could. The frontier wasn't, as Clarence Black had said, grown

188

up yet. A man's actions were his own affair so long as they didn't materially injure others.

Frank paid for the ale and left the Whitsett House. He squinted against the sun's glare and crossed the road to Hugo Lesser's blacksmith shop. The smith saw him coming, ran his massive, thick paws down the shiny, scarred leather apron that hung from his waist, and waited. There was discomfort on his face. He made an effort at smiling, but it was a poor one, so he let it go and stood still, waiting for Frank to speak.

The sheriff regarded the blacksmith with a sober expression and didn't jockey with his conversation. "Hugo, why in the devil did you let them stampede you like that?"

The blacksmith made a wry face, shifted his pale eyes from the sheriff's face twice before he could force them to stay there. "Clarence . . . Frank. He had it all down in black and white. All legal and . . . such."

"Hugo, there's no law written in this country that gives Clarence the right to bust in on George and make him change his way of life."

"Well," the blacksmith said doubtfully, wishing he was miles away and still traveling, "he had a real good name for what George's doing. It's . . ."

"Morality," Frank said gruffly.

"I reckon. He only said it twice. I never got a chance to repeat it to myself. Them women were making too much racket." The pale eyes went over Frank's features. "He's plumb right, too, Frank. George's making a spectacle . . . sort of."

"How about the Whitsett House, Hugo?"

Lesser's face turned a stained, rusty color. His eyes gave way instantly and couldn't be forced back to the sheriff's face.

Frank shrugged. It was useless. He was wasting his time. Clarence had ramrodded a foolish, harmful enactment through the town council and was going ahead with it in his usual dogged, blind way. The sheriff turned away without a nod at Hugo Lesser, and strolled down the plank walk toward the little café sandwiched into the long, narrow space between Eaton's livery barn and Levitt's Emporium. He ate chili and beans and washed the fiery stuff down with black coffee. He had paid his check and was rolling a cigarette when someone entered, spurs making soft music in the stillness of the café, and dropped down on the bench next to him. Frank looked up, saw the florid, open face of the big, burly man next to him, and nodded. Sean Reilly was the owner of the Whitsett House. He was a flamboyant man, loud, hearty, quick-tempered and big-hearted. Clearly he was in the café for a purpose, since his own establishment had a superior dining room operated in conjunction with his hotel upstairs.

Frank smoked and ignored the huge saloon owner beside him, waiting. Reilly's dark eyes shone expansively. He was a good friend and a terrible enemy.

"Frank, boy, what in God's name is Clarence up to now?"

The sheriff didn't bother to answer. It was a preliminary and needed no bolstering. Sean would get on with it at his own pleasure.

"Listen, Frank. You've got to stop Clarence. If he gets this thing rolling, boy, he'll have a foothold."

Frank understood then. He turned slowly, deliberately, and looked at the big man with no show of friendliness. "Sean, you had a chance to sit in on the town council. Why didn't you?"

"Frank, I've got the business to look after. I don't need no prestige. That's all anyone ever joins one of the tomfool organizations for. You know that. Look at 'em, by God! Every last one of 'em's a poor man longin' to have the dignity of officialdom on their backs. Hell! You don't find a solid businessman with money on them councils . . . ever. You know that."

"All right, Sean. Call it any way you see it, but remember this. Those four men make the ordinances. If you're too big to sit with them, then you're laying yourself open to whatever they decide. Now, you're worrying because Clarence's getting this morality campaign of his rolling. You've had several years to buy him out or run him off. You didn't do a thing."

"But, Frank," Reilly protested, "who in hell would ever take Clarence Black serious?"

Frank shrugged. "Evidently a lot have made the same mistake. That doesn't change a thing, Sean. He's within his legal rights . . . the way he worked this thing . . . and the Lord help those of you who are contrary to the way he calls his shots."

For a long moment Reilly didn't answer. He sat sideways, astraddle the bench, looking at Frank. After a bit he nodded his head slightly. There was a decided hardness in his eyes now that didn't escape the sheriff.

191

Frank raised a hand and tapped the big man's arm with one finger. "Don't make any mistakes, Sean," he said softly, understanding the malevolence in the rich man's face well enough. "Clarence's within his rights in what he's done. Don't get faulty ideas."

Reilly's eyes came back to focus. They settled stonily on the sheriff's face and held a blank but pleasant look. He didn't utter another word, pushed up from the bench, nodded crisply, and stalked out of the café.

Frank swore to himself, paid for his dinner, and went outside. Blane Eaton was standing outside his livery barn rolling a limp cigar around in his coarse mouth. He nodded solemnly at Frank, who ambled down beside him.

"Say, Blane, I'd appreciate it if you'd send one of your drifters or hostlers, or someone, up to my office and let me know the second Clarence Black gets his horse and rides out of town . . . toward Potter's Valley."

Blane Eaton's cigar hesitated in its gyrations, held still for a moment, then sagged, forgotten against the heavy, sulky underline of the man. Frank looked around, saw the strange, startled way Eaton was looking at him, and froze in sudden understanding. They faced each other for seconds before Eaton spoke hoarsely around his cigar.

"You're about an hour and a half too late, Frank. Him and that cussed night man of mine rode out of here that long ago."

"Toward Potter's Valley, Blane?" Frank asked in a horrified tone.

The liveryman nodded without speaking, reading the conflict in the sheriff's face and knowing why it was there. Gossip traveled fast in Buelton, especially when the doldrums were on the land and not even a horse thief would come out long enough to ruffle the stifling *ennui* of the country.

Frank walked back toward his office. Time had ceased to matter now. It was like holding his breath under water, feeling eternity passing above in lightning flashes that he couldn't begin to arrest, the whole thing happening in seconds that seemed endless. There had been a vague hope with no real basis but existing inside of him nevertheless, that George would come to his senses before 3:00p.m., before Carrie's stage came in. He went on past the office, turned down the worn lane in the weeds at the side of the building and leading to his lean-to stable. He went inside out of the sun and smelled the strong ammonia and manure odor of the place. His bay horse looked over the partition at him thoughtfully, rocking his jaws sideways as he ate, then, deciding the man thing wasn't going to take him out after all, he lost interest and went on eating from the manger.

Frank leaned against the wall and battled mechanically at the fierce, drab little stable flies that swarmed to investigate him. He hooked a thumb into his watch pocket but didn't take the timepiece out after all. Time wasn't important now. Not any more. Clarence had been at the Boxed C for a good half hour. He and the whiskey sot who was Eaton's night hawk. Whatever was going to transpire was either being enacted right now — this minute — or it was all over.

His stomach was like lead. A memory of George Carpenter down in Tucson one time, years back, came up unbidden and vivid. There had been an argument over cards — a far lesser thing than what George and Clarence would be arguing about right now — then George's unpredictable temper had exploded. When the smoke had cleared away . . .

Frank spat earthward and eased down on the saddle pole, feeling for the cantle of his saddle to steady his balance. It wasn't the same George Carpenter any more, in a way. The owner of the Boxed C was a man temporarily out of his head. It put Frank in mind of a dying prospector he'd found one time in the Mogollons. The man was full of craziness and too far gone to nurse back. He'd waited until the prospector had died and had buried him. This was sort of the same thing, except George's frenzy would wear off — unless he did something serious while he was still unbalanced. That was what was making Frank's insides knot up. Clarence was more than a fool. He was a fanatic. An ignorant, blind one. Belligerently he would challenge George's right to his way of life. George, on the other hand, knew only one way to offset something like this. Frank spat again, fished around aimlessly for his watch, and pulled it out by the little thong that dangled inches below the watch pocket.

Scarcely looking, he pushed in on the stem and let the covering that protected the white enameled face fall back against his thumb pad. 2:30p.m. He stared,

194

incredulous, then raised the watch and inspected it, doubting even though he understood that time had turned against him. The small, industrious sound of the thing reassured him. He snapped it closed and exchanged somber glances with the horse, whose indifference had turned to curiosity.

It wasn't 1:00 p.m., which would have meant he might have caught Clarence and kept George from serious trouble. And it wasn't 3:00, when Carrie's stage would come rumbling in. Even that would be better than having it 2:30, which only meant that Frank had to sit there, helpless to move in any direction, and sweat for a dragging, stifling half a damned hour, just thinking. He spat again for the third time and, for lack of anything else to do, put his hands to work making a cigarette he didn't want.

The air in the lean-to was still and muggy. Sweat ran under Frank's shirt like miniature rivers with lacings of salt. It tickled and itched at the same time. He rubbed himself now and then, and smoked. The time went by like he knew it would, and he was still sitting there, hunched over like a sick buzzard over poisoned carrion, when the sound of insistent boots clumping toward his office around in front, with spurs ringing violently in falsetto emphasis, brought his head up. He listened, still preoccupied, heard the boots enter the office. A voice cried his name in thickly muted urgency. He shoved off the saddle pole, spat into his palm, and carefully drowned the cigarette, palmed it until he was back outside, then dropped it on the path and ground it deliberately and savagely into the dusty, hot earth, and walked slowly back around to the duckboards and into the office.

He looked at the two faces in front of him, both white and drawn in spite of the flush of sweat that made each feature sticky and unclean-looking, greasy. He recognized the night hawk from Eaton's and Blane Eaton himself. Irrelevantly he noticed that the liveryman's shirt, plastered to his obese, heavy-breasted chest, was giving away the man's excitement by the way it radiated each monstrous, uneven beat of his sluggish heart.

"Want me, boys?"

"God Almighty!" Eaton said, cutting off his hostler without a chance, alert with a morbid eagerness to be the first to break the news. "Carpenter shot Clarence down an' killed him!"

Frank crossed the room without glancing at the liveryman again. Eaton's face, with its excited, almost eagerly pleasant look, angered him so that his hands shook. He turned finally and sat down, fixing the man with a cold stare.

"Were you there, Blane?"

Eaton raised his head a little in astonishment. "Why ... you know I wasn't. You talked to me not more'n ..."

"Then get out!"

Eaton took it like he had been struck. Even staggered a little under the impact of the look that went with the words. Then he turned abruptly and went out of the office, leaving the door partly open. Frank swore irritably, got up, and closed the door and motioned the night hawk to the bench, and sat down again. "You rode out there with Clarence?"

"Yeah."

"Why?"

"Well . . . he asked me to. Fact is, he paid me five dollars to go along. If I'd known what was . . ."

"I reckon," Frank said dryly. "What happened, exactly?"

"Well . . . we rode into the yard. Clarence . . . Mister Black . . . had this damned paper he was going to serve on Carpenter."

Frank winced. Clarence hadn't asked him to serve the paper. He had done it himself because Frank had told him he wouldn't do it. For once, fate hadn't pushed him into doing what he was dead set against — or had it? Maybe it hadn't because it had known there wouldn't have been a killing, or certainly less chance of it, if Frank had served the paper. He writhed with inner turmoil, pondering over it. The hostler was talking and Frank brought himself back with an effort.

". . . forget a lot of it, but they argued anyway, then Clarence fishes out this paper and makes to lean over and hand it to Carpenter."

Frank interrupted: "Neither of you got off your horses?"

"No, I told you that."

"All right. I wasn't listening. Go on."

"Carpenter laughed then, not pleasant, just a sort of laugh, y'know." Frank nodded. "He wouldn't take the paper, an' Mister Black got mad as hell."

"Did he cuss Carpenter out?"

197

"Not exactly. Not no names, y'see, just cussed and raised hell in general."

Frank pictured it in his mind's eye. Clarence, bombastic, excited, and dealing in the words that were his trade, George standing there in the yard getting that awful white look to his face that he got when he was burning up inside. He shook himself again, listening.

". . . Carpenter commenced calling him then. Not loud. I didn't think that's what he was saying, his voice was so quiet and all, then I understood and froze with my hands in plain sight on the saddle horn."

"Were you beside Clarence?"

"No, by God! I was off to his right about ten, twelve feet."

"And?"

"And . . ." The man's eyes were big. He was reliving it all over again. It was so fresh he could still smell the salty, sulphurous odor in the air. "And . . . then Carpenter told Clarence to go for it. I don't know what possessed Clarence . . . Mister Black . . . but he ducked a hand for his coat pocket and Carpenter cut him down." The dull, inflamed eyes stared over at Frank without seeing him. "Black's horse shied out from under him. He was hit anyway. He fell like a drunk, all solid and unbending." The man's eyes focused on Frank's nickel badge, a circlet with a small star inside of it. "And Carpenter went up, lowered his arm, and fired that second shot, but I figure Mister Black was dead from the first one. Leastways he never moved after he hit the ground."

"Did you get down and look at him?"

The hostler looked astounded and shaken. His mouth opened and closed twice before he answered: "God, no!"

"Carpenter throw down on you?"

"Yeah. He says, calm as hell, you want in, pardner? I shook my head like hell, too scairt to say a word. He nods at me and says . . . 'Vamoose then.' I did. Come right back to town and told Blane. He brung me up here."

Frank felt the sickness rising inside of him again, like it had in the lean-to. He turned slightly so he wouldn't have to look at the hostler. The sounds of Buelton drifted in, softened, to them. Finally he nodded back at the man.

"You figuring on leaving town?"

"No. I live here. Got a family."

"Good. Stay handy. I might need you again one of these days."

"Not to go out . . . there . . . again, I hope?"

"No, just as a witness. That's all. You can go back to Eaton now."

The night hawk arose, nodded awkwardly, and left on stiff, unnaturally acting legs. Frank smiled sardonically, ruthlessly at the man's obvious fright, then his mind was pulled back from its bitterness by a rumbling sound that made the office quake a little, and a weary voice crying loudly: "Stage's in! Stage's in!"

CHAPTER
THREE

Frank crossed the office in three large strides, threw the door open, and left it that way, but he didn't step outside. There was no need for that quite yet.

He stood unobtrusively under the overhang that supposedly shaded his building and watched the coach settle back a half turn of the wheels, ensconced in a dirty cloak of its own dust that arose gently, gracefully, then reluctantly settled back to earth. The driver hitched the lines around the high brake handle with a weary finality that spoke volumes, leaned far over, and fished something small, massive and compact out of the leather boot beneath his high seat and grunted under the weight as he lowered it to a waiting clerk with black arm socks from sleeve to elbow on each arm. The clerk staggered off around the stage, heading for the office. The gun guard, disdaining to help the grunting handlers who wormed up the back of the stage to unlash the baggage, turned sideways, measured the distance and clearance, and leaped lightly down, his carbine held aloft like a man plunging into water.

Frank saw the nigh door open after several moments of jarring at it because it was stuck, and the passengers began to clamber down. The first and second were

200

men. One, obviously, was a cowboy afoot. The man's sheepish, ashamed look was a story in itself. Frank smiled thinly. He had either lost or gambled away his outfit because no saddle was on the coach's top. The second man was just as plainly a drummer, even to the battered sample cases. Then Frank's throat tightened a little. Carrie got down. She was every inch as he would always remember her, calm, poised, and half smiling her anticipation. His throat tightened even more. The ash-blonde hair was perfectly in place in spite of the rigorous ordeal of riding a thorough-brace coach all day and all night. He stepped down reluctantly, watching her, drinking her in and feeling her image grow in his heart again, as he walked slowly across the roadway to her.

"Carrie?"

She turned, looked quickly at him, and smiled. It made her even more radiant and alluring. He shook his head a little ruefully. It was incredible how she looked so young and lovely.

"Frank Girard. What are you shaking your head about?"

He looked for some significance in what she said but forgot it in an instant. She couldn't know. Out of the corner of his eye he saw Hugo Lesser and several other townsmen standing a short way off, up by the horses' heads, watching them with expressions of absolute morbidity. He edged around so she wouldn't see them. It was apparent they wanted to speak to the sheriff.

"Carrie, you get prettier every day. Did you know that?"

The blue eyes flashed gratitude at him. "Thank you, Frank." She moved back on to safer ground then. "Was George working? Did he ask you to see me home?"

"I reckon, Carrie," he said, feeling the new sweat popping out over his back and chest and shoulders. "Let's get in the shade." He was turning to lead the way to his office when she stopped him with a hand on his arm.

"My luggage, Frank."

"Oh," he said vacantly, looking up at the baggage still on the coach's roof. Maliciously then, on the spur of the moment, he turned squarely and faced the town councilmen who were still watching them uneasily. "Hugo, take care of Missus Carpenter's baggage, will you?" He saw the surprise flood the blacksmith's face and smiled wickedly, vengefully, before he turned, hooked Carrie's arm in his own, and propelled her across the road and into his building.

The office always had seemed drab and shoddy to Frank, but with Carrie standing in the center, looking around with interest, it seemed positively grimy. He went over and sloshed the coffee pot. There was no resounding echo of liquid at all. He looked at the thing like it had struck him and put it back down. His tongue was clamped to the roof of his mouth and his feet were sticky inside their boots.

"Frank?"

He turned, went back by the desk, and shoved the chair around for her without answering, just levering up a forced smile so palpably insincere that he blushed.

202

"Frank?" she said again. "What's the matter?" It was said quietly, patiently, like a mother asks her child what calamity had befallen, not believing anything could really happen that was as serious as his face said it was.

Frank wanted to swear but he didn't. He frantically fished out the tobacco sack and began to create a cigarette.

"Carrie . . . aren't any of us perfect. George's got quirks like all of us."

He knew he was all wrong, finished the cigarette, lit it, and couldn't avoid her eyes any longer. With a deep, bracing intake of breath he raised his face, saw the wonder and uneasiness stirring in her glance, and looked beyond her to the dirty wall.

"All right, Frank," she said. "I'm prepared. What is it? What's happened?"

"George killed a man." He dropped his glance quickly to give her a second to get back her control. He had misjudged her, though.

"Who was the man, Frank?"

It came out so quietly, evenly, that he was startled a little.

"Man named Clarence Black. A lawyer here in town."

"Yes," Carrie said. "I know who he was. I've seen him. What . . . ? How did it happen?"

"Listen, Carrie, God knows I'd rather lose a leg than tell you this. Before I do, I want you to promise me something."

She was getting pale now, white and tense-looking up around the eyes. Her handsome, soft mouth was setting, too. The determination in her was predominant now.

"What is it, Frank? What kind of a promise?"

"Promise me, Carrie, that you won't go away. That," he ended miserably, lamely, "that you'll stay here in Buelton for . . . well, a while anyway, until the thing's over." He was looking into her eyes and feeling the pull of her. There was a strange feeling in him that she was actually helping him say these things, sustaining him some way, silently, like he had never been sustained in strife before. It was a fleeting, peculiar sensation and he clung to it.

"Frank, you're asking a lot." The dullness in her voice didn't escape him. Her glance had fallen and was resting on the black, holstered gun on his hip, sagging menacingly from the worn shell belt.

"Well, Carrie, I don't want you to leave until . . ." He stopped there, wondering exactly why he didn't want her to leave, and finding confusion in his own mind.

"Until?" she prompted without looking up from his gun.

He shrugged. "I don't know. Just . . . for a while, anyway."

She nodded gently, raising her face to him. "All right. You have a reason, I know. I promise then, Frank, but it won't be easy, staying in Buelton with all the talk that'll be going around . . . is going around right now, I imagine."

He hadn't considered that aspect at all. His jaws clamped together, making a thin, cold line of his mouth, then he shook his head minutely to himself, and looked back at her again. "George's got a girl living at the Boxed C with him. A 'breed girl, Carrie. He asked me today to meet your stage and tell you he's through."

It was the hardest thing he had ever had to say in his life and the reaction was no better. His chest felt like it was full of boiling tar and his hands were slimy with palm sweat.

Carrie didn't move. Frank remembered how he'd had to wear a mask when Black had been in the office, and walked abruptly over to the little stove, turning his back on her so she wouldn't have to suffer as he had, especially when her anguish was so new and nearly unbearable, and he'd borne his own for over a year, since her marriage to his old riding partner. While he made a new pot of coffee, he thought it might be better if he kept on talking. It should take some of the curse off what he'd already said, relieve the shock maybe.

"Clarence got the city fathers to pass a morality ordinance of some kind, Carrie, then he took the paper out and was going to serve it on George. They got into it and George killed Clarence Black."

"Was it self-defense, Frank?"

The sheriff turned and looked at the back of her handsome head. The ash-blonde hair was soft and radiant in the cool light of the room. It dawned on him that she was thinking of George's defense. He put the coffee pot down and stoked up the skimpy fire he'd built in the stove before he answered. The astonishing, almost incredible loyalty of Carrie Carpenter struck him under the heart, and hurt.

"Not as I get it, Carrie, it wasn't. In fact, I knew Clarence Black pretty well. He . . . never carried a gun. Didn't believe in them."

"Is she beautiful?"

"Yes," he said honestly. "She's awfully pretty, Carrie." He almost added that she was young, too, but flinched away from the implication in time.

The silence grew then, between them and all through the room. It became a solid force he could almost feel, and felt a helplessness before it. Inwardly raging at George and the dead lawyer as well, and the girl, Irene Cobalt, too, he stood by and ached to be able to help Carrie over this tough part of life that had come to greet her on her homecoming. But he was a man's man with none of the finesse or polish required at this time. Wisely he excused himself, went around in back, fed his horse, and smoked a cigarette before returning.

Carrie looked up and smiled her understanding and appreciation when he came back through the door and shot her a quick glance.

"Frank . . . I didn't know you were . . ." She stopped in midsentence, looking at him, then nodded. "Well, I guess it would be better to just say I didn't know you. Don't know you . . . There have been times when I wondered why you avoided me . . . us . . . but I didn't say anything about it. Both you and George seemed to be drifting apart anyway. I just let it ride. But . . . you're very understanding, Frank. I had no idea." She stood up then, smiling at him, looking him fully in the face and seeing the question in his eyes.

"I'll keep my promise, Frank . . . if that's what's worrying you." She saw the wonder die out slowly and a different look move up, then he went past her with mock horror and snatched the burning coffee pot off the little stove, and looked at the steam coming out of its spout with disgust.

"Carrie, some day I'm going to remember this thing and take it off before all the coffee boils away."

She didn't laugh, but the look on his face was so boyishly intent and over-acted she could have, except for the heart full of ache inside her.

"Frank . . . what do you suggest?"

He put the pot down when he answered. "Well . . . you might get a room at Missus Murphy's boarding house down the road." She didn't say anything and he started floundering again, wondering where else she could stay. Not the Whitsett House, of course. Not Carrie, as pretty as she was and alone now.

"All right. I'll do it." She still looked at him as though her thoughts were struggling clear of the miasma his words had forced them down into. "Will you come to see me . . . from time to time, Frank?"

"Yes'm. Every chance I get." He was a little breathless when he answered and crossed the room to hold the door for her. Swinging it open, he came face to face with all four members of the town council. In fact, Hugo Lesser's huge paw was almost on the panel when it opened. They exchanged startled, dumb stares for a second, then Frank's face darkened. Turning his back on the townsmen with a deliberate coldness, he smiled at Carrie.

"I'll drop by as soon as I can, Carrie."

She held out her hand. He took it and held it, looking at her eyes, then let it go. His head turned slowly as she went past the four stolid faces under the overhang, then he saw her luggage piled on his stoop and looked sardonically at Hugo Lesser.

"Hugo, send one of these . . . men . . . along with Missus Carpenter, will you? She'll need someone to tote that baggage."

Lesser's face got that rusty color again and his pale eyes flashed warning fire. They exchanged glares like strange dogs for a few seconds, then the sheriff nodded his head once, coldly, and his lips seemed scarcely to move when he uttered the one word.

"Now!"

Hugo turned, bobbed his head at the luggage, and glared at a small, thin-chested man who seemed anxious to be anywhere but where he was, anyway, and the three remaining councilmen entered the office and went stolidly to the bench and sat down uncomfortably.

The sheriff went over to his chair and dumped himself into it with a wry look. "You've come to tell me Clarence Black was killed by George Carpenter . . . and for me to hit the trail. Right?"

Only Lesser had an answer. The other men just nodded microscopically.

"I reckon. You got it from Blane's man, that it?"

Frank nodded thoughtfully, watching Lesser's face. "Hugo, George fired the shot that downed Clarence, but he isn't the one who caused his death. You know that."

Lesser's face gradually registered understanding. There was surprise there and weak, very weak, anger.

Frank didn't give him a chance to answer. "You didn't think, Hugo, when you authorized that restraining paper. You let a bunch of damned women stampede you into the god-damnedest blunder of your life, didn't you?"

"I had nothing to . . ."

"Like hell you didn't!" Frank spat at him, leaning across the desk, seeing the pale, tense faces on either side of the blacksmith, and ignoring them completely. "You just the same as killed one man and forced another to ruin his life." He remembered Sean Reilly's remark about city councilmen and nodded slowly. "Why? Well, I heard a pretty fair description of you boys today. Little men with a longing for prestige, and getting it in jobs they aren't any more fitted for than roping wild horses. That's you, Hugo, from the damned top of your thick head to your boots." He saw the other men working up their courage to say something and waved a hand at them, letting his eyes drop from the blacksmith's face in scorn. "All right, boys. I know what you're going to say. Am I going after him? Well, yes, that's my job. George hadn't done a damned thing he didn't have the right to do before Clarence went out there like a horse's behind and got himself killed." His shoulders rose and fell. "Clarence would've stopped one sooner or later anyway, you know that as well as I do. But the way he did it makes grief for a lot of people . . . and Clarence Black wasn't worth it, boys. Not worth one tear from Carrie Carpenter, or one drop of sweat from the man that killed him."

"Now, then," Hugo rumbled indignantly, "just a second there. Clarence was a lawyer. Carpenter . . ."

"Was a cowman, a Westerner. Hugo," the sheriff said dryly, "this country would be a damned sight better with fewer lawyers and more cowmen. At least cowmen feed folks, and lawyers . . . well, they live off the grief of others. Like buzzards, Hugo." Frank stood up and rammed his hands in his pockets. "All right, like I said I'm going after him, but I hope to God you . . . you *hombres* lose a little sleep over what you've done. You sure as hell ought to."

Lesser turned to his companions, apparently seeking a measure of confidence from them. Neither man would meet his eyes. He arose and stalked toward the door. His face was greasy with perspiration and blanched white like an old shoeing apron. The other two followed him out like wraiths. There was a macabre humor in the way they went, one behind the other. Frank waited until the door closed behind the last man, then he deliberately spat on the floor, and went over by the rifle rack, took out his carbine in its saddle boot, palmed it, worked it dry several times, and very methodically loaded it and lay it across his desk.

The late afternoon was cooling off a little when he went around to the shed and saddled up, buckled the boot so the carbine butt was inches from his right hand, swung up, and headed north out of Buelton again, toward Potter Valley.

People watched him go and knew why. Not many glances stayed on his face. There was the bitter knowledge among the men who saw that Sheriff Frank Girard was taking the hardest trail any lawman ever had to ride. The sundown trail of a partner turned outlaw. No one said much even after he had passed through town and was small in the distance. There wasn't a thing to say. The course of action differed in many minds but none spoke of it. Some would have thrown down the badge, but that wouldn't have solved anything. Frank knew it as he rode, because he had considered it. Hell! There'd be a reward likely, then others would take up where he'd refused to go. This way, if he got the chance to talk to George, at least he stood a better chance of talking him into surrendering than a stranger would. And a posse of bounty hunters wouldn't even try. Surrendering might not help because he'd be tried by the circuit judge, but at least it was a chance — his only chance now — and it was less final than the bullet that would find him if he resisted a posse.

The Boxed C looked sad and deserted when Frank wound down the wagon ruts from the road and went into the yard. The gray eyes saw Clarence's body lying there with flies exploring it. No pity showed in them. He swung down wearily, tied his horse, and, skirting the corpse, went directly to the house. It was empty and full of the solemn loneliness that houses get when people have left them for all time. There wasn't a thing in the place to indicate anything more than hurried flight. He grunted to himself, went outside, and looked out over the yard, shrugged, and stalked toward the barn.

Frank was emptied of the allure of the chase. Usually, since he had become a lawman, he'd felt a small exhilaration each time he'd gone on the trail of outlaws. Now was no such feeling. He couldn't have defined the jumbled sentiments inside himself if he'd tried. Nostalgia and sadness were there in great measure, and a reluctant, almost rebellious determination, too. Combined, they made him anything but his ordinary calm, shrewd self.

Inside the barn was more evidence of quick flight, then he saw the little hint he'd half-heartedly hoped he'd never find. The telltale leavings of careless, hurried, and upset hands that were invariably left by every killer. Mute and sure testimony of the direction of flight that he needed to track them. The *alforjas* were still hanging beside the pack harness. No rider would have failed to take a pack horse along unless he knew where he was going and that the first stop with supplies was close.

Frank went back out to his horse, swung up, and circled the yard until he cut fresh horse signs, then he set out slowly, riding head down, beginning the first leg of his monotonous trail, the tracking of the killer.

Day waned slowly and, actually, after the smoldering ball of fire had gone and the long summer twilight was on the land, it got hotter. Frank rode and sweated, following tracks that were indistinct at best because of the iron-hard earth, and never more than barely visible, but going northwest a little, toward the distant mountains with their purple blanketing of trees, like formidable sentinels that stood between civilization and the virgin uplands of the back country.

An idea was forming in Frank's mind. He had taken the half-breed girl with him. If he didn't have dual tracks to convince him, he had George Carpenter's character, which he knew well enough. With Irene Cobalt to guide him through the mazes of the trackless forests beyond, there was a better than even chance that the law would never find him. Too, the fact that they were traveling light meant she was leading the way to a cache, or a cabin of relatives, or to some reasonably close, secure place.

Frank reined up on a bony ridge and let the reins sag. Somewhere ahead, in the immensity of the land, were two dots, two moving, fleeing riders heading for sanctuary. He made a wry face and nudged the bay. The animal went down the little slope dutifully, almost willingly, and Frank smiled his understanding. Evening shadows were coming in fast now. The horse knew they'd camp shortly.

The last crushed, dead grass sign of a passing horse faded out finally and Frank let his animal pick its own course so long as it held northwest. He studied the country around about with calculating eyes, saw the eminence he was looking for, and reined toward it. It wasn't especially high, but at least it topped any others within riding distance. At that it was high enough to make the horse grunt as he zigzagged up the side and finally attained the barren, windswept top where some battered, shaggy sagebrush was striving fanatically for a foothold in the eroded topsoil.

Frank swung down, loosened the *cinchas*, hunkered in front of the horse and made a cigarette, lit it behind a carefully cupped hand, and held the little fiery end inside his fingers. Distance had become deceptive with the fast-failing light and gloom, more than peace and repose, seemed to come in on the wings of the early night, but it was cooling off and Frank's horse, at least, was thankful for this small favor.

The sheriff made himself comfortable finally, confident he was alone for miles in every direction. He lay back with the reins looped around one arm and his arms under his head. The night came pleasantly, sadly, and opened up its tapestry overhead with the myriad little holes that let eternity shine through. With it came memories that haunted the lawman. Remembrances of team roping times and dances and big laughs he and George Carpenter had enjoyed together. The sickening recollections of hearty thumps on the back and practical jokes, and hundreds of little spontaneous things that men do when they like one another. Each hurt, too. Frank grunted and let the cigarette die between his lips, looking owlishly, unblinkingly up at the sky.

He thought of Carrie and wondered why she'd gone to Wagon Mound in the first place. No one had ever made that clear to him. It didn't matter, he supposed, really. Just another facet that contributed to the whole. He thought of the amazingly calm way she had taken the dual blows of Black's death and George's defiant infidelity, and wasn't altogether certain he admired it so much, after all. She had seemed almost inhuman in her shocked acceptance of the thing. Oh, there had been pain in her eyes, and astonishment, too, but not regret — or something — he wasn't sure what, but, anyway, she had accepted it too calmly, too capably. He wondered if, maybe, Carrie wasn't too damned capable. It absorbed him, this new way of looking at the beautiful woman, and he lay there pondering it until long after dark.

Finally, with a tired shrug, he sat up again, narrowed the gray eyes, and swung his head slowly, carefully around the horizon, and back again. He had to do it three times before he saw the infinitesimal pinprick he was looking for. There was no particular elation in him when he identified it, either. In fact, he growled to himself deep in his chest as he got up stiffly and brushed off his pants. No man would cook a supper in the reaches of the night when he was on the run. Just a woman would insist on that saving grace to an otherwise primitive existence — and only a man in love would allow it. He gave the front cinch a tug, tongued the half-breed buckle into place, and ran an indifferent finger under the poop strap, and swung up. The horse held his ears back, waiting and expectant.

"All right, dammit to hell," he said quietly, as though the horse would understand. "Let's go."

The night was grim with grotesque shadows that let him ride over them, then raised from the earth silently, swept over him, and went back to their ageless patterns of flatness again. It took hours to get anywhere near his destination, and, when he eventually got there, some distant coyotes sporting over some carrion beyond a few miles, in the forested slope, made the night seem alive. They made their half-humorous, half-derisive little barks that rose into a crescendo of yapping and ended on a high, chilling key and hung there, then died away in coughing barks again.

Frank stopped when he knew the strange camp wasn't far ahead. He had taken a fix on the location by a clump of bony, sere rocks. After hobbling his horse, he leaned against a still warm boulder and removed his spurs and hoped with all his might that the camp would prove to belong to trappers, buffalo hunters, travelers — anything but Irene Cobalt and George Carpenter. He grimaced again, thinking how many gunmen he'd trailed and how they invariably kept running until a bullet, a posse, or exhaustion dropped them. But it wouldn't be that way with a lusty man like George who had this irresistible girl with him, this new, savage love. He cursed helplessly and reached up to yank the carbine from the saddle boot. His thoughts were unpleasant as he felt the cold steel with its oily efficiency sliding into his palms.

Whether he knew the man he was trailing or not wouldn't make any difference. It should, but it wouldn't. Any man would have acted the same way under the identical circumstances — unless he was filled with ice water instead of blood, and, if that had been the case, he probably wouldn't have been where George was anyway. It was life on the frontier reduced to its lowest denominator, the masculine need, demand, for love and a mate.

He went due north from his horse without glancing back. Ahead was an undulating little land swell left behind after being created by some ancient sea's march over the land. Frank kept it between himself and the camp on the other side and knew why George had allowed the campfire. He had thought they were far enough away, and behind the little hill, to avoid detection of the spindly little flames. He shook his head. Partly that would be like George. Partly it would be his understandable giving in on a point to the girl, too, because love was blinding him as well as making him emotionally unbalanced. Hell, if the old George had been thinking then, he'd have known a lawman would strike for a high point and watch for the fire.

He angled up the slope of the small swell and smelled the aromatic faintness of wood smoke before he had reached the top. It, too, was a nostalgic essence, distilled from the same smell of cook fires that he and the killer had shared. Cursing himself, he went to his knees and crawled carefully, shoving the carbine ahead, until he was on the skyline, then he went low on his stomach and sidled in among the brush, letting his eyes become accustomed to the new depth of shadows, and studied the camp below.

The last doubt disappeared when he saw the powerful black horse George had broken, and treasured so highly, grazing lazily, a shapely hulk of darkness against the lighter shades of the night. He raised up cautiously, saw the two bedrolls made into one large, roomy affair with dirty ground sheets around the outer edges, and gripped his carbine tighter for a moment. Bitterness flecked his eyes. Of all the treasures on earth, the one that was leading George Carpenter down the trail to destruction was probably the least remunerative and most exacting and over-valued — a woman.

He raised himself to one knee, shouldered the carbine, eased back the hammer, and caught the ghostly glow of the big bedroll over his front sight, let it run quickly down the length of blue barrel until it was fully in the Buckhorn sight up close to his face, and yelled out.

"George!"

For a moment nothing happened. It never did and Frank knew it wouldn't. Like riding a green colt the first time. Mostly they stood, frightened and motionless. It was the second time, after they'd thought it over, that all hell broke loose.

"George . . . dammit . . . get up!"

A head came out of the bedroll. Frank knew its outline instantly, even with the mussed hair and abrupt, shocked appearance.

"Who's up there?"

"Me, Frank Girard. Get up and keep your hands from your body."

Another long, aching second dragged by, then the bedroll heaved and a man appeared. He was bootless and shirtless. He was like a statue in the weak, moist light of a Comanche sickle moon. One tip of the huge scimitar was tilted upward. It'd hold a power horn all right. That meant it was going to rain, the Indians said.

Frank neither saw nor cared. He was watching George Carpenter like a hawk, over the sights of his carbine.

"Walk clear of the bed, George."

"Frank . . ."

"Don't say it, just walk . . . and keep your mouth shut!"

Carpenter stepped clear, staring up at the ridge toward the voice, but unable to identify the man at all in the gloom.

"All right, Irene, you come out, too."

"She ain't decent, Frank," George said keenly.

The carbine was getting heavy. Frank hated the beautiful half-breed girl like poison right then. Not just because she was a serious complication in the capture of Carpenter, but because she was the cause of all this as well.

"I don't give a damn. Irene!" He yelled it with unmistakable hatred in the name. "Get out of there and don't make any fool moves. Dressed or undressed, roll out . . . now!"

"You god-damned . . ."

"Shut up, George!"

They were like wolves waiting for the girl to emerge. When she came out, Frank's mouth pulled down sardonically. She wasn't decent at that — but she was indescribably beautiful, too, in the eerie light. A partly clothed goddess with amber-gold skin and with every outline of an exquisite body highlighted softly, sensuously by the night. Her face was turned up toward the ridge, the dark eyes seeking him, searching with lips parted in concentration and nostrils flared out against the breath that came from her in excited, aroused little pants.

Frank forced his attention back to George. "Irene . . . get your clothes on . . . but do it in plain sight and don't reach for the gun I know is in that bedroll."

The girl hesitated, canting her head a little to see him, then shrugged and turned gracefully, bent over, and began to dress methodically with no sign of self-consciousness.

CHAPTER
FOUR

Frank relaxed a little but his arm still ached from holding the carbine aligned. George Carpenter shuffled his feet a little.

"Frank?"

"Yeah."

"How about me putting my shirt on?"

The sheriff switched his glance back to the girl before he answered. She was coming erect, clothed and still searching for him on the ridge. Unconsciously he nodded his head.

"All right, but don't try anything, George."

The killer didn't answer. He moved slowly back to his clothes, yanked into his boots, and was getting into his shirt when he glanced up at the ridge with a sideways look.

"You see Carrie?"

"Yeah. I don't want to talk about it."

Carpenter absorbed this in silence as he finished tucking in the shirt. Frank saw him glance at Irene, then the girl turned sideways, stepping in so that her body was between them. Her face was raised toward Frank's hiding place.

"Sheriff . . . would you kill a woman?"

Frank leaped up then, frantically, knowing exactly what was next although he'd never faced it before. George Carpenter had a gun in his hand that shone wetly as he ran crazily out into the darkness.

"Stop, George . . . damn you!"

The carbine blasted a hole in the stillness and echoes of the thunder chased each other down the night. Frank saw a blur of movement. The girl was running then, too, but not in flight. She threw herself squarely between Frank's twisted, raised elevation and her lover's route of flight. The carbine arced down to pick up the fleeing man — and caught the full swelling of her chest in the sights. The apparition hung there, faintly opalescent and rigid.

The seconds raced by like great black wings beating softly in the darkness, then George Carpenter was swallowed up and gone; even the sound of his pounding boot heels on the packed earth were lost.

Frank's face was twisted with anger and indecision. He had — for a wild moment — considered killing the girl. Not just because she impeded his downing of Carpenter, but because of the evil within her that had caused this tragedy as surely as Hugo Lesser's monumental stupidity had. Then he let the carbine sag and stood there, wide-legged, in plain sight, staring down at her. Irene didn't move. She was still rigid and shaken, looking up at him. It was an endless time, then he moved down the slope with weary legs and stopped a few feet from her, saying nothing and making no effort to control the viciousness that was rolling inside him.

222

The girl's shoulders sagged a little. She raised one hand as though in half-hearted defense, and let it drop. "Now . . . he's gone."

Frank didn't answer. He jerked his head toward the campfire. She stirred sluggishly, walked toward it, and turned, facing him with a wondering, quizzical expression on her face.

Frank leaned on the carbine and studied the girl. What she had done took courage. He could have killed her easily — actually thought of it for a second, in fact, to clear the way for the shot that would bring George down. He looked at her features and strove to see behind the impassiveness, but all there was seemed like dawning fear, perhaps, or wonder about him. He straightened up and sighed.

"Why?"

"What do you mean?"

"Why did you do it?"

She shrugged slightly. "You know why. So he could escape from you."

"No," Frank said evenly, "I don't mean that. I mean why would you risk getting killed so he could escape."

"Because I love him."

Frank made a wry face at her. "You two don't have love. It's not love, Irene, when you take what you want and to hell with the consequences. That's sort of animal-like. Passion, I reckon, but it isn't love, I don't believe."

"With us it is, Sheriff."

Frank thought perhaps she was right. With them that's exactly what it was. Both were primitive. They

223

could only have love of this kind, savage, violent love, like wolves have, and cougars. Animal love. The girl's blood was attuned to nothing higher and George, for some inexplicable reason, in this one respect was just as Neolithic as his woman — his beautiful half-breed woman.

Frank jerked his head at the bedroll. "Make it up. I'll catch the horses." He went away without another glance at her. He felt the stare she gave him as he went out, got the animals, returned, and saddled them up. Together they threw the bedding onto the pack horse. Frank tied a Turk's head in his lariat through the rein hole of her bit on the other horse and motioned for her to get up. She hesitated, one hand on the horn, looking up at him.

"Why do I have to go along? I didn't kill anyone."

He smiled bleakly. "No, but you damned near did when you let George get away. In my eyes you're as guilty of Black's murder as George is. Guiltier, in fact. Mount up."

She still didn't move. The dark eyes were wide and speculative, then she shrugged. "All right . . . but you'll waste time and never get George now."

He unslung his quirt, hefted it by the thong, and measured the distance between them. "For the last time, mount up."

She read the intention in his face, turned angrily, toed the stirrup, and was astride.

Irene started off toward town and he followed, but they only went as far as Frank's horse, then he switched mounts, leaving the animal with the bedroll fastened to a tree, and jerked his head at her.

"Come on."

She looked surprised. "But . . . not that way to Buelton."

"To the devil with Buelton. He's afoot, Irene. You think I'm going to miss this chance?"

She still held back so he unslung the quirt again and lashed out lightly. Her horse jumped ahead. The girl's eyes flashed fury at him, then she stayed ahead, erect in the saddle and refused to look behind at him.

His unconscious mind relayed the information that there was a chill in the air. It meant dawn wasn't far off. This caught his attention. He hadn't thought about time at all, but the whole thing didn't seem as though it had used up more than a few minutes of the night. Dully he recalled the long, slow ride to the campfire. He raised his eyes and speculated on the distance to the forested slope, smiled thinly, and reckoned it too far for a man afoot to make it before dawn

He rode in a large circle from the camp, quartering every grassy area, searching for tracks. Even if it hadn't been so infernally dark, he still wouldn't have found any because the earth wouldn't take an impression even heavy as a man.

Finally he motioned toward a land swell between the forested uplands and the camp, and followed Irene's horse up the little eminence, swung down, and waited for daylight. He didn't dare turn the horses out, so he loosened the cinchas, slipped the bridles, and hobbled them where he could see them constantly, and sat down, the carbine cradled across his legs.

The girl walked over, hesitated, studied his bleak face, and finally dropped down near him. Together they sat in discomfort, each conscious of the presence of the other, and waited. It must have been three-quarters of an hour later when she spoke. The sound was almost like blasphemy in the virginal purity of the pre-dawn.

"Sheriff?"

Frank grunted, an indistinguishable sound with no express meaning at all. He didn't even look around at her, just kept his vigil on the dark land, waiting.

"Is his wife . . . pretty?"

Frank looked around then with a stare that would have wilted the summer sun. Carrie had asked the same thing. Was that all women worried about, when men were dying and being ruined because of them? He felt a fulsome gorge of disgust and animosity come up into his throat. "She's beautiful . . . and decent . . . and . . . and another woman."

Irene looked at him startled, wide-eyed. The silence descended again and threatened to stay, but she broke it. "You don't like women, Sheriff?"

"I didn't say that."

"No, you didn't, but you might as well have. It's all over your face. In your eyes, too."

Frank swore lustily without looking around. "Well, I'm beginning not to like them." He jutted his head at the darkness. "What's George . . . out there somewhere . . . got to thank you for? You're a woman. What've you done for him . . . or his wife . . . or for that matter me?

226

Nothing but bring tragedy with you." He looked around at her and glared. "You say you love George. By God, it isn't love when you'll deliberately make a man ruin himself for you."

"What is it, then?" she asked fiercely, giving him stare for stare. "Love is suffering, isn't it?"

"Not on your lousy life" — he was going to say "girl" but it didn't sound right; lady didn't fit any better, so he settled for her name again — "Irene. My idea of love is something inside you big enough to make you sacrifice it, if it's impossible or if it's going to make people suffer and unhappy. That's the kind of love I know, Irene, not this damned bundling into a bedroll and killing unarmed men because they get in your way."

"Mister Black had no business . . ."

"I'm not saying Black had any business in what he did. I'm saying you're kind of love isn't love at all. You . . . neither of you . . . had enough guts to give up something, use what you call love for a higher purpose than getting a damned fool killed and another damned fool ruined forever."

Irene Cobalt looked straight at the sheriff without speaking, without seeming to breathe even, she was so still and motionless. Then she sighed, let her gaze wander to the horizon where a thin, dazzlingly sharp edging of pink was slicing across the heavy, purple underbelly of the night. Her face was silhouetted that way when Frank stole a look back at her. It irritated him, that stoicism, blank impassivity that hid every vestige of her thoughts. He turned back and leaned forward, actually with very little hope, watching to see what the new daylight would disclose in the sweep of land around them.

He was still squinting into the half light when Irene crept closer to him and spoke again.

"Sheriff . . . I'll give him up. I'll give him up if you'll let him go."

Frank didn't answer. There was no need to answer, and, besides, it was getting light enough to see the countryside now.

She went even closer so that her shoulder brushed against his, and leaned a little. "If you'll let him go . . . Please, Sheriff."

Frank turned his head abruptly. The shock of her breath on his face made him freeze. He didn't know she had come that close. They looked at each other for a single, tense moment, then the girl's head lowered quickly, violently, and her lips closed over his mouth. It was a poignant, delicious feeling and Frank's mind swam in a gentle sea of incredulity and shock, then her arms were around him, not tenderly, but with the aroused passions of a savage, with the desire to hurt him and be hurt by him.

It was like fighting his way to the surface after plunging into an icy lake. Frank made the efforts with increasing violence until he was free of her, leaning on one arm, looking down into her face. It wasn't disgust, either, that he felt, but a wistful sense of relief. She lay framed in the splendor of her black hair, looking at him without blinking.

228

"Well . . . ," he said finally, when the turmoil in his veins had subsided a little, "what was that for? To bribe me?"

She lay there saying nothing for quite a while, just staring up at him, then she made her head quiver negatively. "No. It . . . was started that way, Sheriff Frank. It was supposed to . . . but it changed. It changed."

Frank's eyes held her glance and contained it, pinioned it. She made no effort to escape the nakedness she felt under his look, either.

"You're nothing but a damned savage, that's all. I wish George could see you now, waiting for a man . . . just any damned man."

Frank's face was white from the thought of what she had done to George Carpenter — and Carrie. He didn't know he'd gone too far because he wasn't thinking of Irene Cobalt any more, just something intensely evil that she represented.

She struck him with an open palm. His head jarred sideways with impact and reality returned in a flash. Swinging in fury, he saw her sitting up, the dazzling light of the new day burnishing the wonderful beauty of her large eyes. He had to grip the gun tightly to keep from striking back, then he grunted deeply in his chest, and got up without another word and walked a little way from her, stood motionlessly studying the land with anger boiling inside him where something less violent had been before.

The land was still in every direction. There was no sign of movement but he watched closely anyway for a long ten minutes, dissecting shadows and clumps of brush and trees until he got his reward with no sense of elation, only a grim triumph that arose out of contempt for his old friend. The little moving thing was heading as straight as an arrow for the distant tree-covered side hill. George was moving with a dogged persistence that indicated he was traveling on guts more than physical ability. He wasn't taking advantage of the ground to conserve strength. He was working desperately and directly to his goal. The blindness of exhaustion was driving him and Frank knew it from watching the man's progress. He turned to the girl and saw her staring at the speck in the distance. He grinned like a death's-head at her.

"Take a good look, Irene. There's a man out there. You're the cause of him being there like that. Do you like seeing him running for his life, like a damned crippled wolf?"

She got up and walked over beside him without answering, dark eyes fastened to the fugitive. Her voice was doubtful, uncertain, and only partly believing.

"Is . . . that George?"

"Yes, it's George." Frank looked back again, feeling ironic in his mind. "That's the way he's always done things. Direct, straight for the goal like he's running for his life now." He turned toward the horses. "Come on."

They mounted and rode down off the hill, striking out due north. Frank considered it best to parallel the fleeing man until they were above him, then bisect his trail and come back down on him from between him and the trail to safety in the trees.

The morning brought out its warmth and spread it lavishly over the range. Frank felt drowsy with the heat sifting through his shirt and warming the tense muscles along his sides and back. He concentrated on George in order to stay awake. Occasionally only did he glance at the girl. She was slumped in the saddle now. He couldn't tell whether it was weariness or dejection, and didn't care much either way. His mouth was a slit set in the unclean-looking stubble of tawny beard. Sheriff Girard looked like what he was finally, a lawman on the trail of no return.

It took the man a good three hours of hard riding to offset Carpenter's night long flight, but they did it, and, when Frank swung west in a large arc, then began the downward trek that would bring them in close to Carpenter, he felt his old resentment coming back. A stout heart can't close its eyes so quickly to the hours of comradeship between two virile men. The tug between friendship for the fool ahead and the oath he had taken as a lawman was tearing the heart out of him.

He was riding, narrow-eyed and morose, when the first shot rattled through the new day. Without flinching, Frank swung down, jerked his head at Irene, who was as pale as the dawn itself with blue circles under her eyes. He said nothing as he stood in thought behind his horse.

The horses were Carpenter's salvation, and they could also be the sheriff's undoing. He deliberately slipped the bridles off, made them fast to the saddle horns, took his carbine from the boot, and slapped the animals on the rump and watched them lope back toward town, heads high and tails extended. Irene flashed him a bewildered look but said nothing.

Frank studied the girl. "You want to stay here or go to him?"

She blinked at him, startled. "I . . . don't understand."

"No," he said coldly, "I don't reckon you do. It's like this. I don't want any part of you. If you follow me, you'll give out or get killed. I won't waste a second on you now." His eyes were bitter. "You can go to the devil . . . or George. You're a drag to both of us now. Take your choice."

"What if I stay here? Will you come back for me?"

He shook his head. "Irene, you can rot right here for all I care. For all the law cares. Like you said once, you haven't committed a crime. Not in the law books anyway. But you're guilty as hell to me. There's no way I can punish you except by leaving you here and that's not much punishment . . . not for what you've done anyway."

"But if I go to George . . . ?"

"If you go to George, you'll suffer, too, believe me. You'll see the end of something that's not pretty. You'll see the reward he's going to get for letting you ruin him. Maybe it won't change you any, but it'll give you a pretty sorry memory to pack around with you the rest of your life. Make up your mind. I haven't got all day."

His eyes were flashing over the land as he talked, guessing, probing, and estimating where the warning shot had come from. He had it narrowed down to a slight bluff with some bedraggled old junipers on the crest, or the side hill that led up where sage was thick and rank.

"I'll go to him."

Frank smiled bleakly. "Good. At least he'll have something to . . . to . . . well, I reckon you could say inspire him now. Go on." He raised his arm and pointed toward the hill. "He's over there somewhere. Keep in plain sight. He'll recognize you. Move out . . . and . . . nothing, damn you . . . just tell George I won't fire until he shoots first. That if he doesn't give up and come in with me, he'll never leave here alive." The tortured eyes were alive with anguish. "Try to make him come in, Irene. That's the least you can do. And . . . one more thing . . . tell him for me . . . s'long."

It was hours later when Frank got his answer. A single shot that coughed George's defiance at him. Reluctantly he moved forward, using the shadows and brush as aids in stalking the killer of Clarence Black.

The die had been cast and, actually, Frank had never really thought George would surrender to him anyway. But there was the decency that told him to give his old partner every chance. It was all done and past now. The hardest part was ahead. He went ahead cautiously, not exactly believing George wanted to kill him, but knowing he would, just as he knew that he himself would act the same way. In fact, it was only the little nickel circlet with the star in the center that placed them so vastly apart now.

Remembering the thing, Frank removed it thoughtfully. Not because of any change in his resolution but

233

because it invariably reflected sunlight. He dropped it into a pocket and wormed within rifle range of the juniper knoll, saw no movement, but lay in a bank of leaf mold near two askew, stunted old oaks, and aligned the ridge over his sights.

Movement was slow in coming. The sweat began to annoy him, running under the forehead band of his hat and coming down greasily over his face. Some deer flies found him and buzzed in delighted astonishment, then the sunlight reflected off metal up above, and Frank fired.

The duel was uneven. A carbine against a handgun. For a silent moment Carpenter's return shot didn't come, then Frank knew George had him pegged although the pistol wouldn't carry the range accurately. The thunder of the shot was clear as a bell, but the slug dropped many feet short. Frank mopped his face with a sleeve and swore irritably, raising up, peering against the dazzling brilliance and squirming closer to a tangle of brush that presaged the ascent to Carpenter's ridge.

George's keenness was equal to Frank's persistence. He fired the third time. Just one shot, sparingly and accurately. Frank flinched at the sting of the slug along the outside of his leg and stared down at the long slit in his pants and the bloody scratch beyond. His look was one of grim humor. First blood for Carpenter. He raised his head, his gray eyes flat and venomous-looking, and called out.

"George, cut it out! You can't make it! Throw the damned gun down and come off of there!"

"I'll make it!" Carpenter shouted back instantly. "Don't you worry! Be smart, Frank, move out!"

"Listen, George . . ."

Bang!

Frank ducked instinctively when the bullet hit a rock somewhere close by and ricocheted off into the day with a tearing violence that made Frank's hackles rise. He whipped up the carbine and pumped two shots into the ridge without aim. They drew no answer and silence settled in again. Talking was useless. The sheriff began writhing uphill a little at a time, grinding his teeth at the scorching heat, the insistent, dragging thorns of brush that clutched and tore at him, and the bitterness that made him go ahead.

He was as high as he dared go, with an open area close by that he knew George Carpenter's eyes were watching like an eagle, when he heard the first, distant rumble of sound. Wondering, he turned as far as he dared, twisted, grunted against the unnatural position he had to assume, and stared out over the range through bloodshot eyes crinkled against the sweat.

Horsemen were riding hard from the direction of the Boxed C. Frank swore to himself and watched them. It was obvious from the way they rode that they were following the tracks of Frank's departed horses. He wondered who the men were until they were close enough for George to fire out into them, then he saw. Sean Reilly was leading the posse. There were eight men in it, all armed to the teeth.

Fury seethed in Frank. He watched the posse men scatter like quail, some throwing themselves from their horses and scuttling into the brush, others using the horses as shields, and Sean Reilly himself, big, massive, and red-faced from exertion, reining up out of pistol range and staring toward the ridge where George and the girl were.

Carpenter called down to Frank with a cynical ring to his voice: "Your friends come to back you up, Frank?"

"I didn't send for 'em! They came on their own hook!" He turned back and faced up the hill. "George . . . don't be a damned fool! Toss your gun down! They'll kill you! That's a lynch mob, not a posse!"

Carpenter's thin laugh wasn't pleasant. "Frank, you couldn't keep them from hanging me and you know it!"

"Like hell I can't! I'm the law here! Not Reilly and his cut-throats!"

"I reckon," the killer said laconically. "Try and make them believe it!"

Frank swore heartily. "I will! Hold your fire until I can talk to them! You'll see!"

Carpenter didn't answer right away, then finally he spoke: "All right! I'll give you free passage back down the damned hill!"

Frank knew a spurt of elation. "George! If I send 'em back, will you throw that lousy gun away and come in with me? Listen, you may not get off, but at least this is your only chance!"

The answer was slow in coming, but it came: "Won't promise a thing, Frank! Let's see how you make out with the Whitsett House gang first! Personally I don't think you got a chance in a hundred!"

"Your word on the shooting until I get off this damned hill?"

"You got it!"

Frank stood up, flexed his muscles, and shook his head to shake off the droplets of sweat that ran down his nose. He was fortunately stooped, brushing the dirt off his clothing when a carbine boomed and cut brush to his left. He dropped instantly, furious, and glared at the posse men who were hiding in the brush now, one of their number leading the saddled horses beyond gun range.

George Carpenter laughed dryly. "That's all the answer you need, Frank!"

"They don't recognize me! Hold it a second!"

The sheriff stood up again, warily, with his eyes glued to the land below for the telltale shimmer of a bearing gun, saw none moving, and hailed the posse men identifying himself.

There was no immediate response, or gunfire, either, so he angled down the hill, struck the flat, and walked boldly toward the clump of scrub oak he had seen Reilly take refuge in.

The big saloon man came out cautiously, darting apprehensive glances up at the ridge where George Carpenter watched.

Frank was blazing angry but strove to hide it. "Reilly, what the hell you doing out here? Who authorized you to form a posse and . . . ?"

"Don't need no authorization, Sheriff. We're doing our duty as citizens."

Frank regarded the big man apathetically. "Wasn't it you that told me yesterday Clarence Black was in the wrong? Weren't you the one that was mad as hell about what he did?" The sheriff's eyes were wide in anger. "Then what in hell're you trying to do now?"

"Listen, Frank." Sean Reilly's florid face was mottled with heat rash and excitement, but his eyes weren't affected apparently. He gave stare for stare with the lawman. "Clarence did a dumb thing, but that don't excuse Carpenter, either."

"Well," Frank said sarcastically, "you're the judge, now, huh? Just what exactly is your axe to grind in this thing, Sean?"

"Justice is all."

Frank's anger exploded then. "That's a lie and you know it. Get on your horse, Sean . . . you and your trailers, and get back to town. None of you is deputized and I'm not asking for help."

Reilly's mottled face went a little pale. He stared at the sheriff with a surprised, awry flame of anger shooting out of his eyes. "You called me a liar, Frank?"

"That's the truth. It isn't supposed to hurt. You know it's the truth, too. I don't know what your idea is and don't give a damn. Mount up and take your crew with you. Now!"

Frank knew an eruption was coming and was prepared for it. He faced Sean Reilly like a mountain lion faces a bear — with confidence in his speed and dexterity against the crushing, overwhelming brute force before him. But Frank Girard had made a fatal error in strategy. He was facing his enemy unmindful of the man who arose out of the brush directly behind him and swung his clubbed carbine in a glistening arc that slashed against his head and knocked him crazily sideways, sprawling, his hat sailing away like a wounded bird, and unconsciousness descending as though the darkness of night had returned, fallen over him, encompassed him completely, and borne him away into a world of infinite blackness — and peace.

CHAPTER
FIVE

That is how Carpenter's Ridge got its name, which it bears to this day. The only dedicatory audience at the naming was the red-eyed, stubble-whiskered man who stood like stone, staring up at the absolutely motionless, sagging body of George Carpenter, where it hung suspended from the largest of the two juniper trees.

Frank's headache was the kind that gathers all the contributing factors — like sleeplessness, hunger, physical pain from George's bullet that had creased his leg, and the awfully drained, emptied feeling that was in his heart — and molds them into a despairing illness that is next to dying. He felt how weak his knees were but refused to let them bend. Carpenter's head was sideways on his neck. The sheriff made a low, barely audible moan, and dropped his eyes from the specter on Carpenter's Ridge. He turned away from it, looked around, and knew he was alone. There was a strange horse tied in the shade. He looked at him objectively, then remembered. It was George's good black horse. Dully Frank knew this was Sean Reilly's macabre joke. He made a cigarette and smoked it all the way down, ground it out, turned deliberately, and went up the hill.

He was breathing hard and George was heavy, but he cut him down and staggered down to the black horse and lashed him across the saddle, climbed behind the cantle, and struck out for Buelton.

The ride was a nightmare. He could hear George's colorless laugh, then the words: Frank, you couldn't keep them from hanging me and you know it! He hadn't been able to, either. One thing stuck in the sheriff's mind as the shock wore off. Why had Reilly done it? Frank had seen murder in the saloon man's eyes the time they sat in the café and discussed Clarence Black. In fact, he had let Reilly know he had seen it by warning him off. Then why had he organized the lynching of the man who killed Black?

Early evening was making the harshness of Buelton into a mellow setting of old buildings with delicate shades, when Frank left the body at the undertaker's with explicit instructions on the quality of the coffin and funeral arrangements, then, knowing the town was alive with speculation like a doctor knows a patient's pulse before he touches the flesh, Frank struck out for the Whitsett House.

He was inside the doors, standing, straight and relaxed, with eyes narrowed against the contrast in light from the outside's dazzling brilliance to the semi-gloom and coolness of the saloon, when Reilly's voice came at him out of the deathly silence that settled over the indifferently occupied bar. There was a cocked riot gun in Sean's big hands.

"Don't make a mistake, Frank. The boys got out of hand. I'm sorry."

241

Frank's eyes didn't widen when they focused. "Put that gun down, Reilly."

"Frank, I . . ."

"Put that gun down!"

Reilly's hands tightened on the murderous weapon; his big face with its usual look of confidence and expansiveness and good nature was splotched with uncertain resolve and a tincture of mixed fright and fear.

"Reilly," Frank said evenly. "For the last time . . . put that gun down!"

"No, by God!" Reilly said. "You . . . didn't get him. The posse did. We did what you was out to do. There's been no crime committed . . . on our side. Frank . . ."

Frank's face was white; the gray eyes were rabid. "You son-of-a-bitch, Reilly. Not a damned one of you was deputized. Hanging Carpenter was murder . . . that's the law. Now, put that gun down or . . . shoot it!"

The sheriff was moving when he spoke. Men rumbled in fright and fought to get clear. Fortunately there weren't many patrons in the place; it was too early.

The gunfire was deafening. Somewhere, a long way off, a woman screamed into the dusk and Frank's gun was vomiting death. Reilly's scatter-gun erupted with a deafening blast. One of the louvered doors was torn literally from its spindles and soared out into the roadway, making startled pedestrians jump and swear with astonishment. But Frank, wise in the ways of his trade, wasn't where the blast struck. He was still crab-stepping when he got off his second shot, saw

Reilly stagger, fumble at the trigger guard with fingers growing numb, swivel the gun frantically, and blow off the second roar of the gun that ripped siding off the wall and broke a window with concussion.

Frank went across the room and fired his third shot with the deadly purpose of a man immune to reason or mercy. Sean Reilly went down behind the bar in a heap. The sheriff skirted the men who hadn't moved, seeing their ashen faces and glassy eyes as a sea of minor obstacles, then he was looking down at the saloon owner.

There was a long moment of pure reaction, when no one moved or spoke, before he holstered his gun, went over, and knelt by Reilly. The blood coming from his chest, near the collar bone, was enough. The man's lung was pierced, high. Death wasn't far off. Frank looked at the face, saw the drained, bluish cast to the lips, and looked into the stricken eyes.

"Why did you do it, Sean?"

"I . . . I had no choice. You'd've . . ."

"No. I mean why'd you lynch George? You didn't like Black, but George wasn't anything to you. He killed a man you didn't want to live anyway. Why, Sean?"

"Boxed C. I . . . want it. It's . . . a natural . . . for what I have in mind."

Frank was surprised. It made sense, but it was new to him. He read the truth in Reilly's face and wagged his head in incredulity. "By God . . . I had no idea. Listen, you could've bought it. Why didn't you try?"

"I did. Four times. He . . . wouldn't sell. I . . . sent the girl out there. She . . ."

Frank's pure astonishment made Reilly stop. They traded stares for a moment. There was foamy blood around his mouth now. He was slipping fast.

"You sicced that 'breed girl onto George, Reilly?"

"Yeah. She would take him away, make him sell the damned ranch. Place for cattle . . . smuggling . . . anything. Good . . . place." The lips still moved but words didn't form or come out. Then the fingers of death began to gather the man's soul slowly. Frank watched, hunkered down, seeing every little movement and knowing the shadows were growing longer each second, longer and deeper — and darker. He pushed up, saw the silent ring of eyes fasten on him, and looked at the men.

"You boys with Reilly's posse that hung George Carpenter?"

Four men shook their heads emphatically. Two didn't move at all. The sheriff nodded to them. "Put your guns on the bar, boys. That . . . or else!"

Two guns went on to the worn planking with dull little harsh sounds.

The sheriff knew the riders by sight. He nodded to them. "Move out. Head through the door and over to my office. First blunder'll be the last."

Buelton knew what was going forward in the Whitsett House. The point of speculation was the outcome. When Frank came out with two unarmed riders herding along ahead of him, carelessly turning his back on the big saloon, there could be no doubt about what had happened. Questions were unasked because sight presented patent answers in advance of the words.

244

Frank put both his prisoners into the strap-steel cages that served for jail cells in the tiny room behind his office where the heat was stifling, and went back to his desk. He had gotten the names of the other men in the posse with no effort and had them on an envelope. He read it twice, then pocketed it, and sat down. There was a lot more than a let-down to it. There was the nagging knowledge that the entire thing had been planned right under his nose — and he had completely missed any part of it.

He thought back to Reilly's obvious fury when Clarence Black had butted in, and understood it now. Sean hadn't anticipated Black's nosiness. That was why he was so enraged when Black had ridden out to the Boxed C to break up George's romance with the girl, Irene Cobalt. Frank went back, in his mind, over the little things he recalled now, and swore angrily to — and at — himself. The girl had been Reilly's final attempt — outside of a last resort to a gunshot in the night — to acquire George's ranch. What the dead man had said about wanting the place hadn't altogether made sense, but that didn't matter. Whatever the reason, for running cattle, smuggling, which he'd mentioned, or any other of a hundred reasons, the fact was unalterable. He had wanted the place badly enough to see George lynched for it. That alone mattered.

And the girl? Frank stood up, fished for his tobacco sack, twisted up a cigarette, lit it, and stalked around the office. That fitted, too. Fitted like it should in all respects. Maybe Sean had known what would happen. Must have, in fact, or else he wouldn't have sent her. It hadn't backfired at all. He had known the girl would fall in love — half-breed fashion — with George. Probably he knew George pretty well, too. Frank spat on the floor. Reilly was poor with a gun, but he had had a head on him, at that. Frank carefully pieced the whole thing together as dusk turned to the abrupt, descending blackness of night. He didn't light his lamp. The darkness was a friend — for a while — then it became a portentous thing, swollen and crowded with pathos and memories — and a flashing-eyed, hard-living ghost with its thumbs hooked in the shell belt the way George used to do. He got up quickly and went out into the night.

Buelton was alive with men. The sheriff stood back under his overhang and felt the mysterious pulse every small town has to its lawman. The idling ranchers standing in the coolness, talking instead of gambling and drinking. The lack of boisterous laughter and wild shouts.

Down by Eaton's livery barn some itinerant freighters were encouraging two drunk Indian trappers to imitate cougars and wolves, but aside from the easy laughter of these strangers, a sense of foreboding, of unnatural tension hung over Buelton. Frank wrinkled his nose at it and went down the plank walk to the café, went in, got some hasty stares, then was ignored completely by the diners. He left orders for the feeding of his prisoners and went out again. It seemed as though buildings stifled him now.

He studied the envelope in the gloom, then struck out for the tar-paper shacks at the south end of town.

Two were close and he had little trouble getting the inhabitants to walk down to his jail with him.

The hours rolled by somberly. When the last of Reilly's posse men were jailed, Frank knew the news had traveled fast. The tempo of the town was changing again. The riders for the big outfits were pulling out. It was apparent the men were leaving with reluctance and under orders. A pall of suspense was building up. Frank ignored it with bitter determination, and, once the last of the lynchers was packed into the two little cages, he took his carbine from the boot again, tucked it under his arm, and stalked through the quiet town to the stage office, wrote out a message, and handed it to the agent, face up.

"Want to read it, Lew?"

"Well, not 'specially, Sheriff, why?"

Frank shrugged. "Thought I'd offer you the chance before I borrowed an envelope off you and asked you to send it to the county seat on the late stage out."

The agent regarded his unblinking eyes for a moment, then flushed his indignation. "By God, Sheriff," he said. "I don't get involved in nothing. Mind m'own damned business. Find that's a full-time job." He handed over the envelope, watched owlishly as Frank sealed the thing, and handed it back. "You want it delivered over there?"

"Yeah, to the circuit judge, care of Sheriff Sanders."

"All right, Frank, I'll send it out in about an . . . an . . ." — the man scrutinized his watch with mental reservations about the unpredictability of horses in general — "half an hour or so."

Frank nodded, and turned back the way he had come. The agent studied him idly, eyed the significance of the carbine, and put the envelope on his desk like it was something that might poison him.

The last duty of the day was growing solidly in Frank's mind. There was telling Carrie. He'd known all along it was his sole responsibility and resented it just as he had resented being involved in George's fiasco before the killing of Clarence Black. But the thing got no easier to do with the passing of time. He ran a hand along the blunt edge of his jaw, felt the whisker stubble, and grasped it as a good enough excuse. He glanced up once, toward Carrie's boarding house, then turned and went back to his office where he could shave.

Shaving wasn't unpleasant generally, but now it was fused with ways of phrasing what he had to tell George's widow. It became a complex, agonizing job that was over too quickly, in spite of its distastefulness. He dallied by washing his face and hands and wincing at the face that looked back from the mirror at him. A harsh, bitter face with haunted eyes. He left the jail without going near his prisoners and lugged the carbine with him. There was a savage sense of defiance akin to a challenge in the way he walked and looked — and felt. If the townsmen wanted to take up for their friends, Frank Girard was ready. He walked the full length of Buelton and turned in at Mrs. Murphy's boarding house, remembered the carbine only when the worthy, stout, and red-faced landlady opened the door, looked once, then looked again.

"Sheriff Girard," she said matter-of-factly, as though introducing him, not acknowledging his presence. "Come in."

Frank stepped into the parlor and smelled the aroma of Boston baked beans. It reminded him of his own appetite that, until the smell came to him, hadn't been more than an unconscious thing weighted with the indifference and anger that lay dully within him.

"You want Missus Carpenter?"

"If you please, ma'am."

The landlady eyed the gun acidly. Frank set it in a corner, and turned back. "Well?"

"Well," Mrs. Murphy said, looking up into his face for the first time, and letting her glance rest on his eyes. "She ain't here."

Frank was shaken. He heard the finality in Mrs. Murphy's voice. It held him rigid. "She's gone?"

The landlady nodded solidly. "Yes, sir, she's gone. Left town on the noon stage."

Carrie had promised to stay. To wait. Frank stood still, trading stares with Mrs. Murphy while the impact hit him, settled into place, and stayed there. He turned slowly, reached for the gun, and draped it under his arm again before he turned back with a small, forlorn hope.

"She leave a message . . . for me?"

"No, nary a word to anyone. 'Course, she may be back. She knew about her husband. In fact, we talked about it for a spell when she was in the parlor, getting her room."

Frank's ire was rising. Mrs. Murphy was one of the type Frank had hoped Carrie could have avoided, the tongue-wagging variety of gossip that every small town nourishes. He shot her a venomous glance, and turned to go.

Mrs. Murphy went past him, opened the door, and stood aside, still looking into his face with her blank, generous features.

"She didn't seem more'n a little sad and a mite relieved to me, Sheriff."

Frank didn't answer. He didn't trust himself. He nodded at the woman and went out into the night, through the gate, and swung south, heading back toward his office again. The music of his spurs kept apace with the hollow sound of boots clumping through the darkness.

Carrie had distinctly said — had actually promised — not to leave Buelton until — he'd forgotten how long she'd promised to stay or what he'd said exactly — but she'd promised, anyway, and then she had taken the stage. The stage.

He crossed the empty roadway, ducked under a hitch rail, and entered the stage office. The agent looked up, nodded his uneasy recognition, and Frank thought the man's face assumed a hint of an uncomfortable, strained look.

"George Carpenter's wife . . . she left on the noon stage . . . that right?"

"I allow," the man said laconically, looking up.

"Where was she bound?"

"Wagon Mound. She bought a ticket that far." The agent raised and lowered his shoulders slightly. "After that . . . I don't know."

Frank nodded. Carrie had just come from Wagon Mound. She'd never said why she'd gone there in the first place and he hadn't asked. Until now, it had been none of his business anyway. He regarded the agent speculatively and wanted to question the man. Instinctively, though, he knew it was a waste of time.

"Thanks."

The agent nodded, then frowned. "Sheriff, you want her in connection with . . . something, maybe?"

"No. Not any crime. She had nothing to do with Clarence Black's death . . . or her husband's. It's just that . . . well, she told me she'd stay in Buelton for a while." He rocked his head tiredly. "Reckon I can't blame her, though. Talk. It's hard enough on a man, but a woman . . . well, that's asking a lot, I expect."

"Yeah," the agent said undecidedly, glancing behind himself at some luggage below the counter, out of Frank's sight, "I reckon. Well, g'night, Sheriff."

"S'long."

Frank went out of the stage office with his full load of bitterness. He walked to within 100 feet of his office before he sensed a man standing in the shadows under his overhang, waiting for him. He glanced up, saw the bulk and shape, and made a wry face.

"What the devil do you want, Hugo?"

Lesser flushed under the scorn in the lawman's voice but the night hid it. He opened the office door and stood aside. Frank entered without glancing at the

251

blacksmith at all. He crossed the room, lifted the lamp mantle, and lit the thing, turned it down when the untrimmed wick began to smoke, and shoved his carbine back in the boot before looking at Lesser.

"Well?"

Lesser seated his mighty bulk on the wall bench and showed his acute discomfort. He formed words and tasted them and discarded them in favor of others. While he was floundering, Frank sank down behind his desk and made a cigarette, remembering his hunger as he lit up, and looked over at Lesser.

"Come on. I haven't eaten all day, and I'm hungrier than a bitch wolf. Spit it out."

"Frank . . . you got to turn them boys loose."

"Not on your life, Hugo. Not a chance. Listen. I was elected to do this job and I'm doing it. They were accessories to a murder, Hugo. They'll face a court and a jury. I've already sent a letter to the circuit judge over at the county seat to put them on his itinerary. He's due over here tomorrow to commence holding court."

Lesser's eyes bulged. "You . . . already sent him word, Frank?"

"Yeah. Not only that, but I've also sent for the loan of a deputy from over there as well. Figure some of the boys might want to get their friends out of here."

Lesser's head lowered a little. He regarded the dirty floor with a desperate stare. "Frank, you hadn't ought to have done that. Listen, them posse men . . ."

"Posse men like hell. Lynchers. That's what they were. Just plain lynchers."

"You were Carpenter's friend. Folks wondered if you'd . . . well, do your duty."

Frank snorted. "That's bull and you know it, Hugo. They had no reason to think I'd do otherwise. I told you and your lousy council I'd do it. I've never lied to you. You had no reason to doubt me. I said I'd go after George, and I went."

Frank stood up and showed the bloody scratch on his torn Levi's. "That's George's trademark." He sat down again and leaned over the desk, staring at Hugo Lesser. "Reilly's boys knocked me over the head when I told 'em to mount up and ride off. That's resisting the law. They took and lynched George without any authority to act at all. That's murder. Then Reilly resisted arrest this afternoon . . . and he's dead." The sheriff scowled slowly at the big man. "You don't understand how serious this damned thing is, Hugo." He sat back and smoked for a moment, still watching the blacksmith. "Hugo, you're dumb. You're so darned dumb I feel sorry for you. Sean Reilly played a game all his own to get the Boxed C. Well, he almost made it, but not quite. It was Reilly himself who sicced that 'breed girl on George Carpenter."

Lesser looked up, dumbfounded, trying to make sense out of what the sheriff was saying.

"So, in my eyes it loads up about like this. You let a fool herd of mares stampede you into allowing a bigger fool to butt into a man's private life, where he had absolutely no right at all. Then there was this girl Reilly sent out to work on George. She did everything she was supposed to . . . and more. She fell in love with him."

The sheriff's use of the word was colored with rancor and innuendo. "Then ... the biggest damned fool of them all killed Clarence Black and lost everything he owned in this world, including his life, because of it. All right. Reilly didn't see how he'd get the Boxed C after all this gun play began, so he seized the best alternative he could salvage out of the mess and rounded up an illegal posse, rode out, knocked out the duly authorized law, and lynched the culprit. Now, Hugo, there's a whole dog-goned chain of lawlessness ... and it's going to stop right there." Frank flagged with his cigarette toward the door that separated his office from the loaded jail cells beyond. "And those men in there are going to be tried for the crimes they committed ... so help me."

Lesser shifted his weight a little. The bench groaned its dire protest at his heft. "Frank, you got some of the local townsmen in there." He said it in weak protest, making a pained grimace when he did so.

"And they're going to stay in there."

Hugo changed his tactics. He recognized the sheriff's keenness of mind and gave over trying to argue the men out of jail. He tightened the skin around his small eyes and stared. It was a rôle that suited him better anyway. He always ran aground when he argued, but his great physique was something he knew how to use to full advantage.

"If you don't let 'em out, Frank, I'll take the keys and do it myself."

The sheriff shifted just a mite in the old chair. A single black gun barrel peered over the desk at Lesser's ample mid-section. "All right, Hugo. You got a chance to be killed. Join 'em, or just back down. It's your play, pardner. Call it!"

Lesser eyed the gun and the face above it. There was absolutely no compromise in either. He sagged again, flushing all the way to the roots of his coarse hair. "Dammit to hell," he said disgustedly.

Frank came close to a smile. "Hugo, what in hell's behind your idea about getting these lynchers out of here? Who put you up to it?"

"The whole town's up in arms, Frank. There's going to be trouble. The council had an emergency meeting and voted them *hombres* have got to be turned out."

"And if I refused . . . what did they vote about that, Hugo?"

Lesser shrugged. "No one knew exactly what to do in that case."

Frank tapped with one hand on the desk top and studied the hulking, thoroughly abject, and miserable blacksmith. He had a sensation of watching retribution in the making.

"Hugo, you go get the councilmen and bring 'em over here. I got an idea that might solve this whole damned thing."

Lesser looked up quickly. Relief spread out so vividly it was like a sun burst after a squall. "By God, Frank," he said, arising. "By God. I'll be right back."

The sheriff watched him clear the overhang, then he went over, closed and locked the door, and strolled to his gun rack with a savage, twisted smile. Justice, after a fashion, was at long last coming into the picture. He checked all of the guns, saw they were loaded, and left them in place. He went over to the jail room door, opened it, and squinted into the darkness. Several frightened and angry faces, scarcely distinguishable, looked at him. No one said a word.

The usual bedlam from the saloons didn't come through the walls to him. Buelton had something far more intriguing to occupy itself with this night.

Frank rummaged around in his drawer, found what he was looking for, and covered the objects with an old Wanted poster on his desk, then he arose and paced the room, thinking of Carrie, until he heard men walking toward his office.

He listened closely, feeling the hair along the back of his neck rising slowly.

"Frank? It's Hugo. Open up. Me and the boys, Frank."

When the town fathers filed into the room, they had difficulty meeting his level glance. The fact that the sheriff was wearing a triumphant, ironic little smile didn't help any, either.

Lesser nodded agreeably. "Well, what's your idea, Frank? We're all interested."

The sheriff let a moment of silence go by, then he nodded and raised his right hand. "Do like I'm doing, boys."

Bewildered but willingly, the men raised their right hands. Frank swore them in somberly as deputy sheriffs and, before the amazement had died out completely, handed each man his badge and rifle, then waved indifferently toward the wall bench.

"Sit down, deputies. I don't reckon Buelton's gunman element'll care to tackle the whole damned town council and the sheriff . . . all duly sworn to uphold the law of the community, and armed to do so."

One of the councilmen almost fainted. His eyes rolled back and the carbine dropped loudly to the floor. Hugo Lesser's jaws worked methodically, rhythmically for some time before he spoke, then he roared blasphemously and jumped up.

"Sit down, Hugo!"

The sheriff's handgun waited, steady in his palm, until the man's cries of outrage had been stifled, then the hammer raised with a sickening *clicking* sound, sharp and ominous. Lesser regarded the gun. It had killed a man only a few hours before. He sat down. All four of the deputies stared in fascination at the weapon, unaware of the bitter glow of victory in the level eyes above it.

"Listen, boys, you bought quite a headache for all of us today. Especially you, Hugo, and I don't aim to let you forget it. In the interests of law and order, you're going to hold off the town tonight, if the town's foolish enough to try bucking all five of us, locked in here. Don't run out on me, boys. I got the right to shoot you down if you do." Frank nodded easily. "I'll do it, too. Especially you, Lesser. I'd sort of like gunning you down, damn your lights! Now shut up and relax, if you can, and let's just listen. We want to be ready when they come."

CHAPTER
SIX

The night was quiet enough to hear leaves whispering, but Frank gathered small consolation from the apparent lethargy. He fought sleep and hunger with monumental valor and bent to the task of his dual duty grimly. The councilmen were like statues. They smoked once in a while, rarely spoke, and frequently eyed him with malevolence, but the sheriff was committed and persevered. He listened to the town and kept his eyes on the men in front of him.

The strain was increasing with the hours until sleep seemed the most likely to triumph. Frank fought with everything he had. If he dozed, the very deputies sitting with him would turn the criminals loose. If he stayed awake — he didn't think he could do it much longer — and was a failure at repelling from the outside friends of the men he had in jail, he'd lose that way, too. The sensation of having eyelids made of fine emery cloth persisted, then his sluggishness dropped away. Men were coming; their voices arose over the dull sound of their cumulative feet pounding the packed roadway.

Frank sat up and held his rifle across his legs, listening. The sound was close. He turned and looked with a saturnine expression at his deputies.

"You want to talk to them . . . or shall I?"

He got no answer and expected none. It was a courtesy, that's all. Technically they were his superiors, in a sense his employers. Hugo Lesser's round, heavy face was toward the locked door as though it stood between him and Hades.

Frank got up and went to the door, standing a little sideways so he could watch the councilmen. The mob was on the duckboards now, slamming down their booted feet like nothing could stay them. The sheriff smiled thinly when he heard them milling around outside. The rumble of many voices died away and the conversation, indistinguishable to the men inside the office, seemed limited to two or three men, then a pistol butt struck the door arrogantly and a voice called out.

"Open up! Come on. Open it or we'll break it down." There were a few encouraging grumbles from the mob.

Frank stepped away from the door, watching it in case some enthusiastic drunkard should let fly a salvo.

"Clear out, boys. You're only making it worse. Don't obstruct justice."

The same voice ignored what Frank said when it growled back at him: "You going to open it up, Sheriff, or do we blow it off the wall? Listen. We've come for them fellows you jailed. They hung a murderer and that's no crime to us. Let 'em out or we'll do it for you. Open up!"

Frank levered the carbine, saw the horrified looks linger on him when the hammer made its metallic, loose rattle, and eyed the councilmen coldly. "Boys, there's five of us in here. You blow that door down, and, by God, there'll be at least six of you won't walk away with it. Now get to hell back home!"

For a moment nothing happened. Evidently the mob was caught flat-footed by Frank's assertion that he wasn't alone.

"Who's in there with you, Sheriff?"

"All four of the city fathers. Deputized and sitting here, armed and ready."

"You're a liar!"

Frank lifted the carbine's snout a little. "Call out, Hugo. Make it loud. Each of you follow him. Hurry up!"

Lesser's face was white beneath its sheen of perspiration. He licked his lips and darted glances helplessly around the room. There was no succor and no alternative. He cried out, telling his name and reiterating that he was armed and deputized. The other men followed suit like automatons, each facing the door and avoiding Frank's glance.

Again the silence came down and this time it lasted for quite a while. When the spokesman opened his mouth again, a good deal of the truculence had gone out of it, but the anger and indignation were still there.

"You boys, get the devil out of there. Hear me, Hugo? Listen. Girard's got innocent men in there. We don't aim to stand by and see 'em used like this. Come on out, Hugo, and bring the others with you."

Frank shook his head and answered before Hugo's ponderous mind could form the right words. "Not on your life. You boys want a war, just start shooting.

You're bucking the duly constituted authority of Buelton. The circuit judge'll be here in the morning, along with Sheriff Sanders' deputy from the county seat. You force a battle here, and I'll arrest every mother's son of you, and have you tried. This isn't any threat. There's been murder done. You want to get into it up to the hilt, just start shooting. You're deliberately obstructing justice. That's a prison offence. Think it over. Either shoot or shut up, and get to hell home. All of you!"

The silence grew longer. Frank could imagine a few back on the fringe of the mob slipping away, uneasy and suddenly aware of the implications of what they were doing. It was a long, tense wait, then he heard the mob disintegrating and knew he had won. He looked at the councilmen and sighed, letting the weariness come back again.

"Well, that's it for now, boys." He went back to the desk and put the carbine across it. He felt the slipperiness of his hands for the first time then. "Now you know right from wrong. I'll undeputize you and let you go. In return, I insist on your influence to keep that mob from coming back." He was watching Hugo as he spoke. "It's like this. If I'm wrong, the judge'll let me know damned quick. If I'm right . . . well, at least you'll have been on the right side for once in this mess. Want to give me your word you won't bring the pack back again . . . or do you want to stay here all night?"

Hugo's hatred was making his face twitch. He glowered at Frank, unable to understand fully just how he had been so effectively defeated, and just beginning to understand where he now stood with the men outside. His cheeks were gray. He turned away from Frank without a word and looked at the other councilmen. Two of them got up and walked to the door, ignoring the blacksmith and nodding to Frank Girard. One spoke for both.

"All right . . . right or wrong, we got no choice. Frank, I admire your guts. I hope you're right in this."

The sheriff nodded his head in acknowledgement of the oblique compliment and looked at Lesser and the single man still on the bench.

"How about you two?"

The remaining councilmen arose. Lesser was undecided out of belligerence alone. He knew he was left with no alternative, but that didn't cause his anguish nearly as much as what was waiting for him beyond the door. In the bleak, cold eyes that were ranged along the plank walks of Buelton, shining out of angry, set faces, limned in dark shadows. The man beside him nodded glumly and went over by the door, too. Hugo was left alone. The fire went out of him so suddenly it surprised all of them, the sheriff included.

"Frank . . . I . . . quit. God Almighty, I quit!" He flung the gun from him wildly, tore at the badge, and flung it aside, too. His eyes were wild-looking and saliva was at the corners of his mouth. The tension had broken what no man's gun or fist ever could have done. Frank said nothing. He was shocked and not a little embarrassed at the abrupt show of weakness. He jerked his head at the door and one of the councilmen opened it. All four went out. Hugo Lesser was the last to pass through. Then Frank went over and slammed down the bar again, listening to their footfalls in the quiet night.

He made up a pallet on an old cot in the office and dropped down on it. One cigarette and some brooding thoughts, and then he resigned himself to the demands of his body. Shrugging to the possibility of further annoyance from the townsmen, he let sleep come. With it came the quandary and mystery of Carrie's broken word to him. He could see her looking at him as though they were on opposite sides of the desk. Neither of them spoke; just their eyes talked in an ageless language that defied interpretation. Frank tossed in spite of his weariness. The hours went by like old men heavily burdened, dragging leaden feet slowly. Carrie's apparition left its impression of sweetness and sadness — and an uneasy hunch inside Frank's head that she had the best of reasons for leaving.

After he awoke, the thought persisted. It was a puzzling thing to him. She had given her word; nothing else could matter. Still, he wondered. Could there have been something, after all, as important — more important, in fact — than her oath to him?

He shaved and cleaned up with the mystery in the forefront of his mind. He was still pondering it, wistfully hoping there would be something that would absolve the beautiful woman of the condemnation he had formed around her memory, when the prisoners began growling for attention.

He went into the tiny cell room and listened to their angry demands for food and release, their harangues and dire prophecies. It was all in the nature of his work and none of it was new or original. He listened stoically, still thinking of Carrie, then told them shortly he'd have their food sent up, and walked out, slamming the door against their furious tirades.

Hunger now took precedent over his other troubles. He unbarred the door and went out into the new day's sunlight and carefully locked it from the outside before striking off for the café. Buelton appeared quiet, still immersed in drowsiness in spite of the high sun.

At the café he ate eggs and ham and golden-brown fried potatoes with as much relish as he could with Carrie in his mind like a fever. He recalled her bowed head when he had told her about Irene Cobalt and George. But the memory persisted that her grief wasn't actually sorrow so much as resignation and — from her appearance — relief. He finished eating and shook his head to himself. Could she be different than he had always thought her? Was there a callousness — selfishness — or something akin to both behind the beautiful features? What else could it be when a woman returns to her home and finds her husband not only a murderer, but unfaithful as well? Shouldn't the reaction have been different?

He arose, grunted dourly, paid the café waiter, and shuffled through the doors to the plank walk beyond. Instantly he knew the quiet of Buelton hadn't been inspired by lassitude.

"Girard!" The man was invisible. Hidden strategically and well, purposely. Frank flattened against the safety of the wall, raking the town for his enemies.

"Girard! This is your last chance. Turn 'em out!" The sheriff knew he had no chance, exactly as the hidden gunman said. He was not only fully exposed, but the closest place to seek cover would be Eaton's livery barn, and beyond a doubt it was either occupied by his foemen, or at least covered by their guns.

"You got a second to make up your mind, Sheriff. Hurry up!"

Frank took a long chance. The only way he saw open to him. With slow and deliberate steps he walked out into the middle of the road. Looking for the carbine was wasted time. The six bullets in his six-gun would have either to seal his doom or bail him out.

A handgun roared and dust flew at his feet. It was a spiteful shot by a hiding assassin. Frank's gray eyes narrowed and his mouth pulled down.

"That took guts, pardner. Let's see if you got any more. Step out into plain sight. Meet me halfway."

The taunt lay in the air for a long moment and received no answer. Frank stopped talking. He was directly in the middle of the empty road opposite the Whitsett House.

"Sheriff, you're a damned fool. There's two of us. Walk to the jailhouse and turn them boys loose and we'll forget the rest of it."

Frank laughed mirthlessly. "Two of you. Well, why don't you come out like men, then?" He was going to say more but didn't get the chance.

"You fool!" The man's tones were getting edgy, scratchy. "We can kill you right now and let them boys out ourselves. You ain't got a chance. Either you'll let 'em out or we will. But they're coming out."

"Mouthy buzzard," Frank growled dryly. "For the last time I'm going to tell you this. There's more'n enough trouble piled up over Black's killing. He wasn't worth George Carpenter's death, let alone anyone else's. The man behind the whole consarned mess is dead. I killed him for resisting, just like I will you, if you don't rope it and ride off."

Someone laughed harshly. Frank knew it was an antagonistic bystander and nodded without looking around at the sound.

"Yeah, maybe you'll kill me. Possibly will. But then there'll be two more for the judge to try. You fools think two of you, or ten, or a hundred can bluff the law? You can't. Down me and Sanders'll be here from the county seat. There won't be ropes enough to hang all of you. Now, mount up and slope. The judge'll be here before long. Don't make things worse than they are."

"You said that last night," a thin, piping voice cut in from the opposite side of the road.

Frank had both his attackers spotted now. He couldn't see either man but he knew pretty well where they were hiding. He spat scornfully, then raised his head again. There was pure anger in his face now. "All right. We can't argue this out, so let's shoot it out, if that's the way you want it. Come out into the open . . . unless you're too damned yellow."

It is a rare fighting man who talks much. Verbosity is an enemy to courage. Frank waited, sweating, with the balled up insides of a man facing eternity. The level

266

gray eyes were drawn, narrow and thin, above the flaring nostrils of his face. The wait was torture compounded. He knew a bullet could cut him down any second, and expected it to as well. Probably the only thing that saved him from a dry-gulching death was the fact that the assassins were local men; public opinion would condemn the sheriff's murder in spite of the antagonism against him. Buelton standards, like all frontier ethics, dictated the essential demands of fair play and a chance for any and all men who faced death.

Frank's wrath and tension made his voice unnecessarily loud when the waiting was pyramiding inside of him into a gorge of overpowering uncertainty. "Come on out, you yellow bushwhackers! Let's see if you're as good in the open as you are behind a building!"

Contrary to the gunmen's expectations, the sheriff hadn't been subdued. He had them where they had hoped to have him, challenged and called.

There was no alternative now. One of the men shouted thinly to his companion across the road: "Ready, Ace?"

"Hell . . . yes!"

Frank went for his gun as soon as the second man answered. He was wringing wet and the back of his throat felt like a plank of green pitch pine off a new log. His poise was jarred for a fraction of a second when the man on the west side of the road came out on horseback. He recognized the man afoot, who came from directly opposite the site where the rider emerged. It was a brother of one of his prisoners, a known hardcase, drunkard, a sullen, troublesome *hombre*.

267

Frank's first shot made the walking man stagger, then the air was blown into turmoil by gun thunder. Frank concentrated on the staggering man, letting his wet thumb slide off the dog of his pistol twice and seeing the man standing there, stupidly, until the second shot snapped his head back and he flung his gun away in a careening effort to hold his balance. The man's knees refused to concede defeat, though, and he hung there, bending forward a little from the waist, hat gone and black hair hanging. He must have been unconscious or close to it, because the second slug had pierced his head and blood was dripping abundantly from over one eye, but he seemed to be looking down at it incredulously.

Frank's gamble had been on the mounted man's horse and fate had nodded. The animal was terrorized by the explosions and fidgeted, nostrils distended and eyes red and rolling. The rider got off two shots, one twenty feet wide and the next closer but still harmless, when Frank turned away from the unarmed gunman and tilted his barrel up for the third shot.

The rider was swearing in his high, cracking voice and arcing the gun down overhand for his next shot when Frank fired. The horse gave a convulsive leap, spun crazily in a sunfishing maneuver that made the rider's aim impossible, but also presented a poor shot for Frank who abstained, knowing only three slugs remained in his gun.

The animal's mouth was a mass of red. The bullet had shattered its jaw. Like a waspish streak, the mounted man leaped to the ground, landed kneeling, and fired. It was a smooth, expert gesture and Frank knew, even before he stared at the yellow tongue of flame, the slug had his name on it. It had. He fought to preserve balance after the impact, wondering in the back of his mind where he had been hit. There was no pain — yet. He lowered the barrel and let go with his fourth shot. The kneeling man went over backward, rolled sideways with a piercing, keening scream that broke over into desperate, sing-song profanity, and propped up his firing arm.

The next shot felt like someone had roped his right leg and yanked it out from under him. Frank went down in a sprawling dive and the man's next shot cleared his head by three feet. Lying prone, facing the small target of the downed gunman, the sheriff's pistol came up slowly, froze in position, and hesitated for the thousandth part of a second that seemed like twenty years, then roared and kicked against his thumb pad. The gunman glared at him but didn't fire. Slowly his gun drooped, then dropped, and his head went down much slower, reluctantly and stubbornly, as though the brain beyond knew that surrender to the stealing lethargy that was sweeping over the body below would never allow the man's body to raise itself again. It was a bitter, one-sided battle fought inside a man's head, and battled out to the final act with all the grimness of utter finality, until the head was only inches from the dust, then it dropped suddenly, bounded a little, and a sort of sob came up from the dirt, muffled but discernible.

Frank raised his eyes, saw the horse standing a little way off, head hanging and legs spread, blood streaming

269

from the nose and mouth. He raised his gun. It had grown incredibly heavy. He used both hands to steady it, and fired. The animal didn't even flinch, just took one tentative step forward as though testing the earth, then crumpled with a sodden sound that sent up dust devils.

Someone shouted exultantly. It sounded like it was miles off. Frank looked back at the other killer and saw that, sometime during his preoccupation, the man had fallen. The flatness of the body, with no air in the lungs to hold the chest up, spoke the universal requiem that needed no words. The gunman was dead. Both of them were dead. Their horse, too, was dead.

Frank let go of his gun and pushed it away distastefully and lowered his head until it was lying on his doubled fists, one above the other, holding his head out of the manure-stained road. He lay like that, feeling a delicious relaxation that made every muscle slack and stringy, then the light began to fail. He knew it was death coming, had to be; the darkness came with it, he'd always heard, and the dullness of his mind agreed. He smiled a little, wishing he could tell someone how easy it is to die. No sense of pain, really, no sense of anything — but one agony persisted. Carrie. He'd never know the riddle now, and think what he would, he had gambled she wasn't the kind to break her word. But physically he was done; the loss of blood that made him so wonderfully relaxed and drowsy abated a little because his heart was awakening. It was happening within seconds and Frank Girard never heard the loping boots as men converged on him from both sides of the road.

He didn't know it when they picked him up and bore him into the Whitsett House and lay him on the bar, amazed — profanely so — that he was alive. He didn't hear the men scuttling after the doctor or know that the bartender had detailed other men to dispose of the corpses out in the road. If he had been conscious, his face would have crinkled into that wry little downward smile he had when the townsmen began haltingly to praise him a little, then shamefacedly change their stand on the prisoner question altogether.

It was many hours later before he opened his eyes. The lids were extremely heavy, then, too. It was a sort of half pull to the lids themselves that let him look out at the world. The same kind of half opening eyelids do even in death, and no one was more surprised to see Frank Girard alive than himself — and the dowdy little doctor with the raffish, unkempt Vandyke beard who was sitting comfortably on a cane-bottomed chair, drinking whiskey and water in the warm solitude of the supposed death room.

"Where'd I get it?"

The doctor started, looked around, and shoved the glass away quickly. His red face was startled — almost shocked with the impropriety of a dying man returning from over the edge — and squinted.

"By God, Frank! Well! Maybe you'll make it, after all." The doubt was heavy in the tone, though. The doctor arose with a grunt and went over to the bed, raised an eyelid and peered in, wagged his head in surprise at the caustic look he got, and shrugged as though Nature was making him out a liar — which she was.

"You got one over the knee, in the muscles of your right leg. That's the one that put you down. I saw the battle from my second-story window. Was watching all of you. Figured I'd have the job anyway, and wanted to know what I'd have to be prepared for."

"The other one?" Frank said patiently, but looking anything but patient.

"The other one? Yes, well, you stopped that one with your collar bone some way. It entered here" — he jutted a finger where pain was throbbing sullenly with each beat of the sheriff's sluggish heart, then the finger angled downward — "then it went along your innards, downward a piece, broke three ribs and plowed out . . . here." The finger rested lightly on Frank's coverlets near the end of his chest.

The doctor looked up again, studying the ashen face and bluish lips, pursed his own, and clasped his hands behind his back in his best professional manner.

"Bad . . . you got two bad ones. The leg'll heal quick enough. It's not enough to kill a man or cripple him, either. It's the cussed loss of blood. Man, you were wearing more outside than a man should have inside. Can't replace the stuff. More folks bleed to death than ever die any other way. Someday . . ."

"How long'll I be down?"

"How long!" The medical man was aghast. He squinted myopically at Frank's face again. "You're

272

damned lucky to be alive, boy . . . damned lucky. In fact, you could slide over yet. Time will tell. You'll be flat for a long, long time, Sheriff, I'll tell you that."

"The others . . . they're dead?"

"Can't make 'em any deader. Both were pretty badly shot up, but it was those head shots that finished 'em both. Right through the head, both times." He looked wryly at Frank and nodded with small approval. "Good shooting, Sheriff. Good . . . and fatal."

Frank's awareness kept pace with his returning life. He felt the sickness along his ribs, in his shoulder areas, and to a lesser degree in his right leg. He didn't move because he didn't have the desire or the strength, but he knew, if he could, his body would feel like it was a broken twig in a forest fire.

The doctor still regarded him shrewdly, then spoke again. "You got a young lady outside, wants to see you. Feel up to it?"

Frank's eyes opened wide; the weight seemed less oppressive. He studied the raffish face, saw nothing there to guide his thoughts, and licked his lips with a tongue that felt immense and unwieldy.

"I reckon. Send her in and . . . you stay out."

The doctor nodded understanding and waddled across the room. Not until then did Frank wonder where he was. The room was strange, as were the furnishings. He didn't wonder long, only until he heard the short steps crossing the floor, then he forced his eyes to search out the face he wanted so much to see. But it wasn't that face.

"Irene!" The disappointment was acute.

"Sheriff, oh, Sheriff!" The beautiful dark eyes were swimming in tears. Her face was drawn with grief and bewilderment. She stood looking at him for a moment, then went down on her knees and put her head in her hands, and sobbed on the side of the bed. Frank's apathy had enough life left in it to wish, irritably, she'd cry some place where it wouldn't shake the bed and make those daggers of flame bite into his injuries.

"What . . . brought you back?"

"You," she said finally, snuffling. "You really were his friend. He knew it, too. He told me all about the two of you . . . before . . . before all this happened . . . while we were trying to hold off the posse. He saw them club you. I had to keep him from rushing into them then."

Frank closed his eyes. With no effort he could see George's face. It was wearing that dry, lop-sided grin he affected when something ironically humorous appealed to him.

"Well, he's gone. That's the size of it. He's gone." There were other things he could've said about Carpenter but he reserved them. Things better left in thought and never mentioned. The sheriff opened his eyes and looked down at the girl.

"You didn't have to love him, Irene. That wasn't part of the bargain originally."

"What bargain?" she asked, big-eyed.

"The bargain with Sean Reilly. The bargain you made to work on George, get him to sell out . . . and all."

"Reilly told you?"

274

"Sure. Who else would've? Just the two of you knew about it."

"But I loved him. I couldn't help it."

Frank would have nodded if he'd been able. "Sure, I understand that . . . now." He was quiet for a moment, then: "Irene, you're bad for men. You may not mean to be, but you are. You love easy and give easy, that's dynamite because you're very pretty. I'm not going to warn you. It wouldn't do any good, but I should, I reckon." The gray eyes strayed off her face and looked at nothing, above the black head. "You're always going to cause trouble. I don't think you mean to, really, either. It's just that . . . well, you're built that way. Now . . . do me a favor. Get up and go. I'm sorry for you, Irene, but a darned sight sorrier for George Carpenter, and what you did to him." He looked at the beautiful, alluring face. An ironic light was in his eyes. "I could even love you, Irene, if it wasn't for the fact that I'm already in love. You're beautiful . . . and evil. Like I said, I'm sorry for you, and sorry, too, for the other men you'll ruin before you're too old. Well . . . I preached my sermon. Saddle up and go, Irene. I don't ever want to see you again."

The girl went after a moment of staring at him. She didn't speak at all. The room was as blank as her face, then she turned and walked away.

Frank watched her leave and felt a poignancy in his heart. She would never understand, never in a thousand years.

CHAPTER
SEVEN

The doctor entered the room. He crossed, looking directly at Frank. His glance was curious and professionally interested for the first time. Taking the cane-bottomed chair with one hand, he dragged the thing close to the bed and sat down.

"You've got guts, boy, and something else."

Frank interpreted it to mean a complication. He frowned a little, not so much in apprehension but in displeasure because, since the gunfight two weeks before, he had come to dislike the doctor quite thoroughly.

"What else?"

The round shoulders rose and fell. "Hard to put a name on it. I've seen it before, sure, but never so plain right from the outset. In medicine we call it by several names. The will to live, stamina, resistance, but I think the most fitting name is what the boys at Eaton's barn call it. Guts."

Frank didn't answer. He let his eyes wander back to the partly opened door. The doctor sighed and settled back in the chair.

"Now . . . you take that 'breed girl who came to see you the day you were shot down." The raffish face grinned maliciously. "Well, I heard what you told her." Frank's eyes swung fully to the medical man's face. There was wrath in the stare but the doctor just shrugged again and went on. "Think what you want, Sheriff. I'm a doctor and I've got a patient . . . a very intriguing patient. I don't want anything to ruin his chances. That's why I eavesdropped. You see, that first day was touch and go. Closer than you'll ever know. For that reason I didn't want you upset."

"Doc, get your sermon over with, will you?"

"All right. The point is, along with these guts you've got, there is this other thing. There's a name for it, but I don't know what it is. Anyway, it's the thing that's kept you alive and pulled you through. Now, tell me . . . what, exactly, is in your mind that's kept you hanging on stubbornly, telling yourself you had to get well and get out of here?"

Frank stared at the doctor without speaking for a long time. He knew his mind had been occupied with this remaining problem for a fretting two weeks. Even the trials had come and gone and left him unmoved. That the judge had handed out stiff fines and stiffer jail sentences wasn't really much of a triumph for the sheriff. Even the fact that the town had planned a celebration for him when he was able again left him with nothing more than a cynical acceptance of fickle human nature. There was, indeed, something that transcended everything else, but the thought of disclosing this powerful force to the Mephistophelean doctor was repugnant. Frank shrugged and smiled crookedly, avoiding the doctor's face.

"You figure it out, Doc, you're the dealer in abstractions here, not me. How about letting me walk a little today . . . just for the hell of it?"

The doctor drummed fingers on the edge of the bed, saying nothing. He had an idea that, if he could ascertain the power that had pulled the sheriff through, he'd be able to use it in other cases of near death. But he was only partly right; you can't instill love in a human being. It has to be inspired. It was Frank's love and doubt of Carrie that had kept him from falling into the usual pattern of inertia and discouragement that ordinarily hits badly hurt people. He rarely thought of himself, except to yearn for a horse between his legs so he could strike out for Wagon Mound, find George's widow, and talk to her again.

The doctor didn't bother to answer the question at all. He sat for a moment longer, lost in thought, then arose abruptly and stalked out of the room in grim silence.

Frank watched his back with indifference. He paid no more attention until he heard voices in the outer room, then he watched the door, knowing he had a visitor. It was Hugo Lesser. His body was garbed in the sweaty, dirty clothing of his blacksmith's trade. Only the shiny old leather apron was missing. He entered the room, nodded deferentially at the sheriff, sat down on the doctor's vacated chair, and cracked his knuckles self-consciously.

"Frank, I reckon you know all about the trials?"

The sheriff nodded slightly. "Enough," he said. "The judge came to see me before it started and when it was over. Fines and up to three years in prison all around, the way I recall it."

"Yeah," Lesser said, regarding his thick, massive hands. "There was an oration afterward, too. The judge give it. He said you was right all the way and Buelton was wrong. Well, we'd come to know that, Frank, after the night in the jail. Now the town's paying your bill to the doc. Not just the patching up bills but your keep while you're staying in his house as a private patient as well. I . . . we . . . wanted you to know this, too."

"Thanks," the sheriff said dryly. He was embarrassed by the blacksmith's humility and wished he'd say what he'd come for, and move on.

"Yeah, you're welcome. Now then, Sheriff Sanders come in from the county seat as you know. He's left that deputy, Mister Winters, in Buelton to run your office until you're up and around again, so that sort of settles that end of things for you, too. What I'm saying is that you got no worries and Buelton's anted up a nice poke for you, to kind of show appreciation . . . and all."

Frank's discomfort was becoming acute. He fixed the councilman with a warm glance when he spoke. "Hugo, get it over with, will you?"

"Sure, Frank. Two things. One's official, so I reckon I'd better get that one out first, hadn't I?" Frank didn't answer. Lesser fidgeted a little. "The councilmen want you to fill a vacancy that's come up among the city fathers. Will you do it?"

Frank was mildly surprised. "Who quit, Hugo?"

"Me. I got no business being a city father. Not really smart enough."

Frank grinned wryly. "Me, neither. I wouldn't have the job with a lifetime guarantee, but I'll give you an idea. Why don't you appoint the new preacher that came to town a few months back? The one they call Burying Bill?"

Lesser's face fell. "Well, I reckon we could get him, only the others got their minds set on you."

Frank shook his head. "No dice, Hugo. Another thing. I'm resigning as sheriff. You can pack that back with you, too."

The blacksmith's face twisted in astonishment and pain. "Frank, what in hell're you talking about? Listen, you done a real good job as the law here. Don't let no one tell you . . ."

"It's something personal, Hugo. I had a job to do that I couldn't resign in the middle of, no matter how badly I wanted to. A man's got his beliefs. Those were mine in the George Carpenter trouble. Well, I went ahead and did what I had to do, and it was like being sent after my own brother. All right, I did it and it's over with, but you'll never catch me in a position like that again, believe me . . . no, sir! So take the word back that Buelton's got to appoint another man to fill out the remaining six months of my term, and I'm through. When I get around to it, I'll send over a written resignation."

Hugo Lesser studied the pale, wan face, faded from its normal ruddy coloring by the confinement, and wondered what he could say. The silence lengthened in the room and became an insurmountable barrier the longer it lingered, until the blacksmith knew he could never effectively breach it. He arose finally, still clasping and unclasping his big hands, and licked his lips uncomfortably. Perspiration was out on his body from the perpetually opened pores of his trade.

"Frank . . . I'm awful sorry about what happened. The whole damned thing, from start to finish. Awful sorry."

"Forget it, Hugo," the sheriff said, nettled by the man's lugubrious stance. "I'll see you when I'm up and around again. *Adiós.*"

"I reckon," Lesser said dolefully. "*Adiós.*"

Frank didn't look at Hugo's back when the big man left the room. His eyes were on the ceiling overhead with a brooding, distasteful look in them. He was still like that when the doctor's cherubic wife brought him his dinner. She, a kindly, red-faced woman with merry blue eyes, put the tray down and peered at him.

"Frank, you've got corned beef today."

The gray eyes came down and smiled at her. She alone, of the people who came to the room, treated him as an equal in health. No sick-room manners or tones came with her.

"Ma'am," the sheriff said with a smile, "if you weren't the doctor's wife, I'd steal you."

"*Pshaw!* I'm old enough to be your mother." She canted her head a little and looked at him speculatively. "Sheriff, you do need a wife, though. Have you ever thought of that?"

Frank eyed the tray that was perfuming the room with delicious aromas. "Well, once I did, but it didn't pan out."

"You asked her?"

"Not exactly."

"Not exactly? What kind of an answer is that? You either did or didn't. Which was it?"

Frank's eyes showed embarrassment. "I didn't. Another man asked her first. She married him."

"*Humph!* Did she know you were in love with her?"

He almost said — "Not exactly." — again, but caught himself in time and shook his head instead. "I never told her. In fact, I never took her to the dances . . . or anything."

"Well," the doctor's wife said tartly, "did you expect her to read it in the clouds?"

"No."

The older woman sat down on the chair beside the bed and studied the sheriff in silence while he ate. After a while she spoke again, still regarding him thoughtfully.

"You're a lot better, aren't you?"

"Yes'm. Just about as good as new."

"I thought so. Frank, did you know there's been a lady here every few days to ask how you are? Has the doctor told you that?"

His appetite left him the same moment he felt a lurch inside the prison of his chest where his heart lay. He looked at her, afraid to ask.

"The doctor hasn't told me about any woman. It's . . . that 'breed girl, maybe?"

"'Breed girl? Not this one. She's a thoroughbred." The blue eyes were intent. "Frank, have you tried walking any yet?"

Frank had, but secretly. He didn't want the doctor to know it because he was sure of disapproval. He hesitated long enough for the doctor's wife to divine the truth. She wrinkled her nose at him.

"*Pshaw!* I'm no doctor. I think half of their cures are poppycock anyway. Doctor's told me at supper that you've got something on your mind that's keeping you alive and pulling you through faster than he's ever seen a recovery before. I haven't said anything, Frank, but I think I know what it is . . . this mysterious panacea of yours. Want me to tell you?"

Frank was grinning a little, watching her face. He nodded. "Sure, ma'am. Go ahead."

She accepted the challenge with a brusque nod. "All right. You're in love!"

Frank started suddenly and was silent. The older woman read it all as though he had told her. It was like writing on his face. She smiled and relaxed in the chair.

"All right, ma'am, you've guessed it. Now tell me who the lady is who's been here asking how I'm getting along?"

"Proud to, Frank. It's Carrie Carpenter."

"Carrie!" It was like being kicked twice in the chest by the same mule. First, it had been the overwhelming hope, then the shocking knowledge that it was a reality after all. "Carrie. Ma'am, why . . . doesn't she come in?"

283

The doctor's wife was watching him with astonished interest. He had told her of a love; now she knew who he loved. It was so obvious and so painful that she could feel the smarting behind her own eyes. Like an avalanche it all became clear. The sheriff had come to Buelton with George Carpenter. She remembered that. He had gone after his old partner for murder and that was no secret at all, but she saw through the rest of it now. The finale, sort of, to the love of a deep, quiet man for a woman his less constrained, more dynamic partner had rushed in and swept off her feet and married. She longed for the privacy of her kitchen where she could swear in peace. Profanity, to the doctor's wife, was a delicious vice she indulged in privately as a pop-off valve for suppressed emotions.

She shrugged and looked away from the drawn, pale face. "I don't know, Sheriff, why she doesn't, except . . . maybe it's because it's impossible to get help in Buelton . . . especially when you want 'em to live on a ranch as isolated as the Boxed C."

Frank's forehead wrinkled. "What's hired help got to do with it?"

"Well, you see, Frank," she said, still holding her glance to the opened window where sunlight spread its daylight gown over some rank geraniums below the window. "She's got the baby to think about. It isn't wise to buggy-ride the little thing all over the country, you know, and she das'n't leave it home alone." After a moment's allowance, she turned her head and looked at him obliquely. It was very plain now that no one had spoken of his partner's widow to him. She wanted to make a face over that, too. Men and their strange, warped ideas of manhood! Afraid to mention Carpenter's widow before him. Feeling awkward because they knew how he'd take it, knowing she was alone with a baby now, they'd held their silence.

Frank's stare was wide-eyed with shock. He was quiet for a tense moment, then spoke very softly: "A baby?"

"Yes, a baby. A little girl, Frank. Cute as a bug's ear. I've seen her three times now."

Frank lay back on the pillows. He'd seen Carrie not over three weeks before. She hadn't said anything — he blushed a little — or shown anything, either. Somewhere, then, this baby filled in a void in his mind. That must have been why Carrie had gone away. It was natural for her to do it, under the circumstances. He felt relief overcome and replace the astonishment. That would be the only excuse she could have had, sufficient in his eyes to warrant breaking her oath to him. He even smiled.

The doctor's wife arose and gathered up the tray without looking at him again. "Frank, you didn't answer me when I asked if you'd tried walking any. Have you?"

He looked into the blue eyes and saw the thought behind them. "Yes'm. I've tried it."

"Well, can you do it?"

"Still a little weak, but good enough, I reckon."

She turned toward the door and let the last words drift back to him over her shoulder. "I expect a man wouldn't have to walk far to get his horse. It's at

Eaton's. After that, he'd be riding, and that's easier than walking. The Boxed C isn't awfully far to a riding man . . . is it?" Then she was beyond the door, humming. He could hear her for several seconds after he couldn't see her any longer. The idea wasn't subtly planted and it tickled him. He lay back and laughed. The noise was musical, although obviously not a sound that had come out of him in a long time. It was easy to tell because it was a scratchy, rusty sound.

Frank lay with his thoughts for a while after the doctor's wife had gone. They were pleasant, sunny thoughts that seemed to follow an orderly sequence now. Just one thing didn't fit. The baby. He wondered about it for a while, then grunted, shoved back the covers, and got out of bed. It was his first daylight excursion, although he'd practiced walking many times lately, after the house was quiet at night and his thoughts wouldn't let him sleep.

The weakness was there like it always had been, but the sensation of being top-heavy wasn't as solid as before. He grimaced. It made a difference, having an incentive to be abroad, and just walking to offset the boredom.

He dressed carefully, keeping one ear cocked for sounds of the doctor. He couldn't know the doctor's wife had sent him on a wild-goose chase out into the country in his buggy.

Leaving the house was easier than he had expected. It was simply a matter of going out through the sun-porch door and standing in the sun blast, letting the leaching rays wash over him with their intense warmth. He stood motionlessly for several minutes, looking at the drowsiness of Buelton, then he walked slowly up the duckboards, through town and down to Eaton's barn. The startled glances he harvested as he went along rolled off him with barely any acknowledgement at all. Fortunately no one offered to stop and congratulate him. It was the set, determined look of his mouth and eyes, unbeknown to him, that discouraged it.

Eaton's cigar almost dropped out of his mouth. The small, piggish eyes grew large and round.

"Saddle my horse for me, will you?"

"Sure, Frank, glad to. Hell, yes." The liveryman started toward a stall on the north side of the shady, fly-infested old building, redolent of ammonia and hay and manure with an overtone of sweaty leather and saltiness. A hostler hurried up, but Eaton waved him away, got the animal out, and led it over to the tack room, dragged out Frank's equipment, and put it on.

The sheriff watched with approval. His horse was sleek and shiny from inactivity and the grooming he had rarely gotten when he was stabled behind the sheriff's office in his little shed.

Eaton handed over the split reins and looked questioningly at Frank. "You . . . all right, Frank?" He made an embarrassed gesture with one hand. "If it's something that's got to be done, maybe some of us boys from town could do it . . . you know what I mean."

Frank had never cared much, one way or the other, for the liveryman. He smiled at him, though, in appreciation for the evident sincerity behind the words, took the reins, toed into the stirrup, and pulled himself aboard the animal.

"Reckon not, Eaton. Thanks just the same."

He turned and rode slowly back out into the sunshine. It was a good feeling to Frank Girard, as it always is to born horsemen, to be atop a good horse again in the warmth of summer. He reined northward out of Buelton, knowing and ignoring the many stares that followed him. The word would pass around quickly.

The horse was content, fortunately, to take a sensible gait and hold to it. The long-legged, rein-swinging walk of the frontier that spurned the miles rearward with a steady, consistent regularity.

The sun had made sweat darken Frank's cotton shirt by the time he cut the ridge above the Boxed C. He sat there in the shade for a little while, looking out over Potter Valley. It was a sight that inspired deep admiration for the natural beauty of the far reaches every time he rode the ridge.

Below was the ranch George had carved out of nothing. The deep, purple shadows were getting longer, leaner, and losing their midday depth with the passing of afternoon. Frank watched the sparkling little creek reflect vagrant sunbeams like fingers of molten silver, then he reined out into the heat again, and started down the wagon ruts that led into the yard.

The shade was an ally in the hot land. Frank tied his horse to the same imbedded stud ring in the gnarled, leaning cottonwood tree he had used on his last visit to the Boxed C. He turned away with mixed feelings after loosening the cinch and smiling at the animal's apparent relief to be resting in the pleasant fragrance of the shade.

The ranch had the feel of being owned again, of being lived in and patronized again. It was something vague but certain in the atmosphere. Frank walked slowly toward the cabin's porch, climbed the steps with some effort, and sat down at the top of them, leaning against the porch upright he had used as a backrest the other time, not too long ago, that he was here. He let his narrowed eyes, banked by the squint against the sun glare, roam over the place. He was seeing it as it must have always looked to George Carpenter, until Sean Reilly's half-breed girl had changed it all. It was a beautiful spot. Serene, silent, a little aloof, and immeasurably patient, as though the timelessness was nurtured in the ancient oaks, the skirting of hills in the near distance, and the rolling breasts of land where cattle and horses grazed. He sighed, fished for his tobacco sack, and twisted a cigarette into existence, lit it, and smoked in comfort.

Carrie's voice didn't really surprise Frank altogether, when it broke in upon his somber reverie. He had known that she'd come out sooner or later. That his tobacco smoke had penetrated the house didn't matter. Nor her surprised look when she saw the big black horse George had thought so much of, tied in the shade of the cottonwoods.

"It's cooler in here, Frank."

He turned and looked up at her. She was a statuesque woman, straight and tall and full-bodied, with that inescapable aura of capability and strength. He nodded into her blue eyes and smiled. "I reckon. Don't want to make a lot of noise, though."

Carrie understood and came out onto the porch without a sound and sank down beside him. She was looking over the land, too. Then she turned and faced him.

"Are you supposed to be out . . . Frank?"

He shrugged. "Not exactly." He remembered his brush with the doctor's wife when he'd used those words before. "No, I reckon not. But I'm able, and that's enough for me. Besides . . ."

"Yes?"

"Well, I heard about your baby, Carrie." He looked at her, saw her steady glance on his face, and left it lying between them. But she didn't take it up. The silence grew and Frank perspired a little more because of it. The sensation he'd had once before, that was helping him say something he didn't know how to say, was completely lacking now.

He bobbed his head like a man resolved to doing something unpleasant. "Carrie, is that why you went away?"

She nodded. "Yes. I wanted to tell you, Frank, but you were gone. I wanted to tell you that day in the sheriff's office, but . . . well, it just didn't fit in right then."

"Nothing to be ashamed of, Carrie. You could've told me then."

She shook her head at him. "No, I couldn't. Frank, you were doing something that was emptying all the heart out of you. It was in your eyes and your bearing. How could I have added another sorrow to those you were already carrying?"

He snuffed out the cigarette and spoke with his head lowered, looking at the cigarette butt to be sure it was dead. She saw his profile and had to bite her underlip at the wan, ill-coloring of his face.

"You didn't have to shoulder any more than your share of the grief, Carrie."

She made a small, despairing gesture with one hand, reached over impulsively, and squeezed his arm. "Frank, I'm used to it. You aren't . . . weren't. There's so much you never knew."

"Oh?" he said, looking over at her, wondering. "Well, there's one thing you could tell me, if you would."

"Anything. What is it?"

"I've wondered about you. Well, the way you took it when I told you about George's killing Black, and living with that 'breed girl. You were kind of resigned, I reckon, but you didn't seem to care much . . . Carrie. I've wondered about that. Can a woman turn her love for a husband on and off like a lantern?"

"It wasn't that at all, Frank. I've said there's a lot you don't know. I'll tell you some of it if you insist, but it isn't pretty."

"All right, tell me anyway . . . that is, if you don't mind."

"I don't mind, with you, although I'd rather forget it all like a nightmare." She was silent and somber-eyed, looking at the Boxed C and beyond, then she spoke again, and Frank relaxed in the shade, feeling the unrelenting support of the porch upright against his back.

"Frank, George had done that before."

He was startled and glanced at her, but she wasn't looking at him now at all.

"He'd had other women friends. This girl wasn't the first. As his wife I thought the wisest thing was to act dumb, but after a while it made my respect . . . my love for him wilt a little. There were other things, too. Like his drunken rages and his . . . well, abuse. All these things quenched the love I'd felt for him once." She turned and looked at the sheriff. He saw the anguish in her face and she saw the surprise in his.

"You didn't know any of this, I know. No one did. Oh . . . a few may have suspected, but no one ever said anything. Not to me, anyway."

"Nor me," he said, understanding in a flash why they hadn't. It wasn't a good idea on the frontier to carry tales, especially to a man's closest friends. Every boothill cemetery in the land was occupied by men who had made that fatal mistake.

"Frank, it's hard to say when you stop loving the man you're living with. The thing happens so slowly, so insidiously. But you know, finally, that you can't look at him as a lover or a husband any longer." She shrugged. "Then there's a time when you don't know what to do. To divorce him, just walk out . . . or what. I was in that stage, when I had to go to Wagon Mound."

"I see," he said softly. "The baby complicated things, too, I reckon. You didn't want to bring your child into a world that had taken its father away." He saw her eyes widen in astonishment and nodded at her. "The doc's wife told me about your little girl, Carrie. That's one reason why I rode out here today . . . to offer you any help I could."

"Frank!"

The horror in her eyes jolted him. He raised off the post and looked down at her, feeling the stirrings of the craving he'd always felt when he was near her.

"I'm sorry, Carrie. I didn't mean to say anything . . ."

"Frank Girard! Do you think . . . ? But, this isn't my baby, Frank. It's George's."

The sheriff leaned back against the post again with a stupid, blank look on his face until the meaning of what she had said soaked in. It took a few moments at that.

Her face lost some of its startled look but she still held his glance imprisoned in her look. "That's what I meant when I said I didn't want to disillusion you further, that day in your office. The time you told me about George and this 'breed girl. I got a letter from a girl in Wagon Mound, where George used to trail Boxed C cattle to ship them. She wrote that she'd written George and he wouldn't answer her. She was frightened, Frank, and had no money. Now . . . do you understand why I didn't want to tell you?"

He nodded, feeling the ground slipping away under him. He'd known George as a devil-may-care rider, but this was different.

"I went over there. She had her baby and I paid for everything and made arrangements to have the little girl taken care of until I could come back, have a showdown with George, move out, and take the child myself." The lovely eyes were softening. "Frank, she's the image of her father. I'm in love with her. Maybe there was a little love left in me for George, after all. He's gone now, but I've got his daughter and I love her like she was my own." She reached out and took his hand. "Come in, I want you to see her, Frank. To meet her."

He arose unsteadily and held her hand in a tight grip. "Carrie . . . I'm sorry. I had no idea about this end of things."

"Of course you didn't. I didn't want you to, Frank. You had the kind of a decision to make that takes the heart out of a man, just like it does out of a woman. I made my decision and you made yours. I couldn't see any point in telling you my troubles, when you were bent with your own."

"I'm awfully sorry. You see, I figured you were cold-hearted, the way you sat there and took what I told you with hardly a show of . . . well, outrage, or whatever women do when they see their man going to hell like George did."

She smiled thinly and squeezed his fingers, returning the unconscious pressure of his perspiring fist. "Come on. I want to show you my daughter."

They went into the cabin and Frank's first impression was that the entire place had been subjected to a laborious scrubbing. Carrie pulled him along until

294

he was standing over a little cradle with rockers on it, looking down at a child that was sleeping blissfully in the coolness of the quiet house. He stared at her, trying to see George, but couldn't. She was small, wrinkled, with scraggly dark hair and a nose that looked old and flat. He felt Carrie's eyes on his face and levered up a dismal smile when he faced her.

"There's a likeness, I reckon."

Carrie's eyes twinkled. She squeezed his hand tighter, then, and laughed softly. It made her beautiful face a fitting background for the flash of perfect, white teeth.

"You don't have to be kind, Frank. You aren't used to children. She's not very old. Men don't often think they're pretty when they're this age. Mothers do, though." She pulled him away. They went back out onto the porch and sat down again. He took off his hat and dropped it on to the planking and ran a hand through his hair.

"They do fill out . . . don't they, Carrie?"

This time the laughter peeled musically at him. She half turned and winked, controlling her mirth with an effort. "She'll be the prettiest thing you ever saw, Frank, in about a year. From then on, she'll get prettier."

He smiled ruefully. "I hope so." He thought of Carrie raising George's daughter and the blush began below his shirt and spread painfully up over his face, neck, and ears, until it was lost above the hairline.

"Carrie?"

"Yes, Frank?" Her intuition told her what was coming. She kept her face averted. His agony was plainly in the voice. Looking away might help a little. It did.

"Carrie, George wasn't the only one in love with you when he married you. We . . . were different, though. He had the . . . well, guts to ask you and this other *hombre* didn't."

She said nothing, but that peculiar sensation came back again. The one that made him feel that Carrie was helping him say things, sustaining him in his tribulation. Helping him with some power she emanated.

"I was that other fellow, Carrie."

"I know." It came softly as she turned back and faced him. "I didn't know it at first, but later I did. I'm terribly sorry, Frank. Things would have been so different . . . wouldn't they?"

"Yes, I reckon so. Carrie, it's not too late. I'm more in love with you now than I was before. I know you better, understand a lot of things I never thought about before."

"Like what, Frank?"

"Well . . . character, and things like that. Carrie . . . will you marry me?"

She smiled at him. There was a sheen of something awfully like tears over her eyes. She nodded thoughtfully. "Yes, I'll marry you. I love you, Frank. Like you, I've come to love you since the killing of Clarence Black. It isn't youthful, passionate love and I want you to know that now. It's a different kind of love. The kind that comes with maturity, understanding . . . and mutual suffering."

Frank's shoulder blades were tickling with the perspiration that ran down them. He put out one arm and she swept up against him. He lowered his face, found her mouth, and kissed her. Then they sat without moving until Frank's arm went to sleep and he had to move it.

"Carrie, shall I bring that new preacher out here in the morning?"

She smiled up at him and nodded. "Well . . . you could do it tonight, still . . . if you wanted to, darling."

Frank arose hastily, as red as a beet, fumbling with the brim of his hat, rolling it and unrolling it between his two hands. "All right. I'll eat in town and be right back with him."

"You'll hurry back, darling, but don't eat in town. I'll have supper for three when you bring him back."

He was halfway across the yard when she called to him. He turned and saw her standing like a goddess on the porch, the setting sun bringing out every facet of her beauty, like it always does to a woman deeply and maturely in love.

"I love you, Frank."

He untied the horse, grinning back at her, yanked on the cinch, and swung up, blew her a kiss, bowed low, and spurred the startled, slightly indignant horse into a lope back toward Buelton.